Beneath the Southern Stars

by

Amy Craig

Men and Women of Valor

Beneath the Southern Stars

COPYRIGHT © 2025 by Amy Craig

Cover Art by *Lisa Dawn MacDonald*

The Wild Rose Press, Inc.
PO Box 708
Adams Basin, NY 14410-0708
Visit us at www.thewildrosepress.com

Publishing History
First Edition, 2025
Trade Paperback ISBN 978-1-5092-6260-1
Digital ISBN 978-1-5092-6261-8

Men and Women of Valor
Published in the United States of America

Dedication

To grandparents raising their grandchildren. May their love keep you forever young.

Chapter One

The luxury rental car's forced heat blasted Ann's face. She flexed her fingers on the vehicle's leather-clad steering wheel and waited on a southern Louisiana traffic light to change from red. Shifting in her seat, she lifted a hand from the steering wheel and re-checked her passport and business cards. Customs officers found the heavy cardstock from Bolton's Valor Security and Investigations more credible than her tight, road-weary smiles. If everything went well, she and Ricco would slip into the New Orleans airport before dawn and make their international flight.

A low fuel light flashed.

She checked the remaining mileage estimator and calculated their travel time. The empty intersection teased open, country roads. They'd probably make it.

Leopard frogs called for mates. Their chuckles, as familiar as jazz bass lines, summoned memories, but she kept her grip at ten and two. People romanticized the South, but she planned to ghost it.

The traffic light turned green.

Punching the gas, she blew past Hemlock's weathered, concrete streetlights, wide, oak canopies, and looming, unbroken shadows. Winged insects buzzed the headlight beams like cheap drones. The state had plenty.

Tugging lower her baseball cap, she considered her

partner, Ricco Rotondo, and what he would think of the area's sagging strip malls and foggy retention ponds. The rural landscape retained a gothic charm, but Ricco, dozing in the passenger seat, would never see the appeal of moss-draped trees, Acadian cottages, and free-range chickens. Drool trailed the stubble on his tanned chin. He was a good investigative partner but a lousy travel planner. After flight cancellations interrupted their Houston itinerary, he found an early bird flight from New Orleans.

Figuring she could handle Interstate 10, she drove until a wreck closed the throughway and detoured them into Cajun Country. She should have argued for Dallas!

Too late to turn back, she pushed the luxury rental through the backcountry miles.

Glitching, the mileage estimator flashed.

She rolled her eyes.

It flatlined.

She slammed a palm against the dash.

The console screen went blank.

She muttered a curse.

Ricco stirred.

"It's nothing." Biting her lip, she eased off the gas and considered her options.

A neon sign for Zydeco Fuels promised full service.

If the gas tank held fumes, she needed fuel fast but didn't want to spend a minute longer than necessary in this parish. Shaking her head at the flawed options, she whipped into the station lot. The building's clouded windows and rusted beams undermined its sign's neon promise. Running her tongue over her front teeth, she coasted toward the pump.

Ricco rubbed his hands over his face.

The rental car sputtered and died.

"Gas?" Ricco asked.

"Apparently." Questioning why she ever left the U.S. Navy and its reliable fuel depots, she put the car in Park, scanned the fuel yard, and shook out her aching hands. "I'll be quick."

He cracked his jaw. "Yes, boss."

Securing her gun, wallet, and phone, she left the key fob on the center console and slammed the car door.

Cold, wet humidity cocooned her face and amplified the frogs' calls. An armadillo darted across the lot. Rubbing her upper arms through her thick sweatshirt, she scanned acres of pine trees crowding the corner lot. A soft, yellow glow washed out the stars. Dreamers attributed the glow to New Orleans' nightlife, but the light pollution came from nearby chemical plants. Water access kept the state afloat and slowly destroyed it.

Pulling out her corporate credit card, she faced the pump. Moths buzzed. The overhead lights flickered. A small, worn sticker on the pump read *Cash Only. See Attendant. No Checks.* Shaking her head, she tucked her hair into her hat and made her way across the cracked, concrete lot. Feet warm in wool socks and leather boots, she navigated maintenance hole covers and approached the weathered outpost. Every bit of this place needed a coat of paint. *Had the station always been so shabby?*

She pulled open the door, ignored the squeaking metal hinges, and walked inside. A radio played fiddle tunes through dust-caked speakers, and a heater hummed above scuffed floor tiles. The smells of stale, fried food, viscous motor oil, and volatile gasoline fumes lingered. She wrinkled her nose and glanced at the plastic-wrapped food, sunflower seeds bags, and homemade candies lining the shelves. She hadn't had a praline in ages. Squashing the nostalgic impulse, she approached the counter where a slight man wearing dirty overalls sat on a stool.

He swiped a finger across a glowing e-reader and looked up with bright-blue eyes. "Took you long enough to come inside." His gravely, garbled voice retained a French lilt. Coughing, he slapped a fist against his chest. "Counting your dollars?"

"Something like that." She pulled twenties from her wallet and fisted them. His deep-set wrinkles, large pores, and graying beard suggested he'd worked this station his entire life, but she couldn't place him or his thick, dark lashes. What did her lapse say about her faculties? People changed, but Hemlock's citizens retained their identities like hard-won merit badges. A tourist traveling through town might catch a snippet of Kouri-Vini, think they heard Cajun French, and wonder why their high school French lessons failed them. They would discover high school failed many people.

Instead of worrying about the attendant's provenance, she laid the money on the counter. Scuffed plastic protected rows of scratch-off lottery tickets. Given a windfall, most people bailed. "Forty on the first pump."

The attendant leaned back on his stool and crossed his arms. "You from the plant?"

"Nope."

The heater blew a strand of hair across her eyes.

She brushed away the annoyance.

"We don't see many motorists this time of night. Interstate wreck?"

"You nailed it." Dipping her head, she turned toward the station exit. The sticky floor pulled at her boots.

"Hold up."

Muscles tensed and ready to draw her weapon, she turned and forced a smile. "Yes?"

The attendant narrowed his gaze, brought a hand to his wiry beard, and stroked his jawline like a man who enjoyed jigsaws. "You come through town often?"

"No." She tilted her head. "Any more questions?"

"Lafayette?"

She cracked her knuckles. His voice, as rich and jagged as fried cracklins, and his interest, as meddling as a schoolmarm, kindled distant memories of well-intentioned townies. "Colorado." Weighing the spark of interest in his gaze, she regretted her admission.

Uncrossing his arms, he lifted the money and pressed the buttons on an old, metal register. *Bing.* The drawer popped open. Placing the money inside the slots, he slammed closed the machine and looked up. "Lonely drive. Wouldn't send my daughter out on a night like this. Women go missing."

She wet her lips and thought of the girls she knew. Surely, they'd all grown into strong, capable women. Samantha Eddington shared the attendant's bright-blue eyes, but Ann hadn't seen Sam or her family in twenty years. "Crime spree?"

"Nah, *Chère.*" He winked. "Ain't you never heard of the *Rougarou?*"

Rolling her eyes, she turned her back on the

attendant. Louisiana's werewolf had nothing on the things she'd seen with Valor. Raising a hand in farewell, she walked away from old, familiar possibilities. "Thanks for the warning."

He grunted.

Outside, wet, night air enveloped her. She strode across the concrete expanse. Pushing the pump nozzle into the rental's tank, she watched display numbers turn over. The digits appeared like ghostly, gear-fueled revelations against a black sky. Tipping back her head, she looked for constellations. A satellite blinked.

She slid a hand into her pants pocket and glanced at the station building.

The attendant stood at the door, his silhouette distorted by the cloudy glass. A glowing device illuminated his aged features.

Shit. Nothing should be more interesting than his book. The pump panel marked four gallons of fuel. Five would get her to the airport.

Metal squeaked. The gas station door opened.

She adjusted her stance, free hand poised near her holstered gun.

The attendant leaned on a polished, cypress walking stick and crossed the yard.

Her heart thudded. Peeling out of the lot would alarm Ricco, but she didn't have a choice. Yanking the gas nozzle from the fuel tank, she shoved it into the pump holster and flicked the spilled gasoline from her fingers.

"Ma'am, you forgot your receipt!" The attendant raised a hand. "Hold up."

Ricco stirred in the passenger seat.

The muscles in her legs and arms trembled. She

rounded the hood, dropped into the driver's seat, and yanked closed the door.

"Problem?" Ricco slipped a hand inside his leather jacket.

She missed Reverse and dropped the car into Neutral. The rental revved. "No problem. Needed fuel and didn't feel much like small talk."

The attendant tapped the window.

Ricco considered the old man and scratched his jaw. "Want me to shoot him?"

"No." She pressed the button to lower the window. "Hold off."

"Spoilsport." Ricco drummed his fingers on the dash. *Tap. Tap.*

Chest tight, she thrust out a hand for the receipt and kept her chin tucked low.

The attendant extended his phone.

Recoiling, she almost dropped the device.

"Duckling?" a video caller with cloudy, pale-blue eyes shouted and scratched his whiskered cheeks. "Is that you slinkin' about town like an alley cat? It's three in the morning!"

"Thanks for the reminder, Paps." Dropping her head against the seat rest, she sighed. Her grandfather could grow an impressive beard, but his military background instilled rigid behaviors. She regretted the attendant's call waking him, but he rose with the sun. Dropping the phone to her thigh, she yanked off her hat, thudded her head against the seat rest, and debated her options. Paps, bless his ravaged hearing, did what the croaking frogs, greasy station, and rheumatic attendant failed to accomplish. She missed home. Swallowing, she raised her head and faced him through four inches of softly glowing glass. "Surprise, I'm in Hemlock."

The attendant slapped a hand against his thigh. "Well, I'll be damned." He coughed out a laugh. "Ann Storey, I knew it was you. Never could keep your hair controlled. Wait until I tell Sam."

Pierre Eddington.

Hemlock's entire population would soon know about her arrival, and their tongues would wag. She made eye contact with Ricco, noted his amused smile, and worked her jaw. "We'll be late for our flight."

He cracked his knuckles. "I gathered."

"This wasn't my plan."

Ricco scratched the back of his neck. "I offered to shoot him."

Ann held Pierre's phone out the window.

The attendant grabbed the device and relayed his encounter to Paps.

Ann ignored the man's embellishments and held Ricco's gaze. "I should have let you."

****

Hemlock's hotel options trended toward bed-and-breakfast, but the white structure on Longfellow Street presided over the historic district like a shabby-chic wedding cake. The new owner stripped away the hotel's incongruous additions, painted the aged façade gleaming-white, and replaced a hot, tarmac parking lot with a lush, interior courtyard. Ann remembered cracked, mesh-enforced windows, but black-trimmed, sparkling panes reflected the streetlights. Too bad, she despised the man who installed them. While she waited for Ricco to secure a room from the night manager and grab a quick shower, she messaged her boss, Vince.

—*Travel hang-up sent us through Hemlock. I ran*

into family. Will be late to Venice. Dock my pay.—

Vince ran Valor Security and Investigations and knew she and Ricco should be en route to Italy. A former Army captain, Vince assigned jobs based on employee qualifications and expected results. Ann had admirable skills and a captain rank, but denying her grandfather wasn't in her wheelhouse.

—*Get out fast. I'm more worried about you than the schedule.*—

—*Afraid I'll get homesick?*—

—*Afraid you'll blow up the bayou.*—

Indulging in a smile, she pocketed her phone and reclined the driver's side seat. Vince's light-brown hair, gray-blue eyes, and omnipresent stubble matched his Green Beret training, but he was also a good boss. Former military personnel respected Valor, but they also respected Vince and his dry sense of humor. She wouldn't advertise her south Louisiana boondoggle. He wouldn't make a big deal out of the schedule delay.

Ricco opened the car door and slid into the passenger seat. "You tell Vince?"

"Yeah." She adjusted the rearview mirror.

"He mad?"

"Not particularly. Twenty-four hours won't kill the schedule."

Ricco buckled his seatbelt. "Then why didn't we stay in Houston?"

She glanced over. Ricco smelled like mint toothpaste, cheap soap, and pungent aftershave. His tanned, good looks and combed, black hair gave him a Mediterranean appeal, but he was lethal. She met him at Justin's funeral, beat him at pool, and partnered with him every chance she could. He respected her, but he also kicked cans to see how far they rattled. She shrugged and started the car engine. "I don't like Houston."

"And Hemlock?"

She pulled onto Longfellow Street and dodged a stray cat. "Don't like it, either."

Laughing, he bridged his hands behind his head. "Can't wait for the tour."

"You won't get one." Turning the corner, she scanned the historic district for subtle changes. The buildings looked so familiar she checked the car's rearview mirror and confirmed her reflection. Yep, she was still a strong, capable woman, and this was still a quaint, Southern town. She navigated the rental car down a country road.

The sun came up, and sunlight poked between pine branches.

A gravel circular drive fronted Paps' cottage. Three dormer windows marked upstairs bedrooms. Despite Paps' age, the window glass shone, and the wooden shutters hung straight. If Paps' back ached, at least he took pride in the family stronghold.

She spotted three tri-color Mardi Gras banners on first-floor railings and wrinkled her nose. She'd almost forgotten the carnival season. She glanced toward Ricco for his reaction.

He scratched a thumb along the side of his mouth. "This it?"

"Yep." Stepping outside of the car, she inhaled fresh, country air. Her heart rate hovered near normal, and her muscles no longer twitched for action. Hemlock's isolation could be beautiful and terrifying, but she wouldn't retreat.

Ricco exited the passenger side door and bumped her shoulder. "You got this homecoming."

"Do I?" She glanced over and gave thanks their partnership never deviated into romance. She'd seen his dating game. His moves could use some work, but the dating pool in Summit Springs, Colorado, was shallow. Most people had already dipped their toes into it, too. Bedding Ricco never seemed worth the risk, and having a friend at her side confirmed her decision. If she got too antsy, orienteering and trail running kept her busy. Colorado had unique terrain.

Still, she shifted away and blamed her reaction on lingering claustrophobia. Years of tight quarters made her pine for wide, open spaces and crisp, fresh air. No wonder Valor's headquarters in Colorado grounded her. She never planned to return to Hemlock, and these certainly weren't her terms.

"So, what comes next?" Ricco rubbed together his hands. "Bacon and eggs?"

"Doubtful." They'd located a Pacific-Northwest killer and run recon on drug-making operations, but this stop wasn't a vacation. "As soon as we visit my grandfather, we'll go to Venice. Hemlock is nothing more than a detour."

Ricco whistled. "Deep."

She jabbed an elbow into his left side and left him grinning. He was like a lethal puppy, eager to please and quick to inflict pain. He would have shot Pierre and let her squeal out of the gas station lot, but he wouldn't have recognized the collateral damage. Running out of gas in Hemlock was her mistake, and she owned it.

Climbing Paps' front steps, she pulled a key from beneath a fake rock and opened the cottage door.

Paps snored in a leather armchair. A knit blanket covered his lap.

The room's aged cypress paneling looked as familiar as the freckles dusting Paps' skin, but an adjustable hospital bed waited in the room's corner like an incongruous poacher's trap.

Ricco hesitated at the threshold. "Is he sick?"

"Not that I know." She tilted her head and scanned the room. Labeled boxes held bandages, gloves, syringes, and catheters. Paps might have taken on caregiving duties, but his closest neighbor was half a mile away. She laid a hand on her grandfather's shoulder. "Hey, Old Man."

Blinking, he sniffled and straightened in the armchair. "Duckling, I thought you were a dream." He patted his lap. "Come sit!"

His booming command elicited a smile, but she claimed a seat on the worn couch. "I'm too old for your lap."

"Never." Paps cleared his throat and looked up. "And who's this?"

"Ricco Rotondo." He extended a hand. "Pleasure to meet you."

"Another Valor kid, eh?" Paps adjusted the blanket on his lap. "Well, at least you keep good company. Make yourself at home. Coffee? It's in the kitchen."

Ann stood.

Ricco waved off her unspoken offer. "I can make coffee. Sit and catch up."

Dropping to the couch, she rested her chin in a palm and replayed her last conversations with Paps. Did his cheeks look gaunt, or was the early morning light playing tricks with shadows?

"Annie." Paps smiled. "It's been a minute."

"Has it? We talked last week." She waved her free hand toward the cluster of medical supplies. "What's going on with the hospital bed?"

"Ehh." He shrugged. "Did I tell you the railroad donated land for prairie restoration? Fifty acres."

She wet her lips. He probably pulled strings and had the land donated to the Cajun Prairie Preservation Society. Conservation was a family hobby, but she abandoned her roots to chase international criminals. Unfortunately, launching into interrogation mode wouldn't get her answers about the medical gear. "You have anything to do with that donation?"

"Tax write-offs." He crossed his arms over his chest. "Follow the money."

She tugged an earlobe. "So, who's paying for all this med gear?"

"You heard about the new hotel?"

They could do this all day. She flopped back on the couch.

"New Orleans newspapers did a write-up. Nathan's bringing Hemlock back to life like Longfellow's poem brought New Orleans to national attention."

Standing, she paced the living room. Nathan Charlet, the owner of the pillared hotel, was her high school boyfriend and a Southeastern celebrity. Hemlock and his fans were obsessed with *Evangeline*, Longfellow's most famous poem. Everyone pinned their prosperity on romance, moss, and daydreaming tourists. She preferred calculated risks.

Lifting a taxidermy alligator, she stared it down.

Paps cracked his knuckles. "Nathan's a good man."

Repositioning the gator, she cleared her throat and

considered defining the term. "I've heard."

"Hotel has a spa."

She rolled her eyes. "Really? A spa."

Paps circled a pointer finger and encompassed her face. "You might enjoy the spa."

Laughing, Ricco walked into the living room, cleared his throat, and handed her a coffee mug. "Thought you might need something strong."

She took a deep swallow and watched her closest blood relative squirm. Paps knew damn well she'd never been to a spa. She spent her Navy career on active duty before moving into the private sector. Deploying in and out of the Middle East and North Africa, including a 2007 tour in Iraq, honed her instincts. Paps knew about her work with Valor and seemed unperturbed she and Ricco appeared on his doorstep without giving notice, but the old man was keeping secrets, too. She tilted her head. "What's going on?"

"You could do worse than taking a day off." He rubbed his jaw. "Just sayin'."

What he was *just sayin'* was she should settle down with Nathan, have four sweet-cheeked, Catholic babies, and bake Me Maw's recipes. Instead, she set down her coffee and squared her shoulders. "No Nathan. No spa. Get yourself a pedicure, Old Man."

He laughed and slapped his knee. "Duckling, I missed you."

Duckling. The nickname conjured old memories. She should have flown Paps to Colorado more often. She softened her stance. "I miss you, too, but I have too much going on to listen to bullshit about Nathan. Ricco and I ran into travel complications. I didn't mean to drop in, but I'm glad I did. What can we do to help around here?"

Paps shrugged. "Not much."

"Nothing?" She jerked a thumb toward her partner. "Ricco sucks at pool, but he's a pretty good mechanic."

Raising his mug, Ricco toasted her compliment.

She winked.

Paps straightened in his armchair and visibly swallowed, but he held his ground.

The old, grandfather clock ticked.

She worked her jaw.

Finally, he cleared his throat. "Honey, I have pancreatic cancer. The docs say it isn't good."

Biting the inside of her cheek, she tasted blood. The hospital bed, staged to make a patient more comfortable, lingered in the shadows. Crawling into Paps' lap and laying her head against his chest suddenly sounded ideal, but she no longer had that option. Cathartic tears welled in her eyes. The release might help, but the tears would interfere with her remaining time with Paps. She blinked them back. "How long?"

"Less than a year."

New drug trials launched every year. She had time to find solutions. First, she would meet his practical needs. Tilting her head, she considered logistics. "Who's takin' care of you?"

"I hired nurses." Paps wiggled his shirt collar. "Lindsey arrives at nine."

"Nurses." The term tasted as bitter as chicory root. Instead of burdening her, he hired a home health service. She should have noticed his illness during the preceding year. What did her obliviousness say about her character and her strength? Her career defined her life, but it could take a backseat to the man who raised her. Turning to Ricco, she put aside decades of grit and bravery to linger in a small town where she never fit in. "Go to Venice. I'm staying in Hemlock."

"Like hell." Ricco flopped into an armchair. "I want to meet Lindsey."

Paps cleared his throat. "Lindsey's a man."

Ricco wrinkled his nose. "Well, shit."

"Airport." Ann jerked her head toward the door. "Go."

Grumbling, Ricco slouched toward the exit. "Eventually."

Her partner was a good man, but Ann owed Paps everything. When her adolescence knocked her off course, he offered her acceptance and security. She could blame her parents for their absences, Hemlock's residents for rejecting her tomboy demeanor, or her high school boyfriend for shattering her dreams, but she could always count on Paps. Now, he needed her.

Chapter Two

The next morning, winter humidity seeped past Ann's flannel shirt. She tossed a weighted rope saw over a longleaf pine branch, grabbed both ends of the line, and dropped a limb. Decayed wood hit the forest floor with a muffled thud and broke into brittle chunks. Tossing the largest pieces into a pile, she dusted her gloved hands.

"A widow-maker." Paps sat in a utility terrain vehicle. "Thanks for taking down the branch. You have a good eye."

Coiling the rope, she grunted. Paps worried about his longevity, her well-being, and the weather forecast. She couldn't force his cancer into remission, but she could care for his property.

Towering longleaf pines surrounded her, Paps, and Ricco. Spiky needles carpeted the forest floor and hung from woody shrubs like rigid, brown tassels. Despite the hour, mist floated between pine trunks, a breeze shook the trees' upper branches, and brown needles drifted to the ground. Left unchecked, scrub brush and hardwood saplings would soon choke out the area's natural, grassy understory. She wouldn't let that happen. Before she returned to Valor, she would ensure Paps had an award-winning oncologist. The forest would also burn.

Rubber tires skidded on gravel.

Shading her eyes against the morning haze, she listened and judged the speed of the approaching vehicles. Nothing about their approach alarmed her.

Three white vans made a final turn, cut through the fog, and braked to a stop. The vehicles bore the logo for the *Cajun Prairie Preservation Society*. Paps' army of volunteers preserved Louisiana's natural ecosystems *and* enjoyed flirtatious, caffeine-laced carpools. "Your volunteers are on time."

Van doors opened. Volunteers spilled out.

She dropped her chin. "Damn, why are they all babies?"

Ricco laughed.

Paps scratched his freshly shaven cheeks. "They're old enough to enlist."

She grunted. "I've seen desert goats with more facial hair."

"Have you now?" He canted his head. "I thought Navy brats bobbed around in toy boats."

"Ha!" His slumped posture worried her, but his sense of humor seemed fine. Flexing her fingers in her thick, leather gloves, she stretched the stiff material. A little action would loosen the gloves and her attitude. "Today's a good day for a burn."

"Don't I know it." He scratched behind his ear, spat onto the fallen pine needles, and dropped his gravelly voice. "Don't worry about the volunteers. I taught them everything I taught you."

She groaned. "That's what I feared."

Chuckling, he beckoned the chattering volunteers grouped on the gravel-and-clay road. "Over here, y'all!"

The volunteers approached, holding chainsaws,

fence pliers, axes, and shovels. Some looked as if they worked at the New Orleans port, and some looked as if they paid dues at private gyms, but they arrived armed to defend Louisiana's unique ecosystems. They also deferred to Paps, so they couldn't be all bad. She shifted into position behind him and felt Ricco at her side.

"You think Vince will bill him for our hours?" Ricco's voice hovered near a commander's authority-laden whisper.

She elbowed her partner.

"Mean!" He laughed and pulled away. "I'm jogging back to the cottage for a hat."

"City slicker." He needed the excuse like she needed a suppressor. Given an hour of free time, she would take her shot and go for a run, too. "Don't get lost."

He saluted, turned, and set a punishing pace.

She wished she could join him.

Paps cupped his hands around his mouth and faced the volunteers. "Thanks for coming out! Before we burn the woody invaders, sign a release form. Also, if you partied last night, find somewhere private to empty your stomach. I've seen enough of that shit to last me a lifetime, and chemo drugs make me queasy. The rest of y'all, light it up!"

The volunteers cheered, which meant they knew about Paps' diagnosis before her. Shaking her head, she sighed. "You always give it to dem straight."

He turned and winked. "That I do."

She raised her eyebrows. "Except the part where you hid your cancer diagnosis from your kin."

Rubbing a thumb along the side of his mouth, he

looked away. "I didn't want to burden you."

The moment her parents abandoned her, she became his burden. Forcing him to acknowledge his sacrifices would be harder than getting him to admit he cheated at egg *pâquing*. "You're not a burden."

He kicked a pinecone into the brush. "You're here, aren't ya?"

Recognizing the vulnerability in his gaze, she tabled the issue. Paps loved her, but he was too proud to ask for help. Luckily, she left her pride on the battle field. Researching his diagnosis kept her awake all night and short-circuited her temper, but she wouldn't let sentimentality make her say foolish things. She sought out the volunteer leads she met on yesterday's late-afternoon video call. "Baptiste? Jeanne? You good to go?"

"Aye, Captain." A slight, Black man training to be an electrician, Baptiste turned the key in a front loader waiting beneath a towering pine. The machine's internal combustion engine rumbled. "We'll follow your granddad's signals."

Jeanne tossed her colorful, box braids over her shoulder. "When have you ever followed anyone's signals?"

Baptiste scanned Jeanne's figure. "Baby, I'll follow you anywhere."

"Of course." Jeanne blew him a kiss. "Who wouldn't?"

Ann kept a straight face. Based on Paps' download, Jeanne played music in New Orleans clubs. Her protective, quick-wash hairstyle minimized the effects of her sweat-soaked dancing. Ann liked her, but her flamboyant braids and upfront sass would be problems in Ann's hierarchical world. Baptiste's flirtations would get him in trouble, too. Lifting a machete, she slashed her way through tangled brush. She had better things to do than referee romances. In another year, creeping vegetation would overtake the road, and Paps might be in the ground.

"Baptiste, set us up!" Paps shouted.

Baptiste drove the heavy machinery toward a tangle of vines and woody stems. He cut a path Ann and the other volunteers could follow.

She watched his progress. He had a good eye, but he manipulated the front loader like a teenager driving an arcade game. Good thing the heavy equipment could take the abuse. Overseeing Navy personnel taught her when to intervene and when to let young adults innovate. Given today's conditions, Baptiste was doing fine. Paps was right to give him leadership responsibility.

"He'll take down a tree." Paps navigated the UTV to her side and crossed his arms over his chest. "Maybe two."

Adjusting the handheld torch hanging from her shoulder, she jerked her head toward a split-rail fence marking the property's entrance. "You have spares."

"Huh." Paps poked a stick at the silver wood fence and rattled the rails. "Maybe I do."

Baptiste reached a clearing, idled the front loader, and tapped the horn. "Everyone ready?"

"As long as Baptiste doesn't wreck the front loader"—Jeanne flipped her braids over her shoulder—"we're good."

Baptiste flexed his biceps. "Baby, I'll wreck you."

"Right." Swaying her hips, Jeanne walked into the

woods. "I'd like to see you try."

Smirking, Ann wondered if hearing about their hookups would get old. If she caught them engaging in a quickie during their volunteer shifts, she would have a reason to singe off their short hairs. Metaphorically, of course.

Instead of worrying about what-ifs, she needed to get Paps in a good place and return to Valor. Eying the nearest woody shrub, she ignited her torch. Flames sprang from the nozzle. She pointed the device away from the combustible understory. Looking for Paps, she made eye contact. "You good?"

He brandished a fire extinguisher from the UTV's seat. "Ready and willing."

Raising her torch, she toasted winter wood. Dried leaves crackled, and narrow stems glowed orange before curling into ash. The acidic smell of smoke would linger for days over the forest's damp, base scent. Nudging her boot toe against a spiky, green pom-pom, she adjusted her aim.

Longleaf pine seedlings were short, dumpy green clusters. A tourist might mistake them for grass clumps. When the seedlings grew into saplings, they stood tall enough to weather prescribed burns. She would avoid blasting the seedlings, but like all her lines of work, casualties would occur.

Paps jammed his thumbs in his overall pockets and arched his back. "I'm glad you're here. The stand needs thinning."

She looked into his cloudy, pale-blue eyes. "So, why haven't you burned it?"

He straightened and patted his stomach. "I'm too old and too rich."

More accurately, he was too sick. His puffed breath dissipated. He was the last of a dying breed. He worked for the railroad and purchased acreage to bolster his retirement, but he might not live long enough to enjoy it. Life could be a bitch. Shaking her head, she aimed her torch at a climbing vine and sent the opportunistic plant into the afterlife.

Paps drove off and monitored other volunteers.

After thirty minutes, she checked on Baptiste, Jeanne, and the volunteers. They had the burn under control. Slow, steady progress yielded predictable results. She lifted the torch toward the next strand.

From the front loader, Baptiste waved both hands. "Guidry, sir!"

Her heart thudded. In a flash, she was back in Fallujah, bitter and jaded. Memories of her service rocked her. Shaking off the flashback, she hoped nobody was hurt and sprinted past Paps' lumbering UTV.

Time slowed. A red-cockaded woodpecker hammered a trunk with relentless fury. *Tat-tat-tat!* The bird's aggressive, staccato attack echoed between the pine trees. The animal would drive its beak into the tree bark until it achieved its goal. She understood its compulsion and always completed her missions, too. Skidding to a halt in fallen needles, she counted the volunteers surrounding the front loader and exhaled.

Jeanne pointed toward a pile of debris jammed against a fallen pine snag. Human bones protruded from a fallen tree's white, woody remains.

"Shit." Ann drew a sharp breath. Her heart raced. Tempering her knee-jerk reaction, she inhaled through her nose and exhaled through her mouth. Prescribed burns should help imperiled ecosystems, utilize eager volunteers, and clear her mental fog, but the flames shouldn't involve a murder mystery. Falling back on her training to deal with the deceased person rotting in Paps' back forty, she compartmentalized her concerns about coming home. "Anyone know who that is?"

Tat-tat-tat!

Turning, she scanned the crowd.

Two volunteers hid their faces from Baptiste's grisly discovery.

One held his cell phone and filmed.

She shot him a look and waited for him to stop being an ass.

Jeanne edged closer to Baptiste.

Paps cupped his hands around his mouth. "Burn's done for the day!"

Ann planted her hands on her hips. "He's right. House your tools, grab a coffee, and hang by the vans. The police will want statements. If you have outstanding warrants or reasons to avoid police questions, get lost before they arrive."

Nobody moved.

Interesting. Usually, at least one person runs.

Paps leaned out of the UTV and cleared his throat. "Who put you in charge?"

"It comes naturally." She scanned the crowd of anxious faces. "Sorry."

"I'm kidding." Paps put a hand on her shoulder. "Bad luck finding those remains."

His heavy, comforting touch reminded her of the bone-crushing hugs that cured her childhood ailments. She jerked her head toward the cottage. "I can take care of this mess. You go home and get comfortable."

Releasing her shoulder, he crossed his arms over his chest. "I ain't dead yet."

She pressed a kiss to his smooth cheek. "Okay. Stick around and take it easy."

He barked out a laugh. "Like that's an option."

"Easy's always an option." Pulling off her gloves, she retrieved her cell phone and dialed the police department. While she waited for the call to connect, she thought about the report she would make. The last time she lived in Hemlock, she would have spoken to the dispatcher in a shaky voice, but the armed forces forged her nerves. Reporting the discovery was her only obligation.

The call timer started. "Hemlock Police Department. Lucy speaking."

"Hi, Lucy, this is Ann Storey."

"Annie? Girl, I haven't heard from you in ages! Mayor Eddington said you were in town. Did you really expect—"

Ann cleared her throat. "Lucy, I'm in my grandfather's woods off Highway 2 and Burden. We've found human remains."

"Oh." Lucy switched on her official dispatcher voice. "I'll send officers."

"Thanks. I'll swing by before I leave town."

A pencil tapped on the other end of the line. "You do that."

Ann ended the call. She respected Lucy's professionalism, but she also wanted to throw her phone against the nearest pine tree. Whoever had the misfortune of dying in Paps' woods also took her attention off her grandfather.

Ricco jogged back with a hat on his head and

surveyed the group and their nervous chatter. Sweat wet his black hair, stuck his T-shirt to his muscled chest, and dripped into his frowning gaze. "What did I miss?"

Ann jerked her head toward the bones. "Someone had a bad night."

Crouching, Ricco examined the bones. "Anyone in town missing?"

She shrugged.

"Could be Lisette Hyde." Paps scratched his chin. "She worked at the Southern Hotel. Folks thought she had a falling-out with her boss and ran off."

Ann tilted her head. "I thought you didn't know anything about the remains."

Standing, Ricco pulled out his phone, quirked an eyebrow, and swiped right. "Lisette Hyde? Valor sent out a private investigator to probe her disappearance. No trail. I read the agent's report."

Paps toed a pinecone. "Could be."

"And nobody told me about a case in my hometown?" She expected Paps to issue commands, not skirt direct questions. Cancer diagnosis be damned, she wondered what else he kept secret. "Who hired the private investigator?"

"Nathan." Paps looked up. "Lisette was his assistant."

"You know the guy?" Ricco whistled. "No wonder Vince kept you in the dark."

"Brilliant." She strode toward the coffee dispenser and filled a stainless-steel tumbler with coffee. The drink's bitter, aromatic taste suppressed her mixed-up, tumultuous feelings, the cold, damp morning, and the tragic, macabre discovery. Dousing her annoyance would require a second cup. Vince had every right to keep the Lisette investigation low-key, but he could have mentioned the missing person case out of professional courtesy.

If society volunteers watched her, they would see a leader in control, but if one more person mentioned Nathan's name, she would toss her tumbler at their head.

Jeanne walked up. "Did you used to babysit me?"

"Hell, no." Hearing a Southern drawl creep out, Ann cleared her throat. Mimicking local speech patterns helped with assimilation, but she wanted nothing to do with Hemlock. "If I babysat you, then you'd be better behaved."

Jeanne laughed and picked a spec of dirt from her thumbnail. "Who's Nathan?"

Ann grunted and clutched her drink. As soon as she helped Paps beat his cancer, she would reprioritize her Valor assignments. In the meantime, she should play nice with the natives, Nathan excluded. "An ex-boyfriend."

"Damn." Jeanne shook her head. "It's always the quiet ones."

"Nathan didn't do this."

Pulling back her chin, Jeanne tilted her head. "Girl, you sure?"

Ann ended the discussion with a curt nod. The handsome asshole was many things, but he wasn't a killer. At least, he hadn't been. If Jeanne doubted her assessment, she'd air her skepticism with Baptiste.

Paps signaled the volunteers. "Come on, y'all. Get comfortable. Turn on some music. We'll be here for an hour, at least. If my old joints need a break, yours probably do, too."

While individuals responded to police inquires, Ann and Jeanne discovered a shared love of hot sauces and upbeat remixes. Baptiste finally lured away his girlfriend. Ann bullshitted with Ricco and won twenty bucks off a sports betting app.

Spending a day outside wasn't bad. A gopher tortoise ambled past a cleared spot, Bachman's sparrows traded calls, and crime scene photographers documented bleached bones on the forest floor. Life was rarely perfect, and the crew's disposable booties, bio suits, and single-use gloves lent the scene added gravitas. Mother Nature could reduce a person to his or her essence, but specialists could still catalog the transformation.

Putting away her phone, she watched Jeanne give a statement to Hemlock's lead detective, a swarthy man named Mike Sullivan. His police cruiser blocked the drive, and its lights flashed through the fog like red and blue strobe lights. The effect was overkill, but at least he turned off the sirens. It must be a slow day in Acadiana.

Ricco jerked his chin toward the detective. "You date him, too?"

She tilted her head. "Don't you have a flight to catch?"

He shrugged. "Vince told me to sit tight for a day."

"Remind me to kick his ass."

Ricco laughed.

She strode toward Jeanne and the detective.

Ricco followed.

"Jeanne pronounced like *pick-AHN*," the volunteer said. "Calloway. Jeanne Calloway."

Ann bit back a smile. Southerners pronounced the

nut's name every which way to Sunday. Jeanne's breathy, confident phrasing summoned summer humidity and smooth jazz. She kind of liked the sassy brat.

"She's hot," Ricco said.

"She's taken."

He shrugged. "For now."

Detective Sullivan glanced up from his notebook. "Any relation to Judge Calloway?"

"She's my iron-horse mother." Jeanne winked. "You know her?"

Slipping an index finger into his collar, Detective Sullivan nodded.

Ann smiled. Southern roots ran deep.

Detective Sullivan flipped through his notes. "How long have you been a volunteer with the Cajun Prairie Preservation Society?"

"A year." Jeanne glanced toward the skeletal remains. "Do you think those bones have been there long?"

Ann put together her own estimate. Once a longleaf pine died, foraging woodpeckers tore away the tree's protective bark. As the coating sloughed off, the elements weathered the pine's tender wood. She would bet money the tree fell during the last hurricane season, which meant the snag became a morbid hiding place less than six months ago. Her guess meant little to a police investigation. She would keep quiet and discuss her hunches with Ricco.

"Years?" Jeanne wrapped a braid around her finger.

Detective Sullivan shrugged. "With outdoor exposure, human remains can move through the decay cycle much faster that you would expect. Skeletons don't appear until four to six months after death, but years could have passed. Forensics will formulate an estimate."

Ann traded doubtful expressions with Paps. Raising her eyebrows, she considered amending the detective's window of discovery.

Paps shook his head.

Fine. This was his town.

Jeanne shuddered. "All those nights in the rain, and their kin had no idea."

Baptiste put a hand on the small of Jeanne's back.

She leaned into his touch and pressed her side against his shoulder.

Ann stepped forward to deflect the detective's attention. "Detective—"

He lifted a hand. "We're almost done here."

Biting her tongue, she stared into the pines. Before discovering the bones, she and the society members had burnt less than an acre of understory. Hemlock's police wouldn't release the crime scene before the burn window closed. Longleafs could live for three hundred years, but another meant fire's cleansing breath would have more to burn. She hoped the grasses, sedges, rushes, orchids, asters, and pitcher plants hung on. Could Paps? Crossing her arms over her chest, she kicked a pinecone into the underbrush and listened to the detective's insipid questions.

Gravel flew.

Narrowing her gaze, she jerked her head.

An electric sedan tore down Paps' road. Reddish dust trailed the vehicle's chrome bumper like antiquated exhaust.

Ricco whistled. "Nice car."

She ignored him.

The driver parked, threw open the door, and rounded the hood.

"For the love of..." Ann tipped back her head and stared into the pine canopy. After twenty years, her bruised heart still recognized Nathan. His handsome face graced the cover of countless regional magazines, but his shaggy, rock-and-roll hair hadn't changed a bit. The strands were as black as night and as glossy as a raven's wing. The effect made him boyish and brooding in equal turns. She couldn't care less about his ostrich boots, crisp jeans, or white button-down. His achingly familiar face clenched her heart. "Anything else coming my way?"

The woodpecker's staccato song ignored her.

Dropping her head, she straightened her shoulders. Bones lay tangled between a pale, stripped trunk and leafless, winter shrubs. She still breathed. Standing fifteen feet from Nathan shouldn't be a problem. Glimpsed television appearances suggested he fixed his teeth, worked with a voice coach, and glossed over his youthful misdeeds, but he was still a hick from Hemlock.

Detective Sullivan chased down Nathan.

"Um, you forgot to mention we're talking about Nathan Charlet. He's hot and famous." Jeanne stepped closer and rested a hand on Ann's shoulder. "You know him?"

"In a way." Ann tugged her earlobe. Nathan took her to senior prom, but he knocked up Flannery Timmons at an after-party. The transgression was more than Ann could forgive. His life-altering mistake broke her heart, and misspent youths shouldn't leave scars. She worked her jaw. "It was a long time ago."

"I bet."

"Is that *the* Nathan?" Ricco asked. "Will you introduce me?"

"Introduce yourself, ass-wipe." She shrugged off Jeanne's friendly posture and jabbed a finger into Ricco's chest. "Don't you think you should have told me someone I might have known had gone missing?"

He brushed away her finger. "Why? To get tangled in a place where you don't belong? That's why Vince told me to keep my mouth shut. I followed the boss' orders."

She mentally cancelled Vince's holiday present.

Nathan accomplished a lot, but his platinum credit card couldn't influence her life or dim her heartache. She served her country with distinction and honor, and she reserved the right to hold his vanities against him. Who had time for pretty men?

Compressing her lips, she drew deep, steadying breaths. This day was bound to happen. She hadn't expected to relive high school during an active police investigation, but she would get through it. Instead of fuming, she summoned a polite smile.

Nathan marched past her and approached the forensics team. "Show me the remains."

Ann marked his resonant voice. It had deepened with time.

Detective Sullivan skirted Nathan and planted his hands on his hips. "Stay out of their way."

Nathan flared his nostrils. "Those might be Lisette's remains."

"And you'll help us identify the victim? Count her

bones? Determine how she died?" Detective Sullivan cocked his head and waited.

Nathan paled.

Suppressing a laugh, Ann chewed her bottom lip. Was the scent of death too much for his delicate sensibilities? He needed more than lauded design credentials to solve a murder case. Shaking her head, she turned to Paps. "You have anything else to share?"

Paps shrugged. "I didn't take the rumors for much, but folks said she ran off with a few thousand dollars in antiques and left him high and dry." He dropped his voice. "They were a thing, I heard."

Her animosity toward Nathan ebbed a degree. "That's tough."

"Might not be her. Laborers move through these parts looking for short-term work. Could be anybody."

"You're right." Rubbing a chill from her upper arms, she watched Nathan and Detective Sullivan square off. Officers crunched leaf litter, snapped pictures, and unrolled crime scene tape. Grief would flavor the town gossip for weeks. The tragedy of Lisette's death wasn't her problem, but Paps was. Keeping him comfortable had to be good for his health. "Have you had any water?"

"If I needed a nurse, I would have called Lindsey." Shaking his head, Paps turned the key in the UTV and motored off.

Jeanne approached, holding a phone. "You okay, girl?"

"That's my line." Ann exhaled. "You holding up?"

Jeanne shuddered. "I don't know if crime scene investigation is my bag. How do the police deal with this shit all day? No wonder they're terse. Those bones will haunt my dreams."

"Mine, too." Ann spent sleepless nights reliving deployments. The desert's whistling winds and looming dunes were never part of her plan, but they might have saved her from Nathan's betrayal.

"I dunno what's going on with you and Nathan Charlet"—Jeanne wiggled her eyebrows—"but everyone in the South knows that man. The question is, how well do you know him?"

Ann worked her jaw. Before the Academy and Nathan's fame, she imagined sharing a little house at the edge of the grasslands. His cheating left her dreams as ravaged as Louisiana's ecosystems. She escaped to the Navy and reclaimed her pride. What if life hadn't turned out the way she planned? She didn't need to ruin Jeanne's outlook with her jaded regrets. "We went to school together. Don't let Baptiste meet him. The pair would be insufferable."

Jeanne laughed and swiped right on her phone screen. "Noted, but I want you to hear me spin. Come to the club next week and dance. You'll meet someone hotter than Charlet."

"I doubt it." The acres between the Atchafalaya and Sabine rivers were as unique and special as the days she spent in Nathan's ripped arms. Too bad, like the early European settlers, he'd burned those dreams to the ground. His ancestors destroyed the prairie to plant rice, and Nathan raised his kid. She glanced at Jeanne's finger poised above her phone screen. "I don't know how long I'll be in town."

"Long enough to wait for a body identification." Ricco lifted Jeanne's phone, typed in Ann's number, and returned it. "Long enough to dance."

Ann glared and looked between Jeanne and Baptiste, whose turn with the detective would soon end.

Ricco lifted his palms. "A man can dream."

She shook her head. What else did she have to do? Look after Paps and convince Vince to pause her workload. Hemlock's citizens had a way of muddling through life. She could do better. "Great, we'll drive into New Orleans and hit the club."

"Excellent!" Jeanne offered a hand. "I'll text my number."

Seeing no other gracious option, Ann smiled.

Jeanne linked arms with Baptiste and walked toward the vans.

Ann envied her easy gait. Jeanne had to be in her late twenties, but she retained an upbeat, infectious outlook. Was Ann the only person who'd turned into an old salt? She blew out her breath. If the bones belonged to Nathan's assistant, she would order a flower arrangement and acknowledge his loss, but she wouldn't seek out his company. Gracious living had its limits.

Ricco offered her water.

Twisting off the cap, she saluted him and downed the sweet, cool water. Passing through Hemlock hadn't been her choice, but she would focus on the things she could control. "As soon as the investigation ends, and the police release the crime scene, we'll sort out this mess."

Ricco rubbed his cheek. "We always do."

She butted his shoulder in camaraderie.

Jeanne looked over her shoulder. "You comin'?"

"Yes, ma'am." Ann crushed the water bottle. "I finish what I start."

Chapter Three

The full moon cast long, eerie shadows outside Nathan's bedside window. His linen sheets littered the floor. Shadows traversed the white, plaster ceiling and tangled with a wrought-iron chandelier. Lisette, with her zest for life, should still be alive and helping him run his design businesses.

After Ann's crew uncovered human remains and called the police, news of the discovery spread through town like a brush fire. In the last year, only one person from Hemlock went missing. He'd felt his stomach empty, seen spots, and rushed to the discovery site. He wished he'd abstained.

The skeleton, dusted with white ash, rested in the winter mud like oxidized, lead weights. The bones could have drowned him in the bayou's moss-draped, murky depths. He would have deserved his fate. Helpless, he stood by while the evidence team bagged human remains and took them to a cold, sterile locker. He wasn't a member of the police force. He was a regional influencer who flexed hometown graciousness. If the bones belong to Lisette, then he and Hemlock had failed to keep her safe.

Tossing his pillow to the polished, wide-plank floors, he flung an arm over his eyes and wondered if exhaustion would erase his regrets. Instead of relief, he replayed Ann's cold shoulder. He'd driven to the crime scene, knowing he would see her, but he hadn't known her hardened beauty would gut-punch him. Had she dreaded seeing him? The notion grieved him, and he dragged a hand down his face.

Enough! Throwing his legs over the side of the bed, he stood and stretched his back. Hemlock's churchgoers could hunger for intrigue and assess his haggardness, but they could also get on with their days. Maybe the bones belong to someone other than Lisette.

Padding down the stairs, he flipped the kitchen light switch. White walls, cypress headers, delicate marble, and high-end appliances created a clean backdrop for creative meals. Yellow daffodils in a green glass vase came from Evie, his twenty-one-year-old daughter.

He turned on the coffeemaker. The high-end appliance cycled through a rinse program before brewing a cup. Adding half-and-half to a mug and sliding the vessel under the machine's spout, he dialed a strong, bitter cup of coffee.

The machine spat steam.

"You know, a pot would make more sense," Evie said.

He turned and extended an arm.

She tucked herself against his chest and laid her head on his shoulder. "We drink enough coffee to float a boat, and then some."

Chuckling, he pressed a kiss to her rose-gold hair. She had his green eyes and an engagement ring, but she still smelled like his sweet-cheeked baby. He'd bathed her in a chipped porcelain bathtub and dreamed of making her life easy. Reaching for the first mug of coffee, he offered it.

She straightened, took the mug, and sipped. "I recant. This is damn good coffee."

He summoned a frown. "Watch your language."

"As if I could watch my language." She dropped into a chair at the pale-green breakfast table and batted her eyelashes. "You taught me all the best words."

Reaching for a second mug, he smiled. As if what? As if the 1990s came roaring back into vogue and stayed? As if he would soon lose her to matrimony and New Orleans' sprawling suburbs? Hell, he'd offered to set her up in New York City at a reputable gallery. She'd laughed. Instead of ruminating, he rubbed a hand through his tangled hair, closed the cabinet, and turned his back on his regrets. "When you hit your thumb with a hammer, you can swear until you're blue. In the meantime, watch your language. You're too smart for exasperation."

She snorted and planted her feet on a second chair. "Fair enough."

Her simple acknowledgement steadied him.

She'd blown through her BA in Painting and Printmaking from College of Charleston in Charleston, fallen in love with Huanlong, a medical student, and returned to Louisiana to build a life while Huanlong did his medical residency at a New Orleans hospital. She would build her studio practice and lean on Nathan's lifestyle magazine and resale shop until she no longer needed him. What more could he ask for?

Gripping the warm mug, he looked toward his hotel and imagined his next act. The booming business revitalized Hemlock and anchored his impact on the small town. His older brother ran the plant, but Nathan was part of another generation of Charlet men keeping

Hemlock solvent.

What had success cost him? Flannery raised Evie. He grew his businesses. What right did he have to police his daughter's language? Maybe he should have abandoned his pursuit of success to witness Evie's real-time milestones. Too bad, he missed that chance, but he could only look forward. He cleared his throat. "Why're you awake this early?"

"I could ask you the same thing." She cleaned her nails and looked up. "Anything you want to get off your chest? You look like shit."

"Evie," he growled.

"No offense, Dad. I have some concealer you can borrow."

He set the mug on the marble countertop.

"I mean, you want to talk about the reason you ran out of the hotel yesterday?" She tilted her head. "Or chitchat about the bones they found in the Storey woods that might belong to your assistant? Anything?"

He exhaled and considered the simple joys of life on the road. "Hemlock's publicist doesn't have the bandwidth to counter a murder investigation. I hope the bones belong to anyone but Lisette. She might still be alive…somewhere."

"But"—she chewed her bottom lip—"they're probably her remains?"

He shrugged and dropped into a pale-green chair. "Can't say."

"Can't?" She raised her eyebrows. "Or won't?"

He kicked out his legs and crossed his ankles. "Baby, I just don't know."

She let her shoulders slump.

He took her hand and squeezed it. Looking back,

her teenage years were a hoot. She'd raised so much cane, or Cain, if someone outside Louisiana wanted to be picky, he was lucky she dodged a criminal record. She had enough drama in her pinkie bones to outshine anyone onstage. If her art career fell apart, she would make an excellent actress. She wore flamboyant outfits and nurtured emerging artists. He should follow her lead and let honesty rule his responses, but he still wanted to protect her innocence.

He released her hand and spread his fingers against the painted wood. "Until the police ID the body and arrest the murderer, I'm in the dark. I hope the gossip is wrong. The habitat kids could have found an old cow bone and made a grave mistake, but they didn't. Someone's dead and someone's crying, but we don't know who." He leaned back and let his legs spread. His speech was pretty good. His warning ought to buy him a few days to get his shit together. "Be patient, sweetie."

She stood and dropped her mug into the farmhouse sink. The porcelain clash rattled in the still kitchen. "Daddy, you're lying."

He blinked like a lamb.

"I saw how shaken you were. No dinner. Half a bottle of scotch."

Evie was a charming sprite, but his head ached too much to battle with a warring imp. He rubbed a hand over his face. "You're right, the bones probably belong to Lisette. The forensics lead said the proportions were female."

She dropped her shoulders. "Bummer."

He stood to pull her into a hug.

She bypassed him and pulled eggs from the

refrigerator. "You're still insufferable…"

Ignoring her mutterings, he looked out the kitchen window and watched dawn tinge the sky a light-pink color. Without a beautiful daughter slamming cabinets and clanking china, this time of day was peaceful. Raising his coffee mug to his lips and sipping, he imagined a rich omelet. Crawfish and green onions would go a long way toward remedying his day.

"So, you also saw your old flame?"

He choked and slapped his chest. "Come again?"

Cracking an egg against a glass bowl, she smiled. "Ann? Your high school girlfriend? The woman you were with before Mom? I heard she was back in town. I've always wanted to meet her."

He scratched his stubble. "Have you, now?"

He'd seen Ann's cold shoulder and the defensive brute who stood beside her. She was still as noble and fierce as the day she'd walked onto the football field and thrown her pom-poms. If the high school administrators wouldn't let Samantha "Sam" Eddington play football, then Ann Storey wouldn't captain the cheer team. Sam took the field, and Ann took his heart.

He'd known her since childhood, but when he glimpsed her righteous indignation from the fifty-yard line, he felt his heart swell beneath his football pads. The other women in the stands suddenly mattered less. She was a furious, blonde cheerleader with piercing blue eyes and a stubborn streak a mile long. Courting her had been a cat-and-mouse game that led to prom. Then, he'd fumbled big time.

The timing of their reunion couldn't be worse. He'd failed Flannery, his deceased wife, and Lisette, his missing assistant. Who else could he fail? Locking Evie in a tower seemed like a prudent response, but a tower would sink into the Louisiana mud. Maybe she and her fiancé would like an early honeymoon.

Evie lifted the egg bowl and judged the volume. "Is she still pretty?"

"Prettier." Blonde curls, blue eyes, and a heart-shaped mouth made her a cute kid and a beautiful adult. As she grew, life toughened her cuteness. She was two months younger than him, but her lean, muscled frame and intense, honed gaze warned strangers to stay clear. He was far from a stranger and would still respect her wishes. "Not that it matters. Our relationship was a lifetime ago."

Evie laid waste to another egg. "I still want to meet her. I've heard about her for years. She's such a badass. Who wants to be a debutante when you can be a Navy captain and a special operative? Can she come over for dinner?"

Maybe he *should* look into that tower. He rested his chin in a palm and let his worries for Lisette take second place to his surprise at seeing Ann. For decades, he woke at strange hours and wondered where she might be and what horrors she faced. Guidry, her grandfather, dropped declassified details at community events, but Nathan couldn't linger or ask questions. He cared for Evie and Flannery and made his fortune, but Ann haunted his dreams

"The whole town's talking about her return." Evie closed the egg carton and turned. "I mean, she found the body. What are the chances?"

He rubbed his temples. "Evie, you'll meet her soon enough. Instead of running off to New Orleans for the big Mardi Gras parades, why don't you stick around a few days? Ping your wedding vendors and stay close."

She scratched her scalp. "Um...."

Did they have thesauruses at art school? He raised his head. "How about fixing the lobby mural? I've never seen a spoonbill with three legs."

Evie snorted and pulled a fork from the drawer. Whisking the eggs in the bowl, she added cream and seasonings. "If you hadn't rushed the opening, then I would have painted the whole mural."

"From South Carolina?"

She added Parmesan cheese. "Over a long weekend."

"Right." Pushing back his chair, he stood and stretched his arms over his head. "Well, you can paint the next one."

"The next one? How many hotels can Hemlocks support?" She turned on the gas stove and let an enameled cast iron skillet heat. "You remaking the entire town? Opening an airport?"

He scratched his chin and wondered if he'd done enough. "Maybe."

She raised her eyebrows. "Maybe?"

After learning of Flannery's pregnancy, he remade his life to generate income. A random newspaper interview led to a syndicated column. His precocious, jaded takes on antiques were too funny to confine to newsprint. A store, a television show, and wealth followed. Evie had never known financial distress. He'd never doubted how much he loved her.

Then again, once she stopped wearing pigtails and looking at him with hero worship, he noticed her sass. Must have gotten that trait from Flannery. He crossed his arms over his chest. "Give your Daddy a break and fix the mural?"

"Don't play that card." She poured the eggs into the skillet. Steam rose. "You're thirty-eight years old."

"Almost thirty-nine."

She checked the omelet with a thin, metal spatula. "Maybe I'll throw you a surprise party. Cocktails and charcuterie in the hotel bar. A jazz band." She looked up. "You can wear one of your expensive-ass suits and flatter politicians."

"Fuck me." Shaking his head, he stood and headed toward his room. "You eat the first omelet," he yelled over his shoulder. "After I shower, I'll make my own breakfast."

"Afraid I'll poison you?" she called back.

"Afraid you'll audition for reality television."

She laughed. The refrigerator door banged closed. "Can I use all the crab?"

"Brat!" He padded down the wide-plank hallway. Remaking Hemlock into a day-trip destination for New Orleans tourists wasn't his dream, but having Evie in his life made everything worthwhile. When someone asked him what he wanted to be as an adult, he said he wanted to be a successful father. Having accomplished his goals earlier than he anticipated, he wondered what came next.

Chapter Four

The morning after finding the human remains, Ann sat in Sam's living room and stared at the ugly bison head mounted on her wall. Paps dared Sam to run for mayor and offered the head as a prize. His rifle-wielding ancestor allegedly shot the animal in Kisatchie National Forest. He said the trophy was a good reminder someone had to keep townsfolk in line. They were liable to shoot anything that moved.

Sam took his dare, won the mayoral election, and mounted the taxidermy head where pedestrians could see it through her front windows.

Ann approved. After five minutes of awkward silence and Ann's apology for staying away too long, their shared history anchored their comfort with each other.

"Where do you think he found that head?" Sam swiped a thumb across her phone screen. "Online auction?"

"Possibly." She doubted Paps' trophy was Louisiana's last bison. He probably bought the monstrosity at one of his railroad conferences. She couldn't remember when the shaggy beast arrived, so maybe her kin held the piece since the 1870s. Standing, she stretched her back and considered patting the shaggy beast. "I hope some jerk, Texas cowboy sold that bison for a few bucks. One day, Paps will confess."

Sam laughed and set her glider in motion. "Like, on his deathbed."

The image hit Ann like a sledgehammer. She swayed.

Jumping to her feet, Sam gripped her elbow and steadied her. "I'm so sorry! I didn't mean it like that. It's…"

"I know." Ann turned and folded herself against Sam's ample chest and welcoming arms. Her friend smelled as sweet and familiar as she had in high school, and the familiarity comforted her. Everyone died. If she let Paps' diagnosis paralyze her, she couldn't enjoy his remaining time or the opportunity to rekindle old friendships. Pulling back, she braced a hand on Sam's shoulder. "I appreciate the moment, but why do you still wear that awful perfume?"

Sam feigned slapping her.

She ducked the blow and headed toward the kitchen for a snack. Down the street, a band played zydeco tunes before the Southern Hotel. Pulling back the curtains, she watched hotel guests mill between green, hanging ferns and polished, brass fixtures. Uniformed employees hung purple, green, and gold bunting for Tuesday's parade. If her life had turned out differently, she might be a carefree traveler sipping mimosas before the big show.

"Impressive, isn't it?" Sam adjusted her short, spiky hair. "Magazines tout how Nathan restored the hotel's gracious character, but they omit he offset forty percent of his construction costs by leveraging Louisiana and Federal subsidies. Historic tax credits for the win!"

"Smart." She dropped the curtains and rolled her

head above her shoulders. Her muscles felt tight, but replaying one's life in their childhood bed could do that to a person. "Good for him and Hemlock."

"You see the boutique next door? It's a stylish showroom with custom furniture, fine interiors, and luxe wedding gifts. If I could afford to buy the space, I would move in."

She raised an eyebrow. "The mayor doesn't get discounts?"

"No!" Sam grinned. "The mayor takes inspiration from his showroom and orders Internet knockoffs. Let New Orleans' bougie, uptown bitches pay showroom prices and Hemlock tax rates."

Laughing, she braced her palms against the countertop and savored Sam's homey kitchen and affectionate gossip. The cottage's cypress cabinets and ceramic cookie jars were no longer popular, but Sam kept them for her own reasons. Ann didn't really care why. If she lifted the cookie jar lid, she might find edibles and chocolate chip cookies. Sam could make her own calls. Ann was thrilled to have an excuse to see her old friend.

"When the fashion-forward boutique opened with men's and women's clothing under one roof, you wouldn't believe how much people gossiped. What, like the patrons would get busy in the changing rooms?" Sam shook her head. "The manager, Davies, is a trans man. He rocks a shaggy white-boy mullet so ambiguous that shoppers see whomever they want to see. He has impeccable style."

Sam's loyalties had obviously shifted, and Nathan had assembled a four-acre complex. Left unchecked, Sam might rename the town after him. Ann would be the sole detractor. "And the big barn across the street?"

"It's an events center." Sam slipped on her shoes. "The Evangeline."

She rolled her eyes. *This town and that poem. Who had time to sit under a tree?*

"You know that's his daughter's name, right? Evangeline. She's getting married there next month. The center has room for a thousand guests."

She whistled.

"Events like that will keep the hotel full, the restaurants buzzing, and the traffic streaming." Sam kissed her fingers from her glossy lips. *M'wah!* "Dat boy's my hero!"

Ann lifted a palm. "Can we talk about the murder? The election? Your political consultants?" She jerked her head toward a luxe, leather purse that cost more than Sam made in a month. "Who you're shagging?"

Sam tilted her head and crossed her arms over her chest. "You're still hot for him, aren't you? Like a teenager when her crush gets too close. You'll look anywhere but at the specimen before you."

She rubbed her temple. Old friends had their downsides, like calling her out after twenty minutes of niceties. "You mean I'm the queen of avoidance?"

Sam chuckled.

Her phone rang. Fishing it from her back pocket, she swiped to accept Paps' call. "Yep?"

"I heard from Detective Sullivan. They ID'd the body."

She held her breath.

"Nathan was right to come running. The bones belong to his manager, Lisette. To my way of thinking, Nathan's suspect number one. Never did like that kid."

"You told me to go to his spa!" She rolled her eyes. Nathan might be a privileged jerk, but she doubted he was a murderer.

"That was before I decided to tell you I had cancer!"

"About that—"

"I'm an indecisive, old man."

"Bullshit." Shaking her head, she glanced at Sam. *Lisette*, she mouthed.

Sam raised her eyebrows and pantomimed firing a gun.

Ann shrugged. Streaming series made criminal investigations look cut and dry. She could sell her Valor exploits to a production company and walk away with a fat check, but the victims would haunt her. Linking arms with Sam, she pulled her toward the back door where a path led through the woods to Paps' house. "Did Lisette have family around town?"

"Lafayette," Paps said.

"Detective Sullivan will have someone deliver the news." She opened the back door and swatted mosquitoes from the shadowed doorframe.

Sam held open the door.

Ann stepped on the back porch. "How did you hear?"

Paps cleared his throat. "Duckling, this town can't keep secrets. You want a covert operation? Take another assignment with Valor."

"Right." She pulled in a deep, cool breath. Migrating birds called through the morning mist, and a squirrel mined mulch near a crepe myrtle.

Sam mimed iced coffee and turned back toward the kitchen.

Ann pressed her phone against her shoulder and scratched her neck. "Thanks for letting me know about Lisette. I'll, um…"

"Stay with Sam. Lindsey's here. I'll see you later."

"Okay, love you." Ending the call, she wondered if she could slip Lindsey a bonus. In addition to his daily tasks, he convinced Ricco to rearrange the cottage furniture and make the layout more conducive to Paps' treatments. Keeping Ricco busy was no small feat.

Sam returned with two glasses of creamy, iced coffee.

Ann accepted a glass and sipped the bittersweet brew. Wiping away an errant drop, she channeled relaxation. Paps wouldn't expire today, but how had Lisette ended up in his woods? She snorted. Detective Sullivan's investigation wasn't her problem. She was a former Navy officer and a private operative, not a procedure-obsessed, small-town cop.

Paps called back. "Also, Nathan's hosting a celebration of her life. Six o'clock. Free drinks and small bites. I told him you'd be there."

"What?" She held the phone away from her face and examined it. The call timer climbed. "You intimated he's a murderer."

"Hard to murder someone with a room full of witnesses. He needs all the support he can get." Paps cleared his throat. "You owe him that, don't you?"

"I don't owe him shit." Her history in this town lingered like a bad aftertaste. Small-town niceties like potlucks and wakes endured, but Sam's ceramic cookie jar held cannabis-laced cookies. She knew which choice to make, but she slurped her coffee like a middle-aged office worker who couldn't bear to turn on the computer.

Sam raised her eyebrows.

She rubbed a hand over her face. Hiding was never the right option, but playing nice with her ex was a tough ask. He'd flown past her at the crime scene without acknowledgment. If she avoided him for the remainder of her life, she would die a happy woman. "Nathan won't miss me."

Paps grunted. "He'd do it for you."

He'd done something, all right. His betrayal sent her into the armed forces where she traveled the world and had a thriving career, but history haunted people, too. Caught between Sam's meddling and Paps' guilt, she thought of opponents she faced. Hemlock's citizens gave no quarter during the Civil War. She wouldn't, either. "I'll be there."

"Get showered and dressed. Ricco had your suitcase delivered."

She switched to a video call and waited until Paps' neatly combed, white hair and trimmed, full eyebrows came into resolution. Lindsey stood behind him, arms crossed and swapping jokes with Ricco like the pair were old friends.

"Yes-s-s?" Paps drawled.

"This isn't a date." She narrowed her gaze and waited until all three men watched Paps' phone screen. "If I discover my grandfather killed Lisette and dumped her in the pines to get Nathan involved, Hemlock won't need Detective Sullivan. I'll kill him myself and mount his head beside that leering bison he loves so much."

Lindsey paled.

Ricco doubled over in laughter.

"Roger." Paps saluted and ended the call.

Fighting a smile, Sam sipped her coffee.

Ann shoved her phone into her back pocket. Sipping a cold beer in Nathan's hotel lobby and making small talk with bereaved citizens wouldn't kill her, but she had to be practical. Wearing heels would torture her feet.

Sam set her glass on the porch rail. "What are you thinking?"

Ann glanced at her feet. Three-inch heels would put her toned ass on full display. Hemlock's citizens also expected the shoes. When a person engaged locals in a war zone, assimilation went a long way toward easing missteps. She made eye contact with Sam. "I need to borrow shoes."

"Is that all?" Sam rolled her eyes. "Girl, I have fifty pairs."

"I know you do." Ann grinned. As soon as she left the memorial, she would return to cargo pants, button-up shirts, and wide-brimmed sun hats. Anyone who cared about her double standards could join her for an infamous Navy SEAL workout. She wasn't masochist enough to enter that training program, but bless their hearts, the country needed those who did.

"What else do you need? Pearls? Clothes?"

"Hardly." She owned a few pieces of jewelry, but she could also fire her Sig Sauer P320 9mm pistol with lethal accuracy. Setting her empty glass besides Sam's on the porch rail, she stretched her arms over her head. "Something in my closet will fit."

"Let me get my stuff." Sam gathered both glasses. "We'll get dressed at your house."

Ann tilted her head. "Why mine?"

With a snort, Sam threw open the cottage door and

held the door with her hip. "To keep you from bolting. Inside, Captain!"

"Bitch." Shaking her head, Ann reentered Sam's shadowed living room and wished she drove the rental car or borrowed Paps' truck. Instead, she walked through the cottage toward Sam's SUV. The keys sat in the cup holder. Nobody in Hemlock would brazenly steal the mayor's vehicle. Then again, she never expected to a find dumped bodies amidst pine trees, either. Checking the SUV's mirrors, she waited.

Sam threw a duffle into the back and claimed the SUV's passenger seat.

Ann started the engine.

"So…" Sam said.

"Don't even start." Glancing in the rearview mirror, Ann pulled a pine needle from her tangled hair and put the SUV in Reverse. Sam's eye for makeup would give her a confidence boost and allow her to spend time with Paps and her friend. "Thanks for coming over, but this isn't a makeover."

"Colorado doesn't seem like a place for makeovers." Sam waved to a neighbor. "How do you get laid out there?"

"I manage." Ann navigated the narrow, backcountry roads. "Efficiently."

Sam snorted. "Well, nothing about tonight will be efficient. It'll be gracious and lovely. We're talking tenderloin, crab, chargrilled oysters, spinach-and-artichoke dip…the whole nine yards."

"Right." Nathan's generosity couldn't resurrect his employee. Some of life's disappointments were too painful to buffer with sweet, tender crabmeat. If gluttony eased pain, she would have downed enough hot sauce and raw oysters to sink an aircraft carrier. "I'm sure it'll be lovely."

Dodging a slow-moving turtle, she increased her speed. Road noise soothed her misgivings. She could blame Nathan for everything that went wrong, but he also had a hand in everything she had. Who would have expected her to follow in Paps' footsteps and tour the world?

A cat darted across the road.

Slamming the truck's brakes, she gripped the steering wheel, muscles tight against the sudden stop. Most people would hit the cat and spare the SUV, but toweling cat guts off the chrome bumper sounded less fun than wearing eyeliner. She turned toward Sam. "You okay?"

Sam adjusted an air-conditioning vent to blow more chilled air. "Mostly. Pulled my neck a little." She rubbed her shoulder. "Crazy animals."

"Mostly works." Easing off the brakes, Ann drove through town and passed Nathan's hotel. Her first night back, she dodged the large, white, brick building and its implications. Tonight, she would step through its doors. "I should have sent a bouquet when I had a chance."

Sam planted her feet on the dash. "It'll be fine. It would always be fine. You and Nathan"—she shook head—"nobody believed it happened."

She snorted. "Until Flannery's belly popped."

Sam adjusted the vent. "By then, you were long gone."

Ann drove. Sam was right about one thing. Ann knew how to accomplish her goals and slip away into the night where no one would see her tears.

Chapter Five

Nathan adjusted his emerald-green silk tie in the walnut-framed, dresser-top mirror. His favorite boots lay beside the bed. Their pebbled, ostrich skin and buttery leather felt like home, but he left them on the wide-plank floor. Dignity demanded dress shoes.

"Daddy!" Evie called.

"Sit tight. I'm coming down." Stepping back from the mirror, he ran his hands through his hair, slipped into his navy suit jacket, adjusted his belt, and tied his shoes. A gold watch sat on the dresser. He slid the timepiece on his wrist and buckled the watch's leather band. If Mama caught him sporting a smart watch at a formal event, she would tan his hide. He would let her. Lisette deserved the dignity of a well-dressed man. With a final glance in the mirror, he left his bedroom.

Evie stood at the stair landing, wearing a sage-green sheath dress.

Black was for funerals. Her rose-gold hair cascaded over her shoulder in loose curls, and her dainty, gold earrings and sparkling engagement ring shone beneath the hall lights. For a while, he wondered how he begat a light-haired daughter, then he found he didn't care. Descending the flight, he pressed a kiss against her soft cheek and resisted the urge to crush her to his chest. "Where's Huanlong?"

She took his arm. "At the hotel bar."

"Smart man." Holding open the cottage's door, he waited for her to cross the threshold. Huanlong had a massive, yellow dragon tattooed along his forearm. Born in the Year of the Dragon, he projected the strength, power, and success patients expected from a neurosurgeon. The kid would be wildly successful. Evie loved him, but he was so full of himself, he tipped his hand. Nathan privately called him an eager beaver, but who was he to pass character judgments? When Lisette ghosted him and took a few thousand dollars of antiques as severance pay, he felt betrayed. Then, he filed an insurance claim and hired Valor to look into her disappearance. Obviously, he should have done more to hone his skills at character assessment.

"Sorry about Lisette, for like the thousandth time." Evie dropped his arm. "I liked her."

"Me, too." A hand hovering at the small of Evie's back, he escorted her along the covered walkway connecting the house to the hotel. Mondo grass grew between poured-concrete paving stones. From a guest's perspective, the two buildings seamlessly flowed together, but guest keycard permissions stopped short of his home. "All the gilt accents and clever touches remind me of her. She never met a bedazzled frame she didn't love."

"Were you two ever"—Evie cleared her throat—"um, more than coworkers?"

"You mean, were we intimate? Swingers? Did we like to smash and clap cheeks?"

Evie gasped. Her cheeks colored.

"No, Baby Girl. We were good friends." Lisette would have laughed at Evie's trepidation. She'd known Evie since she wore braces. No wonder Lisette's death and disappearance hit Evie hard. He would have to be more sensitive. He opened the hotel door. "She would have loved how you fixed that three-legged spoonbill with a strand of Mardi Gras beads."

Turning her head toward the lobby mural, Evie grinned. "It looks good, doesn't it?"

"It looks great." He pressed a kiss to her hair. She was too young to marry, too sweet to compete against burnished housewives, and too talented to confine her art to Hemlock. She was also her own woman. He could promote her art in the hotel lobby and give her a soft landing, but he couldn't fight her battles. "Go find Huanlong and enjoy the party. Lisette loved your impish laugh."

She waved and walked off.

Squaring his shoulders, he approached a circular, marble table hosting a large arrangement of flowers and a framed photograph of Lisette. Her Lafayette family would host a wake and a proper burial, but commemorating the portion of her life she spent working alongside him was his privilege. The unknown portion, the reason her bleached bones lay beside an old pine snag, depended on Detective Sullivan's investigative skills.

Guests arrived in a trickle and then a swarm.

He made the appropriate remarks and leaned into his role. His agent described him as youthful and competent, but she made commissions on his success. She also recommended coloring the gray hairs peppering his temples. He liked the silver glints, but he complied. She'd also been right about fixing his teeth, working with a voice coach, and casting his design skills as a down-home perk. Ambling barn tours with sweet-tea-sipping grandmas were more accessible than European buying trips with a couture-loving Mama.

His agent also introduced him to Lisette. His assistant was the gilt foil to his starched linen. He expected her to waltz through the front door any day now, but he'd seen the bones himself. He fingered a tear from the corner of his eye. Man, he would miss her.

The crowd swelled.

Nanette led an entourage into the hotel foyer. She wore a small, black fascinator with a jaunty, red feather. A white, net veil caged her well-moisturized face. The effect signaled old Hollywood glamour, but her train of rambunctious retirees wore matching ensembles. If anyone could keep the celebration from feeling like a funeral, the Merrymakers and their vodka-fueled gaiety could.

"Lisette was such a lovely girl." Clutching Nathan's hands in her papery, soft grip, Nanette scanned the open bar before refocusing her gaze. "She babysat my Kiki, you know?"

"Lisette was awesome." He squeezed her hand and refrained from pointing out that Kiki, Nanette's overfed Maine Coon, could have delivered the deathblow. "We'll miss her something fierce."

Nanette raised a hand and cupped his cheek.

He looked past her shoulder at her peers and their mawkish enthusiasm. If Nanette and the Merrymakers were concerned about Lisette's disappearance, they could have passed out fliers or done something more constructive than buying matching outfits. Before he dumped his grief on an old woman, he tightened his smile and closed his mouth. Once people reached a certain age, funerals were social events and triumphant victory laps. Some people came to this event to honor Lisette's life, and they deserved a place to share their memories. "Thank you for being here."

"Let us know if you need anything!" Nanette dropped the hand from his cheek, looped arms with her accomplice, and moved on before he could turn her platitude into anything substantial.

Hearing the crowd go quiet and then chatter, he glanced toward the doorway and found Ann and Sam wearing near-identical pantsuits. A light-blue, silk shirt brought out Ann's eyes, and a pale-gray pantsuit complimented her sun-kissed cheeks. He hadn't figured Ann for a woman who owned pantsuits, and he had no right to notice how the fabric showed off her shoulders or draped her long, lean legs.

"Nathan!" Sam approached and kissed his cheek. "I'm so sorry."

"Mayor Eddington." He returned the kiss. "Thank you for joining us."

Sam gripped his shoulders. "Tragic. Anytime Hemlock loses a person, we mourn. The town's too small for anonymity."

"Do murders often happen?" Ann asked.

He risked a glance.

Raising her eyebrows, she waited.

He worked his jaw. "I can't imagine somebody disappearing from Hemlock. Someone, somewhere, would have noticed foul play and come after them."

Ann looked away. "I doubt it."

Sam shoved his shoulder. "Our crime rate is near zero, and you know it."

He respectfully inclined his head. "As it should be."

Ann looked back and tilted her head.

Sam held her gaze. "Indeed."

He watched their faces shift with unspoken phrases, but he was an outsider who couldn't speak their language.

Ann nodded.

"Peace." Turning, Sam made a beeline toward her largest political donor.

He cleared his throat, jammed his hands into his pants pockets, and waited for Ann to make the first move. He'd seen her in the pine stand and avoided her gaze like his life depended on it. Losing Lisette hurt, but commingling his grief with Ann's return would have been a disaster.

"Nathan"—Ann rubbed the bridge of her nose and dropped the hand—"it's good to see you. The hotel's lovely. I'm sorry for your loss. I've heard nothing but positive things about Lisette."

He rocked back on his heels. "Like what?"

She chewed on her bottom lip.

Her lipstick would be gone before she finished her first drink. He didn't care. If he could, he would go back to the days of sundrenched tailgate parties and mixed CDs. Did the soldiers she commanded know how she liked to kick off her shoes and let the grass tickle her feet? That, as a freshman, she was a cheer flyer, but as a senior, she was a steady base? He made fists in his pockets. For a brief, dazzling moment, he knew everything about her.

"Lisette was with you when you launched your show. She was like your sidekick, wasn't she? I mean, on the show, she seemed friendly and hardworking."

For a captain in the US Navy, Ann was adorably

bad at small talk. He loosened his fists and relaxed his shoulders. "I'd known her for about a decade. She had a lot to offer the world." He glanced at the framed photograph on the marble table. "You would have liked her infectious, forthright generosity. Everyone did."

"I'm sure." Ann held his gaze. "Is there anything I can do?"

"Like kick someone's ass?" Pulling one hand from his pocket, he rubbed his chin and recalled his payments for a Valor special investigator. Part of him wished Ann came rolling into town, but Vince sent Brandon. He seemed like a nice dude, but he failed to locate Lisette. Ann might have done better. Rocking back on his heels, he wondered if she'd known about the investigation. "You bringing in the special forces?"

"If need be." She tilted her head. "The Cajun Navy seems pretty effective, but I know a few people."

"So, I've heard." The Cajun Navy rescued stranded storm victims. He needed someone to find a murderer. Looking at the crowd forming, he wet his lips and considered his obligations. As much as he would like to stand here and consider how to be friends with the woman he'd first loved, he had obligations. "Thanks for coming. I appreciate it."

"Any time." She winced. "I mean"—she exhaled—"you know what I mean. Take care of yourself."

Hearing the dismissal, he looked away from the woman he wanted to love for the remainder of his existence. As far as life achievements went, maintaining generations of family ties and a design empire were decent accolades, but his heart felt half-empty. Burying his regrets beneath gentility might be his best option. He dipped his head. "You, too."

Chapter Six

"Boy gets better looking each time I see him."
Standing beside Ann, Sam raised her wineglass and
sipped her red blend. "Last year, he hosted my
campaign fundraiser and brought in enough press to
bolster my regional profile *and* my donor base. If he
had tits, then I'd marry him."

Ann laughed and sipped seltzer water with lime.
She felt as conspicuous as the lobby chandelier. Every
time she scanned the room, she found someone staring.
Meanwhile, Nathan worked the crowd like six
generations of Southern hospitality pumped through his
veins. She shouldn't be surprised. She trailed her
alcoholic, duck-hunting father and poled *de skiff*.
Nathan was the old-money, second-son, football star
from the river house. While she patched bike tires, he
admired gleaming antiques and spent petrochemical
profits. How had he pulled together such a fresh,
modern hotel? She squinted at a lobby mural—was the
spoonbill wearing Mardi Gras beads?

"Something in your drink?" Sam asked.

She drained the seltzer. "Not enough liquor."

Sam clapped her on the shoulder. "I know the
feeling. I'm due for a refill."

Absorbing Sam's blow, she worked her jaw and
reconciled her feelings toward Nathan and the success
he brought to Hemlock. Her heartbeat raced, but the

hotel looked good. The old space was a mishmash of bad additions and false walls that housed small law firms, resale shops, and hobby businesses. Like a shabby mall, its only patrons were teenagers on skateboards and old women with too much time to spend.

Now, the hotel's ground-floor public spaces were open and airy. Richly colored paintings shone against white walls like museum pieces. Nathan's taste in women irked her, but she appreciated his design aesthetic. Acknowledging her admiration felt like a betrayal. She glanced at a covered walkway leading to an adjacent house. Somewhere on the campus, a flaw existed. A limpid, carpeted ballroom sat behind double doors. A toilet sported a stubborn stain. Giddy teenagers scratched out tags on prom night. She rattled the ice in her cup. Some events were better forgotten.

Hating where her mind took her, she dumped her ice into a nearby planter, thought twice about the move, and shoved her fingers into the soil to ensure the plant lived. Rich, damp soil coated her fingers. Life moved on. So could she. Arriving at Lisette's memorial exposed her to gossipmongers and rubbed her face in Nathan's success, but she could handle herself.

Sam returned with a fresh drink. "You still with us?"

She folded her hands over her chest. "Nathan's a person."

"And I'm the town's mayor and P.R. team." Sam gestured toward the crowd. "Go ahead and make a scene. You'll feel better."

Will I? She worked her jaw and wished Paps had moved to Colorado. Hemlock was so shaky a flood could swallow the town whole. The 1927 flood tried, but Nathan's hotel survived. Destiny was a fickle shrew. Circumstances pushed together lovers and kept apart others. As a general rule, the fates didn't reshape their lives and toss them cold scraps of professional admiration at wannabe funerals.

"I mean, does he even interest you?"

Ann tilted her head. "All this...stuff...is pretty, but I'm confident he's still a selfish asshole. If I had to guess, he steamrolled Hemlock into a bourbon-infused tax write-off. After he establishes revenue streams, he'll bail for another project. If Hemlock needed a makeover, you should have called Chip and Joanna Gaines. He basically knocked off Magnolia Marketplace and added gold paint."

Doubling over in laughter, Sam slapped her knee.

"You must be talking about my father," a woman said.

Ann ignored Sam's merriment and examined a pair standing behind her right shoulder. The woman wore a lovely, sage-green dress and sweet, gold earrings. She sported Nathan's sharp cheekbones and full lips and must be Evangeline Charlet. Her partner was her same height. He wore a tan suit with a striped shirt, a polka-dotted bowtie, and a silk pocket square. Ann had never seen him before, but she'd never seen Evangeline, either. Adopting a neutral smile, she waited for Nathan's daughter to finish her introduction.

The man thrust out his right hand. "I'm Huanlong."

"Ann Storey. Pleased to meet you." She shook his hand and turned back to Evangeline. "You must be Evangeline."

"Evie. I can see why Daddy dated you." Evie

tapped a finger against her lips. "You must have been quite the looker."

Sam snorted into her drink and hip-checked Ann. "I'll be right back. Business with Nanette the *Duchesse*."

"Traitor," Ann whispered.

Sam flashed her a wide-eyed, innocent look before slipping into the crowd.

Evangeline rubbed a hand over her chin. "I mean, you're still beautiful. I can't imagine you and Daddy together. It's weird, you know? You spend your whole life loving your parents, but the universe holds so many possibilities."

Ann wondered what loving one's parents felt like. She couldn't imagine stretching her love for Paps to encompass a mother and a father. She also couldn't imagine having an adult daughter. "Right."

Huanlong elbowed Evie.

Blinking, Evie shook herself. "Sorry, I shouldn't have mentioned anything about how you look. It's so rude, isn't it? I'm a painter. Sometimes, my visual observations overpower my manners. I've been *dying* to meet you."

"Hopefully not literally."

Evie giggled.

Ann softened her stance. Evie's upspeak and vocal fry matched her youthful appearance. Ann could cut her some slack, but Navy commanders would berate her uncertain habits until she changed them or hid them. Ann remembered having young adult misgivings and felt the urge to shield Evie from life's corrections. "Your dad and I were together a long time ago."

"But you're here."

Ann dipped her head. "For Lisette."

Sam ran a thumb along the condensation on her cup. "Yep."

Evie waved a hand toward the foyer. "But you never knew her. You called her work a gilt knockoff."

"Sweetie—" Huanlong whispered in Evangeline's ear.

Evie opened and closed her mouth.

Whatever Huanlong whispered, Evie had more to say. Ann braced herself for an unfiltered analysis. She considered faking a mission with Ricco, but he had yet to arrive at the event.

"But I didn't say—"

Striding up, Nathan wrapped an arm around Evie and clapped Huanlong on the back. "I see you've met my future son-in-law."

"Daddy! He has a name!"

Evie's stage whisper turned heads.

Ann kept considered Nathan and tilted her head. "What does he call you?"

Nathan raised his eyebrows. "Sir?"

Huanlong chuckled.

Evie rolled her eyes. "Right."

Ann pursed her lips. She'd played nice with Sam and made an appearance from a discreet, leafy corner, but family reunions were above her grade. Nathan's daughter was a delight, but he was still a charismatic, traitorous asshole. "Don't you have guests to greet?"

"Why?" He rocked back on his heels. "Ready to recruit Evie to the society? Pitch her on native milkweed and trumpet vines?"

"That's where your plant knowledge stops, isn't it? You preach curb appeal on national television, but do the dainty boxwoods like the heat?" Leaning forward, she dropped her voice. "Do your buyers have second thoughts about your antiques, too?"

"So, you watch my shows."

She sharpened her smile. "Only at the dentist's office."

"Burn." Huanlong waved a hand like he might dissipate smoke. "I like her."

Nathan turned toward his son-in-law. "Buddy, Ann could eat you for breakfast. One day, you will be a workaholic neurosurgeon. Today, you're my drink caddy." He lowered his voice. "Take Evie to the bar."

Ann stepped forward. "She's twenty years old."

Evie cleared her throat. "Twenty-one."

Ignoring the interjection, Ann stepped closer to Nathan. "I like her."

"Great." Nathan looked back and forth between her and Evie. "However, she looks thirsty enough to put her foot in her mouth, and I've already claimed that family trait."

Huanlong wiped the sweat from his forehead with his pocket square. "It's warm for February, isn't it? Is the AC on?"

Ann smirked and glanced at Huanlong. His Southern demeanor looked fresh enough to mark him as a newcomer. Paps could give him a few pointers. *Pocket squares were for show, and handkerchiefs were for blow.* The old adage startled her. She wondered how long she could stay in Hemlock without feeling its effects. Despite Huanlong's fashions, he and Evie remained independent of Nathan's indiscretions. She turned toward him and smiled. "I like you, too. You should stay."

"You should not. It's seventy-two degrees in this room." Nathan crossed his arms over his chest. "Decide whether you're sick or thirsty, because if you stand here much longer, you'll pay for your wedding."

"Thirsty. Very, very thirsty." Huanlong cupped Evie's elbow and led her toward the bar. "Can they make a Pimm's cup?"

Evie followed her fiancé's lead, but she looked over her right shoulder. *Next time?* she mouthed.

Ann saluted and hoped vague, high school stories and innocent, juvenile schemes would be enough. Until she had a better understanding of Evie's mettle, those were the only parts of Ann's past she would resurrect. Pivoting, she faced the source of her discomfort. He might be an excellent designer, but he was still a polished turd. "Throwing around your weight to keep your daughter in line?"

"Nosey brat." Nathan cleared his throat and ran a hand through his hair. "She used to be shy, but…hell, if she'd wanted an introduction, I would have made it."

Itching for a quick outlet, Ann rubbed together her fingers at her side. She would weed the hotel courtyard before she would seek out Nathan for small talk. "Would you?"

"Why not? You didn't do anything wrong."

"I fell in love with you." The admission tripped out of her throat before she could think twice. Raising a hand, she rubbed her collarbone. The old, soothing habit obscured her regret but not her self-reproach. Why did she say that?

Nathan examined his shoes.

Glancing away, she rubbed her upper arms and wished she hadn't backed herself into this *tête-à-tête*.

Like a stray cat, she would swerve her truck to avoid hitting Nathan, but she wouldn't rescue him from a country road. If wallowing made her petty, taking the high road saved her from jams. She swallowed. "Evie's sweet. Looks like you."

Jamming his hands into his pants pockets, Nathan stared after his daughter. "She looks like her mother." He closed his eyes. "Fuck, I'm sorry for mentioning Flannery."

"Evie paints?" Ann cleared her throat. "Like, professionally?"

"Her work hangs in the lobby. She sold several pieces to admiring guests." He picked up a scrap of paper and tucked it into his front pants pockets.

His old, caretaking habit hung on. She thought of the vibrant, colorful pieces referenced and swallowed. Some things changed. Being in Hemlock could get easier, but she remained in town to care for Paps. "I should get home."

Pulling a hand from his pocket, he stepped back and gestured toward the door. "Thanks for coming."

"Sure." She patted her pockets and confirmed she still had her cell phone and her keys. Sobriety had its perks. "Take it easy. I'm sorry for your loss."

"Thanks. Me, too."

His lingering gaze stopped her. She tilted her head.

Stepping back, he signaled an employee holding a microphone.

Whatever she saw in his gaze, the emotion quickly dissipated. Back in the day, they were each other's biggest fans. She felt his gaze in the hallways, reveled in his pride, and loved him for his quirks.

Then, she hadn't been enough.

"If I could have your attention?" Nathan held a live microphone. "Thank you all for coming out tonight to honor Lisette and everything she contributed toward this hotel. The staff misses her creativity and her organization. I miss her excellent sense of humor."

More likely, he missed her warming his bed. Ann bit her lip and stood in place so her exit did nothing to detract from Nathan's speech.

"Lisette was a remarkable individual. She transformed spaces like this old hotel into works of art. She understood successful projects reflect architectural beauty and the essences of the people who use buildings. She had an eye for things that sparkled and an unique ability to turn ordinary rooms into extraordinary experiences." He dropped his head. "We'll miss her."

Evie approached, took his hand, and clutched it.

The pair looked so similar the sight squeezed Ann's heart.

Nathan drew a sharp breath. "May Lisette's creative spirit continue to inspire us, and may she find eternal peace and sublime perfection."

The crowd clapped.

Wondering if he wrote the speech, Ann headed toward the exit.

"There's my girl!" Paps stood with his railroad cronies and pulled her to his side for support. "Isn't she the prettiest thing? I tell you what, she might be packing heat in a nylon holster, but she's still my little girl."

She savored the moment and leaned her head on his shoulder without transferring her weight. His friends were as familiar as the local speed traps. Pierre, the gas station attendant, looked particularly pleased with himself. "Hi, guys. Nice to be back in town. Thanks for having me. Anything new you want to share?"

The men nervously laughed and toasted her.

Paps kept his arm around her waist.

She stood strong and savored his familiar presence. Instead of fearing his demise, she could treat each day like a gift. Paps' freshly shaven cheeks, pressed linen suits, and crisp smells were as unique as his stories. On Mondays, he smelled like soap and laundry detergent. On weekends, he smelled like pine resin mixed with a gin. Spending time with him felt unexpectedly good.

Using her peripheral vision, she kept track of Nathan. He worked the room, but his hollowed eyes, tight expression, and controlled movements conveyed his grief. She congratulated herself on limiting the fallout from their conversation. Her memories kept her from appreciating what he achieved, but she understood why the other women in the room also marked his presence with bright smiles and knowing looks.

She wished she hadn't needed a cancer diagnosis or Lisette's death to bring her back to Hemlock, but Sam was right about the food. Who could resist the salty allure of garlic, butter, Parmesan cheese, and oysters plucked straight from Louisiana's salty estuaries? Every person had his or her limits. She had yet to find hers, but she could ignore her ex and make the best of the situation.

Chapter Seven

The day after the party, Nathan sat in his office with his laptop open on his desk and his wireless earphones in his ears. He exchanged sound bites with a New Orleans news anchor and touted Hemlock's appeal. After the interview, he closed his laptop and met Mayor Eddington's gaze.

Sam sipped a beer. "I outta make you head of tourism."

He stood and brushed out his wrinkled pants. Sitting for the interview left his legs stiff, but he couldn't bob on the screen like a fishing lure. "I *am* the head of tourism. I boost Hemlock's brand on social media, spread positive messaging, create memorable visitor experiences, and influence consumer sales. When the event center opens, I'll drive convention sales, too."

"And look good doing it." Sam hefted a paperweight. "Too bad those activities make you rich."

"Too bad the tax surplus pads your budget." He stretched his back and ignored her sarcasm. They'd raised this town together. If Sam chose public office over a management role in his company, then he would honor her wishes. "Have you eaten?"

She raised her drink in salute. "I have."

"You'll run yourself into the ground."

"I'll rest when I'm dead." Grinning, she finished

her beer and set the empty glass on a coaster.

He shook his head. "Any more news on Lisette?"

She propped her hip onto a couch arm. "After I'm done navigating state preemption laws, battling inflammatory statements, overhauling hiring processes, auditing police academies, and negotiating union contracts, I'll call Detective Sullivan for an update."

"Right." He spun his phone on the desk and remembered the Valor investigator hired to investigate Lisette's disappearance. His money failed him, but the investigator's report might contain leads that interested the police. Awakening his laptop, he opened a report copy.

Sam shifted on the couch. "Nice turnout last night."

"Hmm."

"You and Ann…"

He raised his eyebrows. "That was a long time ago."

Sam grinned. "We're young, Nathan."

"I don't feel young." Firing off the email, he lifted a pen and twirled the implement around his finger. He'd spent the morning celebrating the *Lundi Gras Boucherie* and wondering if Ann would show. She hadn't, but the long-running tradition let local chefs show off their dishes and slow-roasted pigs. Shaking hands and touting the hotel had drained him. "Feels like I've lived this life longer than most."

"You have, but you're a good man."

Opening a desk drawer, he slipped his laptop onto the green felt liner. "Ann disagrees."

"Does she?" Sam stood. "She's over at the *Duchesse's* Tea Room. Thirsty?"

He resisted looking out the window. "The hotel has a restaurant."

"It's a damn good one, too."

Giving into his impulse, he stood, walked toward the second-story window, and shifted the sheer white curtains. Streetlights fought back the encroaching early twilight, but two figures squared off outside Nanette's Tea Room. Ann wore soft overalls and a pink-and-white plaid, cotton shirt. Nanette wore an outrageous garden hat and a sensible, black suit. Both women planted their hands on their hips and looked more like tested, cautious soldiers than dainty, Parisian ladies. Whether weeds or weather occupied them, seeing Ann alive and well settled his stomach.

Behind her, the cottage wall sported a painted Acadian flag and script letters proclaimed the tearoom had the best tea in Hemlock. Most French preferred bitter coffee, *pastis*, wine, beer, and champagne. As far as he knew, the Tea Room served Lillet, Suze, and Dolin along with their Earl Grey. "Why are they arguing over the garden?"

"Beats me." Sam rifled through her purse. "Weed's the only thing growing in my garden." She snorted. "I mean, like beneath the tomatoes."

He knew exactly what grew in Sam's garden. Letting the curtains fall into place, he listened to the busy hotel's muffled cocktail hour and prioritized his obligations. "Just because Ann and I have history doesn't mean we have to be friends."

Sam swung her keys. "You know why she's back in Hemlock?"

He shrugged. The ache between his shoulders felt tighter. "She's tired of bumming around at the Valor field office?"

"No, you dunce." Sam moved toward the office door. "Only one person could bring Ann back to Hemlock. If you thought about her appearance longer than two seconds, you'd realize she has hard times headed her way."

Scratching his head, he dissected Sam's roundabout communication. Ann and her grandfather, Guidry, defended their privacy like Jean Lafitte defended Barataria Bay. If Sam wanted him to know something *and* maintain Ann's confidence, she should have dropped hints before late-afternoon exhaustion zapped his resources.

Ann transitioned from a tomboy to a cheer captain, but she and Guidry treated their cottage like a refuge. Nathan understood why. Ann's mother skipped out when she was three, her dad drank himself into an early grave, and Guidry stepped in.

He acknowledged Ann broke the town mold, but he loved her quirks and her strengths. Nanette, the self-styled *Duchesse* of Hemlock, couldn't cause her grief. The folksy grande dame costumed for Mardi Gras, but she wasn't about to keel over in the flower garden.

That left Ann's grandfather. Thinking about the possibilities, Nathan felt his stomach drop. He had already caused enough pain in Ann's life. Being an unconscious jackass was an unacceptable evolution. "Shit. I'm oblivious."

Sam held open the door. "Noted."

What good was money if you couldn't accomplish anything? He rushed past, thundered down the stairs, and waved off a concerned valet. A car's headlights blinded him, but he jogged across the street.

Ann's worn overalls triggered old memories. He wondered how many times he yanked her braids and teased about her freckles. She'd teased him right back. Tonight, he would discover what she needed.

"Honey, it's plain cow parsnip." Nanette yanked out a tall plant with huge leaves and numerous tiny, white flowers. The plant's hollow, woolly stem snapped. "Nothing but a weed."

Ann winced. "*Tante,* it's a native host for swallowtail butterflies. You want a butterfly garden? Work with what grows naturally."

"But it's ugly!"

Ann stroked a remaining stalk's broad leaves. "Cow parsnip's the largest carrot family species. Native Americans peeled and ate the young leaves and flower stalks. The foliage is very aromatic." She turned over the leaf and aimed her flashlight on a speck. "These eggs are swallowtails. Patience nurtures success."

Patience was the last trait Nathan cultivated. He cleared his throat. "Evening, ladies. Mind if I have a word with Ann?"

The women turned their heads and glared.

Kiki, Nanette's overfed Maine Coon, threaded between his legs.

"It'll just take a second." He avoided tripping over the cat. The animal often sniffed around the hotel like it planned to install a catico. If he pissed off the creature, he suspected he'd find *offerings* deposited on his doorstep. "I have a, um, landscaping project to discuss."

"Nathan Charlet." Nanette planted her hands on her hips. "You planted two hundred boxwoods in your Ox lot. You turned the space into a damn maze, and you have a bustling hotel to run. What do you need with

Ann?"

Most visitors skipped the historical plaque explaining the logic behind Hemlock's downtown configuration. The town's original grid layout located public squares in the middle of each downtown block. Farmers brought oxen-led carts to town and sold wares from the "ox lots." As buildings framed the lots, and combustion engines outpaced oxen, the commerce courtyards became off-street parking.

His property encompassed the entire block. He'd turned the ox lot into a relaxing courtyard for hotel guests. His cottage and a service alley occupied the block's far side and faced the Catholic church's administrative offices. Locals navigated hidden alleys and skirted street-side parking meters, but they also remembered what he'd done to Ann twenty years ago. He wrinkled his nose. "I need her for a consult."

"Well, get in line, boy!" Nanette eyed another stalk of cow parsnip. "Nothing worse than weeds in a garden."

"We've got, um, an infestation." He shuddered. "It's bad."

Both women furrowed their brows.

Ann tilted her head.

The streetlight lent her a halo.

Nanette waved him off. "Fine. I'll go inside and research butterfly host plants. Maybe the stubborn bugs will eat something prettier than parsnip." Climbing the cottage stairs, her heels tapping against the aged boards, she entered the cottage and turned on a lamp.

Nathan exhaled. The light cast his shadow into the street.

Ann pulled off her leather gloves. "What kind of

infestation?"

He struggled to think of something that could damage boxwoods.

Kiki rose on her hind legs and batted at container plants.

He jerked his head toward the hotel. "Maybe you should see the infestation in person. Join me?"

"I can tell when you're lying, Nathan. Your nose twitches." She crossed her arms. "Also, it's almost dark. What's going on?"

Scratching the back of his neck, he stalled. He needed a haircut, a mediator, and a jockstrap. If he were wrong about her presence in Hemlock, then she might kick him in the balls for meddling in her affairs. "Paps' sick, isn't he?"

She worked her jaw and looked down the street.

"What does he need? We can find him a specialist. If you make a big enough donation, then the research hospitals will open treatment beds." He scratched his scalp. "The East Coast isn't that far away."

Turning, she raised a palm. "Your heart's in the right place. Thank you, but no. We can handle it. He's *been* handling it." She narrowed her gaze. "Without you."

He ran his tongue over his teeth and debated pushing.

"And Sam can go fuck herself." Ann rubbed her hands over her face and smothered a scream. "This is what I hate about Hemlock. Everyone's in your business. People think they're thoughtful, but they're gossiping. Please stay out of it."

He worked his jaw and considered a new approach.

She scooped up Kiki and settled the cat on her hip.

"Privacy's a line in the sand, but everyone's willing to cross that line for a good cause. Trespassing doesn't make them generous. It makes them a bunch of busybody, gossiping, self-righteous…"

A large, black SUV pulled up to the curb. Cutting the engine, the driver opened the door and rounded the hood. She had the pristine, smooth hair common to city dwellers with standing salon appointments. Her silhouette barely surpassed the hood ornament, but she wore a pale-yellow suit, a quilted purse, and old-school nylons that ended in block heels.

The driver walked to Ann, narrowed her gaze, and raised her chin. "Are you Ann Storey?"

Ann brushed a hand on her overalls and extended it. "Yes, ma'am. Can I help you?"

The woman shook Ann's hand. "My daughter, Jeanne, volunteers with the plant society."

"Oh!" Ann smiled. "I met Jeanne. You must be—"

"Judge Calloway." She dropped Ann's hand and adjusted her purse. "Are you aware Jeanne, my errant, headstrong daughter, never came home?"

"Excuse me?" Ann tilted her head. "Last night?"

"No, I haven't seen her since the morning she volunteered." Judge Calloway wetted her lips. "You might be the last people who saw her. I reported her missing in New Orleans, but with Mardi Gras in full swing, the police have limited resources."

Cupping Judge Calloway's elbow, Ann dipped her chin. "I'm sure she'll turn up."

"I'm not." Judge Calloway gestured toward the distant woods. "What if she went missing out here? She's a city girl." Shading her eyes, she stared at the tree line. "You think you reach a certain place in your life and your family will be safe, but they're not." Dropping her hand, she faced Ann. "They're just not."

Nathan slipped his clean, white handkerchief from his pants pocket and offered it. "Ma'am, why don't you come across the street? You and Ann can have my office. It'll give you privacy to talk."

Taking the cotton square, Judge Calloway dabbed at her eyes. "Thank you."

Ann mouthed her thanks and offered Judge Calloway an arm. "Let's accept Nathan's offer. I'll tell you everything I know. Have you talked to Baptiste?"

Judge Calloway lowered the handkerchief and furrowed her brows. "Who's Baptiste?"

"Another volunteer." Ann looked both ways to cross the street and led Judge Calloway toward the hotel's front door. "He and Jeanne were"—she worked her jaw—"good friends."

Nathan tailed the women like an obedient bloodhound. He'd rushed over willing to do whatever Ann and Guidry needed, but she needed him like a fish needed a bicycle. Instead of rushing to her side, he should lubricate Flannery's old cruiser and maintain the bike for Evie.

A woman waved. "Howdy, Nathan."

He half-heartedly returned her greeting and checked the white-painted bike leaning against a stop sign. Vivid flowers adorned ghostly handlebars, and colorful beads draped an aluminum frame. Evie erected the memorial where the maximum number of people could consider how they treated bicyclists. She avoided the rural, grassy spot where a distracted driver veered onto a highway shoulder, knocked Flannery from her bike, and altered innumerable lives.

Quickening his step, he opened the door for Ann and Judge Calloway and pointed toward the staircase leading to the second floor. "Make yourselves at home in the office. I'll send something to drink."

Judge Calloway patted his arm and held onto his handkerchief.

He remembered the searing pain of losing someone he'd vowed to protect, but Flannery's absence weighed because he'd failed her, not because she'd been the love of his life. That woman climbed his carpeted stairs with a dirt stain on her denim-class ass. Losing her was his fault. Surrendering a thin slip of cotton to Judge Calloway's tears wasn't much of a loss, but forfeiting the handkerchief was the least he could do.

Chapter Eight

Ann opened the oiled wooden door to Nathan's office and expected rows of leather-bound books, a brass bar cart, and deep, tufted sofas. Instead, she found sleek, modern lines and indigo walls. He'd enlarged the windows facing the courtyard and maximized his views. Sheer, white curtains offered privacy, but streetlights filled the room and created maudlin shadows. She turned on lights and gestured toward wingback chairs upholstered in green fabric. Subtle, contrasting embroidery gave the fabric a welcoming depth. "Please, take a seat."

Judge Calloway sat and crossed her ankles.

Ann occupied the second chair and imagined her mother searching for her. The image wavered like a silhouette lost in early morning fog. Nanette had been a willing replacement, but Ann never completely conformed to her expectations. So much for second chances. Shaking off the memories, she squared her shoulders and respected Judge Calloway for chasing leads. Leaning across the small, brass table separating their seats, she held the judge's gaze. "What can I do?"

"Tell me everything you remember. Where had she come from? Where was she going? How do I get in touch with Baptiste?"

The judge, despite her age, was sharp. Ann cleared her throat. "I can't tell you how much Paps appreciates

Jeanne's help—"

Judge Calloway rapped her knuckles against the table. "Cut the pleasantries."

"Okay!" Ann wiped her palms along her denim-clad thighs and leaned into the official voice she used to deliver reports to Vince. "She arrived to burn the longleaf pine stand off Hwy 2 and Burden Lane. Less than an hour into the controlled burn, she and the other volunteers discovered human remains."

Judge Calloway tilted her head.

"We called the authorities. Detective Sullivan and his team secured the evidence. Jeanne and I hung around for a while. After she gave her statement, she left with the other volunteers."

Judge Calloway raised her eyebrows. "Did she seem uneasy?"

Ann cleared her throat. "Ma'am, she'd just seen human bones. If she weren't uneasy, then I'd have questions."

"And this crime?" Judge Calloway drummed her fingers on the table. "Could it be connected to Jeanne's disappearance?"

"As far as I know, she and the victim never met."

Judge Calloway snorted. "Aren't you supposed to be some hotshot special operative?"

Ann tilted her head.

"I did my research, too! Think about what else you saw."

Exhaling, Ann considered the sleek office and thought of Nathan's eulogy for Lisette. She doubted he had anything to do with Lisette's death or Jeanne's disappearance, but Judge Calloway was right. Looking for patterns was her job. If she could bring Lisette's killer to justice, she might prevent another young, vibrant woman from going missing. However, looking for Jeanne wasn't her job. She was in Hemlock for Paps and no other reason.

Leaning back in her chair, she gripped the armrests and made eye contact. "People say tragedies happen in threes, but superstitions make us anxious. Don't let your fears rule your response to Jeanne's absence. Did she gamble? Have you checked her socials? I can give you Baptiste's phone number."

Judge Calloway narrowed her gaze. "Give me the boy's number, please."

Ann read off Baptiste's contact information and remembered Jeanne's warm approach toward daily pleasures, hot sauce, and offbeat remixes. She was a hard worker with a good head on her shoulders. Barring nefarious forces, she would turn up.

Judge Calloway slipped her phone in her purse. "She's studying to be an entomologist. Biological control to reduce pest populations. Farmers love her."

"Everybody loves her." Ann swallowed her fears.

"A professor." Judge Calloway cleared her throat. "She'll be a professor."

Hope underpinned Judge Calloway's statement. Ann shifted in her seat. "Have the New Orleans Police tracked her cell phone? Her credit cards? They can pinpoint her last location. Data trails exist, and people don't disappear without leaving a trace. If you can't contact Jeanne, narrow the field." She raised a hand. "I mean, the police."

Judge Calloway stood. "I *know* the police should have updates. They don't." She inhaled and closed her eyes. "I'm sorry. She's my only child. How much for you to investigate her case as a Valor employee? You met Jeanne. You know she's special."

A denial formed at the tip of Ann's tongue. She was in Hemlock for personal reasons, but she also imagined her mother in Judge Calloway's shoes. Old color snapshots bolstered her hazy memories, but no matter their differences, Judge Calloway was the woman with pleading eyes and a missing daughter.

Empathizing with her need to find Jeanne, Ann paced the room. "We should call Baptiste." She copied his contact number from the list Paps gave her and initiated the call. When she heard Baptiste's voicemail recording, she hung up and met Judge Calloway's gaze. "He didn't answer."

Judge Calloway planted her hands on her hips. "Why didn't you leave a message?"

"Umm." She considered her phrasing. "I know how to use a rotary phone, but Baptiste's generation doesn't like, um, voicemail."

"Stop tripping over your damn words and call him back!" Judge Calloway rattled her fists before her face. "You're a professional! He probably thinks you want him to drive out to the boonies and pull weeds. For the love of....his phone will transcribe your message."

She bit back a smile and dialed a second time. When the call went to voicemail, she cleared her throat. "Hey, Baptiste! This is Ann Storey with the Cajun Prairie Preservation Society. I'm looking for Jeanne. She left her, um, favorite hat. I'd be happy to meet and return it. Thanks!"

"Her hat?" Judge Calloway raised an eyebrow and hitched her purse on her shoulder. "Jeanne would come back for her field glasses. Her notebook. Her white shrimp boots." Her voice cracked. "Maybe her hat. What if she's gone?"

Ann opened her arms and slowly approached the older woman.

Head high, Judge Calloway sidestepped the hug. "I have money. If I have to call Valor's headquarters and go through your boss, I will. Consider yourself on the case"—she lowered her brows—"do you read me?"

"Yes, ma'am." Ann appreciated how quickly the dignified woman mended the cracks in her demeanor. If Jeanne matured into a more eccentric version of Judge Calloway, she would laugh about the time she dropped her phone in a festival toilet and spent three days hitchhiking back to New Orleans. If only the case were that easy.

In the meantime, Ann would try her damnedest to find Jeanne. While the carpeted, old pine floors muffled Judge Calloway's departure, Ann dropped into a green, wingback chair. She traced subtle, contrasting embroidery and leaned her head against the chair back. In the quiet study, she could admit the truth. Being back on the clock thrilled her.

Chapter Nine

Nathan sat at the hotel bar, sipping whiskey from a cut-crystal glass. In the room's corner, an acoustic guitarist played modern hits and smiled at hotel guests plotting itineraries. Hemlock's Mardi Gras Festival was the city's largest community event, and five days of street dances, live music, and Cajun appreciations had started. After the Tuesday evening parade, the season would end, Lent would begin, and the tourists would go home.

Weariness slowed Nathan's movements, but he remained alert and scanned the bar. The mural's three-legged spoonbill sported new beads, but the error still bothered him. What else had he missed? Overseeing foundation repairs would have been outside his wheelhouse, but maybe he should have loitered. Even if the construction crew had quizzed him on facials, which he saw as more of a necessity than a topic of debate, at least he would know the building wouldn't fall down.

Toasting the bedazzled bird with his drink, Nathan hefted his to-go container and walked toward the courtyard door to find his rest. Evie and Huanlong were in New Orleans. He had twelve hours until Mardi Gras and intended to eat by the firepit and fall into bed with a pleasant buzz.

Ann walked around the foyer's massive flower

arrangement and tucked her loose hair behind her ears.

He stopped short and sipped his drink.

"I just wanted to say thanks. For letting me use your office to talk to Judge Calloway. I'm looking into her case for Valor."

He puffed his cheeks and exhaled. Missing women were bad for business and humanity. He hoped the New Orleans Police found Jeanne, but Mardi Gras crowd control would delay NOPD officers from determining her whereabouts.

"And thanks for offering to help with Paps." Ann dropped her voice. "Most people don't know he's sick. Please, keep it that way." She glanced at the to-go container and wet her lips. "I'll, uh, let you eat."

He considered the waxed cardboard container he held. Despite the rich aroma of fried food, he'd completely forgotten his hunger, the food, or his weariness. Ann had the way about her. She compelled people to live in the moment, and their concerns fell away. Too bad his beer-fueled impulsivity ruined both their lives. He cleared his throat. "Judge Calloway left twenty minutes ago. What were you doing? Snooping?"

She crossed her arms. "I have not been snooping."

"Huh." He pulled out a French fry and ate it. The Cajun seasoning added a familiar kick. After the pig-fest *Boucherie*, he probably should have ordered a salad. "And what else?"

"And that's it." She turned toward the hotel's front door. "Good evening."

The porter opened the door and stepped back.

"Hey, Annie…" Nathan raised a finger.

She paused.

He could find reasons to delay her exit, but honesty

would get him farther. As far as Evie knew, he and Ann dated in high school, and Flannery stole him from under Ann's nose. He preferred to keep his mythology intact, and he needed Ann's complicity. "You hungry?"

She shook her head.

He swore he heard her stomach rumble. "This oyster po'boy's too big for one person. I'm happy to share."

She looked over her shoulder. "Funny. I was never one to share my food"—she looked him over—"or anything else."

Her reproach wounded him, but he refused to give the town gossips a reaction. Striding up, he leaned close. "You can rile me until you're satisfied, but I saw you talking to Evie at the party. She's my only concern."

"Your only concern? What about your dead employee? Wait." She pulled back and tilted her head. "I'm talking to Nathan Charlet, media darling and Hemlock's savior. Your family is your only concern. You're as selfish as the day is long."

Her controlled anger made him feel no bigger than a minnow in a fishing pond, but they might as well have out their feelings. He thrust his drink into her hand, cupped her elbow, and pulled her toward the hallway leading toward his home. "You can rip me a new one, but confine your fury to my living quarters. If my guests need entertainment, they'll find it in the bar."

"Everything is yours, isn't it?" She ripped free her arm and tossed her hair over her shoulder. Looking at the drink she held, she frowned and shoved the glass toward his chest. "I'm not your caddy."

He pinned the crystal against his shirtfront.

Condensation seeped through the fabric. "Still don't drink, huh?"

She raised her chin. "Alcohol never served me well."

"Fair enough." He inputted his personal code into the hallway door and herded her toward his cottage in Hemlock.

"Couldn't you call me like a normal human?"

"Would you answer?" He slipped past her without hearing her response. "Watch out for the breaks between the paving stones. The Mondo grass is kitschy, but it's also a maintenance nightmare."

"So is this forest of boxwoods. How's the infestation?"

"Cute." He passed the courtyard ox lot, skirted the cottage, and led Ann toward a fenced backyard where two teal-blue Adirondack chairs faced an aged, steel firepit. The vessel was sturdy enough to humor Evie's pyrotechnic tendencies without letting her incinerate the town. Opening the gate and placing his dinner and his drink on the chair's flat arm, he gestured for Ann to sit. "If you're hungry, eat up."

She eyed the firepit, the chairs, and the whiskey. "I'm not staying to eat."

"Suit yourself." He moved the drink to the back porch railing and reached for a split log from the woodpile. Stacking the wood, he added kindling and wood shavings. By the time he found the butane lighter, the po'boy's smell won over Ann.

She sat in the Adirondack chair with the to-go container on her lap and half the dressed po'boy in her hands. Without blinking, she took a bite big enough to honor the governor. "This is good," she spoke around a mouthful of food.

He retrieved his drink and sat opposite her.

"Your office isn't fussy." She started in on the po'boy's second half. "Did Lisette design it?"

Wondering when the last time Ann ate, he sipped his watered-down liquor. He needed liquid courage before he asked Ann to cover his ass. "I wanted open space and lots of glass. When you see people collaborating, communicating, and talking, you do the same. People feed off positive energy."

"I'd feed off friend seafood."

He rubbed a hand along the stubble on his cheek and wondered whether he got a kick out of nurturing her or touting his hotel's food. The obvious explanation felt too painful. He could never have her. Tipping back his head, he stared at the stars. "I painted the room like the dark, indigo clouds before a thunderstorm. The color's unexpected but portent and energetic. You can't rush a storm, and you can't rush life." He risked a glance to see if she followed his explanation. Poetry could land a man in the doghouse.

Setting aside the empty to-go container, she leaned back in the chair, settled her hands over her stomach, and closed her eyes. Her chest rose and fell.

He held his breath.

"Okay, Nathan. Spit it out." She raised her head and peeked open one eye. "What do you want? Where is Evie?"

He exhaled. "New Orleans. She joined an uptown walking parade."

Ann grunted. "Figures."

Watching the sparks rise from the fire, he thought about the bands, poets, musicians, stilt walkers, and artists wowing New Orleans crowds with artistic talents instead of plastic throws. If Evie weren't dancing, she'd be holding the burning flambeaux. He'd be just as proud. "She's danced since she was three."

"And painted." Ann wiggled back into the chair. "Despite the fact that you're a cheating asshole, you seem like a good father."

"Next time, can we skip the asshole moniker?"

She smiled. "It still feels good."

He snorted. In another life, he could have sat across from her for hours while the fire kept them warm, but he only had one life. Clearing his throat, he braced his elbows on his knees, grabbed an errant stick, and sketched designs in the brown grass. Weeds had already turned green, but his backyard lawn was a bristly, bleached doormat. "Evie doesn't know much about our relationship. She might not know her origin story. People have a way of shielding kids."

"I don't plan to tell her." Ann rubbed her eyebrows. "What good would it do?"

He looked up. "Revenge?"

Ann yawned. "I'm glad you think so highly of me."

He felt his heart rate slow. "Some people would do it."

Wearily, she sighed, scooted her bottom to the chair's edge, and crossed her arms over her knees. "I'm not here to destroy the life you chose."

"Okay." He tossed the stick in the fire and watched the wood burn. Confirming Evie's safety should relieve him, but he would do anything to shield Ann from losing Joseph. He was the only family she had left. Despite Nathan's assets, he frowned.

Standing, she stretched her arms over her head. "At

the same time, stay away. When we're together, I remember too much. When we're apart, the memories fade. To quote Rhett, 'I don't give a damn'"—she tilted her head and held his gaze—"about you."

Liar. He smiled and looked past the flames. Firelight washed out her overalls and plaid shirt, but she'd always had a presence. He didn't buy her blithe attitude. Women, bless their hearts, could be as vengeful as wet hens, but he would take her at her word. "As you wish."

She snagged a fry, tasted it, and tossed the remainder in the fire. "I wish Evie the best, but I don't have any interest in upending her daddy-hero-worship. You live your life, and I'll live mine, preferably far away from Hemlock."

"Lisette told me this hotel was too close to home." He stood and dusted his hands. "Maybe I should have listened."

"Women have a way of seeing the world men can never understand. Men have a way of doing whatever the hell they want. I've always enjoyed straddling that line."

Her confidence intrigued and enflamed him. He tossed another errant twig into the fire. Wind often shook loose debris. If a person didn't hold on tight, they might find themselves miles off course. "You don't remember how small towns work. We watch each other's backs. We ask for help."

"I didn't ask for anything!" She drew a sharp breath. "You're the one who keeps butting into my life. If I discover Jeanne's one of your girlfriends, and you're connected to her disappearance, I'll shoot you myself."

"Come again?" He rounded the firepit. If Ann were packing heat, she'd hidden her piece, but he didn't particularly want to die with an empty stomach. "Lisette and I weren't together."

She closed the to-go container and thrust the food into his arms. "Right."

He tossed the cardboard into the fire. "I had nothing to do with those disappearances."

Ann rubbed her upper arms. "Lisette's dead."

"I know she's dead." His voice hitched, and he swore. "Christ, I saw her bones in your grandfather's forest. How many times do you think I've dreamed about you rotting away in the desert sands? Jeeze, give me a break. I'm not your enemy. I made a stupid mistake. For the thousandth time, I'm sorry for hurting you, but you're barking up the wrong tree."

"I know you're sorry." She dropped her shoulders and lowered her voice. "I also remember how many times you said you loved me."

In an instant, he was in the high school parking lot, confessing his mess-up and Flannery's pregnancy. He'd expected tears, but he should have known better. Ann took the news with quiet stoicism, drove away, and cried out her heart on Paps' shoulder. Guidry came at him with anger and outrage. Nathan shrunk into himself, prepared for the beating he deserved.

Instead, Paps swung his meaty fist into the plaster-and-lath wall. "You're an idiot. A damned fool." Shaking off the plaster debris, Paps cupped his fist. "You're doing the right thing, but you'll spend the rest of your life regretting it."

Paps was right. A braver man would take Ann into his arms and find a solution, but Nathan's family drilled duty into his psyche until one course of action remained. Raising Evie was a privilege, but he spent twenty-one years dreaming of a life with Ann. With his daughter gone and his wife a tragic memory, he had freedom to take risks. He drew a deep breath. "I never stopped missing you."

Chapter Ten

Ann cataloged Nathan's pain and let the smoke swirl. His whiskey-fueled nostalgia was palpable, but rubbing salt into old wounds cauterized losses, too. "Bullshit."

He widened his gaze.

Shaking her head, she walked toward the music and the hotel where people cared about gaiety, good food, and happy memories.

"Wait, please. Hear me out."

She hesitated. Listening to his explanations had wasted her time, but she confined her frustration to diary entries, bitter letters, and snarky emails. Too bad, she never sent them. Their interactions around Lisette's death were social, but she'd never imagined his opening salvo would be a smoke-drenched declaration. Raising a hand, she rubbed her collarbone. Why had she allowed him to affect her again?

"Can I just…can we…talk?"

She pursed her lips. People changed, but she should have witnessed the change. The last twenty years between them were a void. When had Nathan laughed about youthful indiscretions and growing wiser? His life choices matured him from a long-legged youth into a Southern hospitality baron, but she had as much insight into his success as any fan. He looked and acted like someone she wanted to know, but her heart still bore scars. What if he chose someone else yet again?

Her traitorous heart kicked into high gear around him, but his effect on her body hardly mattered. She'd learned to override her impulses to dodge a bullet. *Once a cheater, always a cheater.* Men grew handsomer with age but never changed their stripes. She'd be a fool to reopen herself to hurt. Turning, she faced his handsome, smoke-tinged visage. "I don't particularly want to talk to you, Nathan. I thought I could keep things easy between us, eat your damn food, and play nice, but too much has happened. We should keep our distance."

Jogging ahead, he reached for her hand and rubbed a thumb along the top.

She watched his slow, circular motions and felt her heart rate settle.

"Why don't we get a second chance?"

His inquiry's warmth stole her response. Firelight flickered on his achingly high cheekbones, full lips, and square jaw. Too bad his image wavered between the boy he'd been and the man he'd become. She yanked free her hand. "You were the person who knew me the best. We shared everything, and you walked away. I wasn't enough to satisfy you. Why on earth should I think that's changed? How could I ever forget that rejection? I gave you everything."

He hung his head. "I can't change the past, but I can make new memories."

If he'd taken her in his arms in the high school parking lot and promised to find a solution, then she would have believed him. She would have helped him raise Evie. He'd been her North Star and the person she'd always trusted to choose the right path. Maybe he had. Maybe their high school love wasn't the all-consuming emotion poets proclaimed.

Heart-wrenching pain overshadowed her memories of loving him. She refused to subject heart to that sensation. "New memories don't erase old ones. The doubt would linger, and apprehension would kill anything we started."

He let his shoulders sag and stepped back. "Okay."

She swallowed and compartmentalized his declaration from the reason she'd eaten his damn po'boy. She was hungry and needed to mine him for information regarding Jeanne. Town gossip suggested his relationship with Lisette was platonic, and Jeanne preferred the Tea Room to Nathan's hotel. Gossip could also kill a woman. She cleared her throat. "Jeanne's mother hired me to look into her disappearance. You're single. Did you date either woman?"

He ran his tongue over his front teeth. "Lisette and I weren't together. I haven't been with anyone since Flannery. Before her, there was only you." He smiled wistfully. "We were so young."

She lifted a hand and sidestepped him. "Thanks for the confirmation."

He grabbed her arm. "Ann...do you believe me?"

The limits of his relationship with Lisette made sense, but she suspected his question had more to do with his statement. *I never stopped missing you.* Could he atone for his betrayal?

She thought about the painful sacrifices, public whispers, and pointed snubs that must have followed his shotgun wedding. He raised Evie with Flannery, but until Flannery died, his freedom was elusive. Plus, look what he'd built. His hotel and shops pardoned whatever social sins he committed. Each time she rebuffed him, his frustration played out in his hallowed eyes, his tight expression, and his controlled movements. She thought he grieved, but she recognized weariness. He was a wild animal caught in a trap of his own design. She'd blustered through his generosity, accused him of criminal intent, and rubbed his face in her pain like he survived unscathed. He'd certainly come through with a larger bank balance.

Cringing at her critical assessment, she looked toward the hotel's second-story windows where silhouetted people laughed and enjoyed a party. She doubted they could survive Hemlock and wondered if she wanted to.

Family roots intertwined beneath Hemlock and kept the city from sinking into the river's deep, squelching mud. Long-held connections also bound the town's citizens to their mistakes. She and Nathan had their chances to make their marks on the city. She'd run away, but he'd stayed. She could believe he missed her, but *if* she survived giving him another chance, she doubted Hemlock's citizens would bless her happiness. Their history would trail them forever.

Considering his hand gripping her arm, she flexed her lithe muscles. His controlled grip belayed the tension in his shoulders and the lines fanning from his fire-lit eyes. She'd hurled her hurt at him. He'd absorbed her blows. His response recommended his character. A weaker man would make excuses.

She'd grown so much stronger than the starry-eyed teenager who made impassioned stands at centerfield. She'd seen lives lost for ideals and served under live fire. For some reason, she had survived. He had, too.

"Ann?"

She blinked. His hesitant query focused her attention. "Yes?"

He took an audible breath. "You believe me?"

She swallowed. "I missed you, too, but I don't know you. I don't know how much of my reaction is rooted in hormones, in nostalgia, or in wistful thinking. You can't promise things will work out. You're good, but you're not that good."

He laughed and hung his head.

His release sounded tired. Second chances required more than sentiments. They required luck and hard work. Two days in Hemlock meant nothing. She wondered if dawn would wash away his declaration.

"Making time stand still is a big ask"—he raised his head—"but missing you is easy."

"Hah. Ask Paps about the green smoothie I made him drink."

He tucked a stray hair behind her ear. "I'd rather remind you how good we can be. After all this dies down"—he waved a hand toward the Mardi Gras crowd—"let me take you out to dinner. Let me get to know you again."

She cupped his face. The contours were leaner than she expected. She rubbed a thumb along his nascent beard. The hairs were softer than she imagined, too. "Why?"

"The minute I saw you in the pinewoods, I wanted to throw you over my shoulder and haul you off to somewhere remote where we never grew up."

She dropped her hand and considered the trampled ground. Lisette's life ended too soon. Jeanne's hung in the balance. A quick escape from the intimate firelight would be smart. She should leave before she did something stupid like throw herself into Nathan's arms and believe his promises. "Everyone should get the chance to grow up. Right now, I have to find Jeanne. She's no older than Evie."

Nathan tipped her chin. "We'll find her. I hired a Valor private investigator to locate Lisette. He wasn't successful, but he found the stuff she stole. Those leads might help you locate Jeanne."

"I have the report."

He worked his jaw. "Right."

In the distance, a car backfired, and a person shouted.

He cocked his head. "She's not dead. She's missing."

"As far as you know."

He wet his lower lip. "I know we missed the dates and the self-discovery. The romance. We were horny kids who snuck away from our parents and got to third base. I won't fumble again. Let me help you find Jeanne."

"Hell, no." She ducked away before he kissed her or imagined he could aid her investigation. When two people mashed lips and discovered a heady rhythm, their jolt of recognition eroded organizational discipline. She avoided banging Ricco on purpose.

Nathan thought he missed her, but two decades had passed since he called her his sun and his moon. Boy had never been good at astronomy. Now, he was exhausted and tipsy. She wanted stone-cold, sober declarations. A little pain and exertion wouldn't hurt, either, but she definitely wasn't letting him in on the investigation.

"I'll see you after Mardi Gras?" he asked.

"Yeah." Opening the backyard gate, she looked over her shoulder. The flickering shadows made him as handsome and as dangerous as the devil. The corners of his eyes crinkled in wry humor, and his expressive mouth held back a smile. He knew perfectly well she ran away from his declaration, but the spark of life in his gaze assured her.

Whenever she'd bent over wearing a short skirt or blown him kisses in the school hallway, he'd given her the same expectant, amused expression. She could play flirtatious games and keep him at bay with school rules, but he waited in the parking lot and kissed her so deeply that the school safety officer blew a whistle.

When he went after something he wanted, he could be as patient as the day was long. No wonder his daughter was accomplished, his empire was successful, and his looks improved with age. She felt her lips twitch and lingered with a hand on the gate. "You mess with me again, and I'm gone. I'll burn you to the ground, and I won't have any regrets."

He dipped his head. "After Mardi Gras."

She grunted and let the gate clatter. By now, half the town probably knew she'd slipped into Nathan's backyard, but what she did there was none of their business. What would she tell Paps? He and everyone else would say the same things. Look how successful Nathan had become, and look who'd rolled over and considered giving him a second chance to screw her.

Squeezing the frustration from her eyes, she hopped a low fence and walked toward the shadows between the streetlights. In the cool, buzzing woods, a path would lead her home. She would have space to think about Nathan's declaration. He missed her? She spat on the sidewalk.

"Whoa, there!" Detective Sullivan stood beside a patrol car with an officer at the wheel. "You need a ride home?"

The patrol officer snickered. "Had too much to drink?"

Detective Sullivan slapped him upside his head and then crossed the street and met her beneath a streetlight. "What's going on?"

She rubbed her temples. "Nothing. You have any leads on Lisette's murder?"

He rocked back on his heels. "That's police business."

She narrowed her gaze. Letting the police handle Jeanne's disappearance was an option she couldn't accept. "Well, Judge Calloway hired me, and that makes Jeanne's disappearance my business, too."

Detective Sullivan exchanged glances with the patrol officer.

"Night, boys." She whistled and crossed the street into the woods. "I'll be seein' ya."

Chapter Eleven

The prior day was such a rollercoaster of emotions. The minute Ann put her head on her pillow, her memories fled, and sleep cradled her in its soft, restorative embrace. God bless melatonin gummies.

Paps banged on the bedroom door. "Duckling, if you don't rise with the sun, you miss half the fun."

Apparently, Paps expressed his love in other ways. His house-shaking thuds would do his former commanders proud, but they also assured her he remained beyond his grave.

The raps stopped.

She considered closing her eyes. Cancer treatments zapped a person's strength. He ran out of steam. She sat in bed and stared at the ceiling. Instead of sleeping, she should make him a protein-rich breakfast. Maybe fried eggs and avocado toast.

Paps turned the radio to full volume.

"Tyrant." Officers kept their soldiers on tight regimens, but none of them had blared *Radio Acadie* at six o'clock in the morning. Points for Paps.

Cajun, zydeco, blues, jazz, swamp pop, and swamp rock were fine ways to start a day, but she'd rather go back to the dream where Nathan loved her like she needed to feel love. The fantasy was a dream she'd indulged for years, but like a guilty pleasure, she'd never mentioned the fantasy.

"Last chance, Annie!"

She refused to start the day drenched by a bucket of water and swung her feet to the floor. "Okay, I'm up!"

"Better be." He turned down the radio.

The jazz line lingered.

She stretched her jaw. Grinding her teeth was a terrible habit, but her night guard protected her tooth enamel. She scrunched her hands in her hair, stood, and grumbled until she shoved a green smoothie into Paps' hands. "If you let me sleep in, you'd have time to cook bacon and air out the cottage."

"Pancreatic cancer is potentially curable." He sipped the smoothie and grimaced. "This shite, on the other hand, is terminal."

She padded around the smooth floorboards and assembled thick yogurt and farmer's market granola. Local honey added a sprinkle of sweetness. Digging her spoon in the bowl, she raised the first bite to her lips and paused. "Stage IV pancreatic cancer has a five-year survival rate of one percent. After diagnosis, the average patient will live for about one year. Don't be average, Paps."

He slammed the empty glass onto the battered butcher-block countertop. "I have Lindsey to worry."

"Lindsey isn't kin." Spooning the honey-drizzled granola and yogurt into her mouth, she let her rebuttal stand and considered mentioning Nathan's overture.

"I heard you were at Hotel Chalet last night."

She gaped.

"That boy's a heartache waiting to happen."

"You told me to go to his spa."

"I also told you he was at the top of my suspect

list." He pulled whole-grain bread from the breadbox, opened the butter dish, and hesitated. "His family is a work of art. Valerie, his grandma?" He raised his eyebrows and waited for her acknowledgement.

She dodged the bait and spooned in more yogurt. "I knew her."

"Woman remembers segregation as well as I do. Trouble is, I'm not sure whether she learned from her past or longs for its return."

She took a bite. Valerie and Paps had picked at each other for decades, but Valerie had a fulltime nurse. She would be surprised if Valerie remembered her breakfast. The old bat went through vodka handles like they lubricated her from the inside. Ann took another bite of yogurt and held her tongue.

"Valerie keeps a spotless house, but she loves martinis more than she loves people. That boy ran wild while his parents hobnobbed along the East Coast. After Evie was born, they came back to town to help see to her, but they missed raising their son."

She chewed her bite.

"What Nathan did wasn't right, but it's been a minute. Could be he's making amends or he's ready to double his prestige. Half the town's wondering if he'll stay or if he'll go. Now, you showed up. You need a grieving widower in your life like you need a sucker-punch to your head."

Leaning back in the chair, she crossed her arms over her chest. "Is that why you avoided telling me about the cancer? Worried I'd fall into Nathan's clutches...at his spa?"

"Didn't want you worrying." He buttered his bread. "Can't do anything more than what I'm doing,

Duckling."

She puffed out her cheeks. Nathan might turn Hemlock into a Southern amusement park, but her arrival had nothing to do with his success. Standing, she pushed back the chair and regretted the chair's legs scraping the old floorboards. "We had a good, long talk, that's all."

"Good. Where's Ricco?"

"Checking out from the hotel. He has to report to Venice."

Paps stared. "That's it? Your partner's leaving you?"

"In hostile territory no less!" Shaking her head, she dropped her dishes in the old farm sink and braced her weight on the porcelain edge. "I can investigate Jeanne's disappearance without Ricco's assistance. If I need reinforcements, I'll call a Valor operative to cover my back. That's what we do." She looked over her shoulder. "I could have come sooner."

He looked out the cottage window. "No use."

"I deserve the chance to say goodbye."

"Aww, duckling." He whipped out a handkerchief and blew his nose. "Don't be that way."

What way? She wanted to ask the question, but instead of ruining the day with regrets, she blinked away her tears, turned, and clapped her hands. "What time does the Mardi Gras *courir* arrive?"

"They're marshaling on Longfellow Street." He chewed his toast. "After they dawdle taking pictures with tourists, and fall off their horses, they'll arrive around dusk."

"Perfect. We have all day to ready the house."

He scanned the living room. "What do you mean,

ready it? It's been ready."

She eyed the hospital bed and the assorted medical supplies. After Paps passed, would the cottage remain a place she visited? Lindsey and Ricco moved the furniture to set out food, but they superficially tidied knickknacks and arranged old memories. Only family could do that. She pulled out her phone.

—I've got Paps. Can you pick up the catering?—
—No problem—

She cleared off a table and disassembled her gun. The P320 was a striker-fired handgun, but the piece had a very short trigger pull. With each pull, an internal spring-loaded pin rushed forward to detonate a bullet's primer, but the trigger pull didn't draw back the striker, the trigger simply released it. At rest, the P320 was effectively fully cocked and ready to fire. She kept the gun in pristine condition.

Paps walked to the table's edge. "Still have that old thing?"

"Can't see any reason to replace it." She let Paps heft the piece's weight. Users unfamiliar with its quirks ran a misfiring risk, but they could thank gun lobbyists for the vulnerability. Federal consumer product safety regulations exempted firearms, but collectors and frequent users kept each other safe by sharing their experiences at shooting ranges, armory counters, and gun shows. A carrier who wouldn't make eye contact and chitchat probably shouldn't have a gun.

Paps knew the gun was basically cocked at all times. He also knew the hardware lacked external safeties like a manual thumb safety to prevent malfunctions and misfires. Before he let her leave for the Navy, he drilled gun protocols into her head.

Some users weren't so lucky. Gun owners notified SIG Sauer the P320 pistol could fire when dropped. The company launched a voluntary upgrade or modification program. The company's fixes changed the gun's internal design, but accidental shooting reports trickled in. Older guns sent back for upgrades and new guns built with the modified design both failed. Unless she melted down her firearm, the gun could still injure a person. She knew better and was too nostalgic to let it go. "You taught me well."

He spun the gun and smiled. "I suppose I did."

Later that afternoon, Paps peeked under a serving tray's foil wrapper. Steam escaped. "What if the sausage isn't spicy enough? Why can't I eat a *boudin* ball?"

She rolled her eyes.

Pierre laughed. He sat in a rocking chair and smoked a cigar.

She should have recognized him in a heartbeat. As a boy, he learned to make *boudin*, the famous pork sausage with liver and rice. If a Mardi Gras runner had a problem with his *boudin* balls, he'd probably rise from his rocking chair and beat the runner with his polished, cypress walking stick. She was lucky he'd only called Paps.

Paps was lucky he had pancreatic cancer and could blame his culinary doubts on his drug regimen.

The first strains of music crept up the drive.

"*Poulet* and run!" Paps cupped his hands around his mouth. "Get ready."

She eyed the chickens circling a kiddie pool. For a reveler to catch one, he or she had to be good at hiding and good at making chicken sounds. The birds couldn't resist their own calls. Given that Nanette and the other matriarchs were already stirring massive pots of gumbo at the community hall, Ann rooted for the chickens.

"I have to remind myself about Mardi Gras's uniqueness. Our family's been celebrating this season this for generations. It's a way of life. All year, I look forward to the carnival." Paps bit into a sausage link, slapped his chest, and coughed. "*Sacre*, it's good."

Pierre snorted.

Paps swallowed. "Yes, sir. It's right special."

She absorbed the scene and took her place on the porch steps beside the chickens.

Within seconds, the riders and trailers would clear the drive. The chicken throw would be the stop's highlight, and Paps' toast would send the revelers toward their next destination. She spied a runners' tall, pointed *capuchin* hat through the trees. The headgear looked like a fringed piñata horn, but nobody would mistake the rider's garish mask and vibrant revelry for anything but Acadian Mardi Gras celebrations.

Cluck. Cluck. Scratch.

She wrinkled her nose. Any chickens within five square miles of Hemlock should take shelter, prepare to outsmart the runners, or surrender to their roux-based fate.

A fiddler and an accordion player teased her memories with "La Danse de Mardi Gras." Just like that, she was a child excited to see the Mardi Gras *courir* sweep through her front yard.

The number of costumed, masked participants had increased, but they followed the *capitaine* on horseback, foot, or trailer. At each stop, pilgrims sang, danced, and collected ingredients for a communal gumbo. The *capitaine* kept the crew well fed from front porch spreads, and seasonal excess gave way to Lent's somber reflection.

Standing, she smoothed her dress. The revelers wouldn't dismiss Paps' *boudin* balls unless a northerner made them. "Here we go!"

The runners flowed into the driveway in a joyous wave of color, music, and excitement. Horses pranced with riders on their backs, musicians played from an idling tractor pulling a cotton trailer, and tagalongs jumped to the ground, passed out beads, and danced.

The *capitaine* circled his white mare. Someone had braided yellow roses into her mane. Purple, green, and gold fringe lined the seams of the *capitaine's* satin shirt and pants. Mud flecked his horse and his outfit, but he confidently sat astride the animal and surveyed his kingdom. "What can you give?" he asked in French. "Rice? An onion? A chicken?"

Paps lifted the first chicken and tossed the bird into the air. In days gone by, he would climb to the cottage's roof and given the hen an advantage. Today, he tossed the chicken over the porch railing and dusted his hands.

The chicken flapped, landed, and made a beeline for the nearest bush.

As the drunken riders chased the chicken and the hens that followed, hilarity ensued. Bodies thudded to the ground, and dirt crushed into their costumes.

"Make soun' like old Boudreau done fall off his ladder!"

Why did their accents get stronger when they drank? Biting back laughter and the joy of belonging in a crowd, she watched runners scramble for bragging rights. Friendship and tradition compelled them.

Costumed in tattered, homemade fringe, calico rags, satin scrubs, and hand-painted wire-mesh masks, the riders flung themselves into the shrubbery with such abandon that they'd be lucky if they finished the *courir* without landing in a muddy ditch.

Behind the masks, they were Hemlock's farmers, accountants, and lawyers, but they were the few and the proud. Trouble was, if they became successful runners, they also became chicken owners.

While the runners scrambled around the yard and guests looked on, a heavy-duty pickup truck parked a cotton trailer in the drive. The Merrymakers climbed off their trailer and strutted into formation. They wore pink, curled wigs and black, lace bodices over white, button-down shirts. Painted, inexpensive sneakers looked like saddle oxfords, but sequins adorned the toes and their fingerless, fishnet gloves.

The effect was something like watching wrinkled, French poodles invade a Sock Hop. Music blared from a speaker roped to the trailer. Dancers limited their moves to arm motions, line exchanges, and square steps. Despite their age, their bright-pink lipstick and raucous smiles earned them well-deserved attention.

Ann leaned against a porch post and let the chaos in the yard warm her heart. Studies showed that participating in community activities helped seniors form lasting bonds. If cackling like drunken hens and shaking their geriatric hides kept the Merrymakers moving, more power to them and their mental health.

A Merrymaker offered Paps a plastic rose.

Playing along, he lifted the flower to his nose and saluted the dancer.

Ann smiled. She was in favor of anything that kept

Paps smiling.

The *capitaine* circled his white horse and pulled the animal alongside the porch. *"Les Mardi Gras passe un fois par an demander la charité."*

Nathan's deep voice asked for charity with a surprisingly crisp, French accent. Squinting past his mask, she saw nothing but shadows, but she wrapped two hands around the last chicken and offered the hen as tradition demanded.

"That isn't the bird I want." He gripped her arm and swung her into the saddle. "Hold on."

Startled, she tossed the chicken into the air and wrapped her arms around him. "Can't you award your favors to someone else?"

"Who wouldn't pick you?" He kicked the horse into a walk and raised a hand for the *courir* to advance to the next household.

Searching for a way to extricate herself without embarrassing Paps, she tightened her hold. Beneath Nathan's satin tunic, his torso felt solid and well-muscled. He smelled like sweat, fresh leaves, and warm, damp hay. She itched to explore the planes of his abdomen and lean into the heat radiating off his back, but she had no business being there. "Let me down. You can't haul me onto your horse like I belong to you."

"You've always belonged to me." He kicked the horse into a gallop. "Hold on!"

She griped his waist like her life depended on it. Maybe her happiness did. Looking over her shoulder, she found Paps smiling, holding a beer, and wrapping an arm around a Merrymaker. As soon as she extracted herself from this spectacle, she would return to ensure he didn't overindulge.

Paps toasted the *courir*. "Don't be a spoilsport!"

She rolled her eyes and tightened her hold on Nathan. Whether Paps spent the evening gorging on *boudin* balls or drove into town to join the *fête* had little bearing on her predicament, but his hot-and-cold attitude toward Nathan left her as confused as riding double on Nathan's horse. Enjoying the faced-paced ride and Nathan's overheated back pressed against her chest were guilty pleasures. As soon as she put her feet on solid ground, she would tear into him and gave him a piece of her mind.

On the dirt shoulder near an intersection, he pulled on the reins and slowed the horse. One road led to cotton farms, and the other led to town. "I can feel how unsettled you are, but if I don't set a brisk pace, the parade will stall on your grandfather's front lawn, and nobody on the route will know what happened."

She pulled away from his body and tucked her hair behind her ear. Sure enough, the sound of riders flirted with the sound of trees rustling in the wind. "If you needed a sidekick, you could have"—she rubbed her temples—"asked?"

He pulled off his mask and tucked the satin in a pocket. "I don't need a sidekick." Turning, he lifted her and settled her across his lap. "After I watched you leave last night, I got to thinking, do you remember how good we were?"

The horse sidestepped and shook its head.

Smart horse. She looped her arms around Nathan's neck and smiled. "I remember you're a cheating asshole."

He bracketed her hips and centered her on the

bulge in his pants. "I remember more. I'd bet good money you do, too."

She sucked in a breath. He'd matured into a man and left his adolescence in the dust. Attempting to lift her hips, she found his muscles were more than a television gimmick and worked her jaw. "I've never been much of a gambler."

"Liar."

She leaned away. "Also, this is rude. Personal space? Zero."

Grinning, he tapped his heels into the horse's sides and set the animal to a gentle walk.

The animal's rocking gait felt entirely too close to the slow thrusts she imagined in Nathan's arms. Lightheaded from skipping food, overheated from her position, and feeling her sex swell, she shifted her seat.

"You can hate me and still be attracted to me."

Guilty. Looking over the winter-browned fields, she watched a bluebird dart through a stand of leafless pecan trees. *Territorial creatures.* Wasn't she one, too? She could pretend she was with anyone else, but she'd be lying. Nathan always felt like home, and the reasons she stayed away from Hemlock remained valid.

Turning her head, she stared into his green eyes, ignored his heady mix of aftershave and sweat, and replayed her happier memories. The bitter ones still smoldered. Only idiots subjected themselves to live fire without a noble cause. She cleared her throat. "You need to work on your pickup lines."

"We're past the point of pickups, Annie. You're in my lap."

She refused to wiggle. "Why, exactly, am I here?"

"You have the balance of power. I wanted

everyone to see how you affect me. You can ride into town like you're the queen and reject me before the crowd, but this moment is mine." He swallowed. "Do you know how long I've missed you and felt guilty for dreaming of you?"

She knew the allure of dreams, too. Leaning forward, the tips of her breasts teasing his silk-clad chest, she raised a hand, cupped his neck, and felt his rapid pulse. He stared, silent and fluid with the walking horse, but his grip on her hips would leave bruises. Lowering her head until her lips hovered near his, she felt his controlled breathing tickle her skin. One stumble from the mare, and Ann would break his nose. She wet her lips. "Nathan?"

"Yes, Annie?"

His soft response raised the hairs on the back of his neck. She was playing with fire, but she held his gaze, wet her lips, and leaned toward his ear. "Put me down"—she turned and bit his earlobe hard enough to taste blood—"or so help me, God, I will end you."

Laughing, he wrapped an arm around her waist and reined in the horse. "Before you end me, may I kiss you?"

She jerked back and wondered if she should have bit harder. "Did you not hear what I just said?" The disbelief in her voice overpowered her outrage. "Put me down!"

He tightened his hold. "I can handle you."

Few people could. Ignoring his rippling thigh muscles beneath her ass, she lifted her seat. Bad move. Caged by his arm and the horse's neck, the shift pressed her against his swollen cock. To escape, she could duck under his arm, swing a leg over the mare's back, and land on the parish highway, but the indignity would hurt. Six feet to freedom. Why did freedom look so far away?

"Has anyone ever asked you for a kiss?"

Hearing his smug control, she swung her gaze away from the road and raised her chin. His eyes were as green as pine needles, and his black lashes lay thick against his tanned cheeks. All the people she kissed paled in comparison to her memories of his kisses. Attributing stumbling rhythms to bad connections and over-inflated memories, she moved on. "I've kissed plenty of people!"

He stroked a finger along her cheek. "Do any of those people matter? Are you with someone else? I can't get you out of my head."

"Selfish thoughts." She looked toward the sun sinking lower in the sky. A bright-orange glow shimmered behind the trees and faded to pale-yellow. "I'm single, but I don't want your kisses or your attentions."

"Afraid you'll like them?" He dropped his hand and stroked her lower back. "Afraid you'll remember how good we can be?"

"Not good enough," she whispered.

He sighed.

She heard echoes of her pain. Reminding him how much of a jerk he'd been wasn't her plan, but the past kept raising its ugly head. They were different people, and the kisses she remembered belonged to randy teenagers, not mature adults. Raising her fingers, she traced the heated column of his throat. His pulse beat beneath her fingertips, and desire echoed between her wet, swollen lips. She chewed her bottom lip and debated making a bad decision.

He butted his cheek against her palm. "It's just a kiss."

The scratchy caress focused her attention. "I've thought about kissing you again, too. I've wondered if my memories were true. Maybe I overinflated your consequence. Maybe you're just another person on a long, long list."

"Maybe." He slid the hand gripping her hip along her back and tangled his fingers into her hair. "Maybe not."

"Whenever we're together, I forget how much life hurts." Her confession came out in a breathless rush. "Your kisses are—"

"Ann?"

His interruption stole her breath. "Yeah?"

"Please, kiss me."

His polite request undid her resolve. Their embrace would be sweaty and awkward...noses bumping and tongues fighting for control. Her disappointment might purge him from her system. Closing her eyes, she braced for fumbling maneuvers and pressed her lips against his. They felt soft. Frowning, she drew in his scent. His fingers massaged her scalp and coaxed her into more than a chaste peck.

"Kiss me," he whispered.

She parted her lips and pulled in his bottom lip. The teasing, crisp taste of his mouth snapped her restraint. He was as familiar as summer rain. Her desire for his body burned through her control like a wild, aching gust.

"Yes." He tightened his grasp.

His kiss and his rhythm were so pleasurable she

sighed with relief, released her reservations, and chased the connection she craved. Wrapping her arms around his torso, she pushed her body into his. Their breathing matched. She indulged in the smooth slide and slow-dance pleasure of kissing the man she once loved.

"More." He grunted, low and impatient. "I always want more of you." Tilting his head, he changed the angle and claimed what he needed.

No longer in control, she felt the kiss everywhere, as though her body's tight, aching muscles could find release. Panting, she drew away, missed the feel of his connection, and keened. Why had she been without this man for so long? Frustrated, she kissed him until she wondered if she might pass out in his arms and remember his kisses as nothing more than a dream.

He caught her lower lip, pulled it between his teeth with a restrained tug, and released her. "When I saw you in the woods, I missed a step." He kissed her with soft, aching passion and moved a hand over her curves like he memorized her figure's dips and curves. "I've needed you, Ann. I've needed these kisses. I can't get you out of my head."

The smooth, heady pleasure of his kisses made her realize how much she'd benchmarked her lovers against him. Kissing him felt good, but the sensations ruined her. Forgetting him again would be like disregarding her name.

Skimming his lips along her neck, he nuzzled the sensitive spot beneath her ear. "You feel good."

His admission sent shivers scattering over his skin. She could blame her response on the cooling late afternoon air, but nobody would believe her. Between her fingers, his hair felt cool and silky. Against her neck, his jaw was rough with stubble. While he kissed her, he rocked his erection against her sex in a slow, teasing motion that had nothing to do with the horse and everything to do their connection. Anyone who saw them would know she'd given into her emotions on a sunny, desolate, wind-whipped road where all and sundry could see her fall.

He slipped his hands beneath her shirt and smoothed the sides of her waist. "I want to feel your skin," he whispered against her mouth. "I've missed you so much."

"You don't miss me." She'd envisioned this moment a thousand times and never thought the reunion would happen, but she knew how to protect herself. She drew in a deep breath. "You miss my body."

"I do." He dropped his head, pressed a kiss to the swell of her breast, and breathed deeply. When that wasn't enough, he kissed her other breast. "You smell like sex." He flexed his hips and raised his head. "Will you fall apart in my arms?"

His pupils were wide, and his gaze was drunk with lust. Desire thrummed deep in her core, too. What did she look like? A woman who'd forgotten herself, straddled a man's thighs, and wanted the same things he did. What would people say?

"My Annie," he whispered.

She didn't give a damn what they'd say. Slipping a hand beneath his white tunic, she held a palm over his heart. His hot, damp skin thrilled her. She ached to run her hands over every inch. His back and shoulders, rippling with shifting muscles, could occupy her for hours. Her breasts were swollen and her nipples tender and achy. She needed the sweet release he promised.

Struggling to untangle her thoughts and her physical response, she pulled her hands from beneath his tunic and drew a deep breath through her nose. "Wait."

"As long as you want." He rocked forward her pelvis, shifted his hips, and made a sound deep in his throat before kissing the soft spot beneath her ear. "I'll wait as long as you need. Just give me another chance. I won't hurt you, again."

Other things in life mattered more than heady kisses and good sex. She couldn't think of any in particular, but falling into bed with him would send her into a spiraling depression. She planted her palms against his chest. "I said, wait."

"You're killing me." He raised his head. "It doesn't have to be today. Don't shut me out. I'm not stupid enough to make the same mistake twice."

"Sure you are." She hung her head and breathed deeply. In the road, she'd ridden his cock and dry humped him as though they were horny teens in a truck cab with nothing to lose. They had everything to lose, and they knew it.

"This ride was supposed to be fun." He tipped her chin. "A little show to give you the upper hand. Feeling your breasts bouncing against my back undid me."

The horse neighed.

She mirrored the animal's disbelief. "Losing control is what you're good at. You're all in, and then you're gone."

He rolled his eyes. "Come on, Annie, it's not like that."

Raising both arms, she gripped his shoulders, lifted her seat, and swung a leg over his lap so she could dismount along the horse's shoulder. Their kisses were frantic, wet, passionate messes. How could an embrace be so hot and so good without knowing each other? This passion couldn't last. Rocking against him was one thing, but knowing which way the wind blew was another. She'd been about to come from the friction on her clit, and he hadn't even touched her. She slid to the ground and figured she could run back to the cottage in twenty minutes.

Pounding hoof beats cut through the air.

The parade rounded a curve and would soon be upon them. What would she say? They'd made out like teenagers, and she had regrets? Maybe the Merrymakers would let her hitch a ride on their wagon.

Offering a hand, he swallowed and offered a hand. "I won't ask for another kiss. Let me bring you into town to enjoy the holiday."

"Fine." Anyone on the highway who saw their swollen lips would know what they'd done. She needed the cover of wind-whipped hair and beer-fueled laughter. She gripped the saddle, planted her foot on his boot, and swung herself behind him. "For the record, I don't belong to you or to anyone else."

With a nod, he slipped on his mask and turned the horse toward Hemlock.

The *krewe*, laughing and motoring in a weaving parade, cheered their leader.

The mare fell into an easy walk.

She held herself stiff and slapped the mare's flank to send the horse into a gallop. The sooner the parade ended, the sooner she could forget this stop. What was she thinking to let desire rule her decision-making skills? Nathan's interest in sex threw cold water on their relationship and left her a frustrated, steaming mess. After everything she'd been through, she should know better than to let him woo her again. She was in Hemlock to tend Paps and find Jeanne. Everything else was *lagniappe*. Experience taught her life was never easy for people who indulged their whims.

Chapter Twelve

Nathan rode to the Hemlock Community Center and waved at the crowds. Within the hour, masks would be off, horses would be trailered, and spoons would feed mouths. Everyone who rode in the parade or watched the revelers pass would have a grand time, and the live music would continue until the exhausted band quit. Finally, the cleanup crew would collapse folding tables, gather discarded beads, and listen to Hemlock's residents sleep off their alcohol-fueled restlessness.

"Throw me somethin', mister!" Nanette cried. "Ain't I pretty?"

Ann tensed.

He pulled a rose from the mare's mane and tossed the flower to Nanette. She could run her mouth about everyone in town, but she wouldn't add his rudeness to her complaint list. As far as she knew, he'd stolen Ann for a joyride. Everyone was entitled to have a little fun.

"Let's get out of here," Ann hissed.

He guided the horse toward the open field where he could provide clear, cold water and a brisk, drying rubdown.

As soon as the mare stopped, Ann dismounted, squatted, and stretched her thighs.

He swung a leg over the saddle and did the same. Pulling off his mask, he tossed it to the ground and shook out his sweaty hair.

She stood and planted her hands on her hips. "What were you thinking? Are you drunk?"

Well, he started drinking around eight in the morning. Some runners started the night before, but he was too cautious to get wasted while riding through the countryside at breakneck speed. He knew how to put on a show and would play the fool for her benefit. Giving her the chance to publicly reject him went a long way toward evening the score between them and salvaging their friendship. He frowned. Friends didn't kiss each other silly. Never mind his declarations. She hadn't exactly swooned at his feet. He wet his lips and reached into his horse's saddlebags for his water bottle. "I'm not drunk, but booze isn't a bad idea."

"You can't just-t"—she rubbed her temples—"kidnap people from their doorstep. Captain or not, you're still an asshole, and I'm not aching for the gumbo pot. If I didn't know you better, I'd slap you."

"You don't slap friends?"

She planted her hands on her hips. "I don't slap fools!"

He laughed away her insult, but her flushed cheeks and wide eyes were a good indication of her indignation. If he weren't careful, then she'd remand her offer to slap him and give him a solid knee to the balls. He drank water and hoped he found dry clothes before his sweaty, cooling muscles conspired with the chilly, dropping temperatures to make him miserable.

Ann's indignation was good. He'd broken her heart, but he could give her an excuse to walk through town with her head held high instead of her ear cocked, listening for whispers. She was the last person who needed blue-haired, church ladies sticking their noses into her business. Then again, Nanette probably typed out the telephone tree. He couldn't do a lot to save Ann from that relationship.

He capped his water bottle. "About seventy people saw me haul you onto my horse. If that's kidnapping, this town can defund the police. Also, you're too stringy for the gumbo pot."

Rolling her eyes, she looked toward past the milling crowd. "Whatever. I'll find my own way home. Next time you're riding, I'll toss the chickens from the roof."

"Why would you do that to those itty, bitty birdies? Dey gone lan' wit' a splat!" He pulled out a handkerchief and wiped the sweat off his brow. The *capitaine's* satin tunic looked fancy, but the costume started as hot as Hades and ended drenched in sweat. As far as clothing went, the costume was as ineffective as a clown's bikini. "Such vengeance. What'd dem roosters do to deserve your wrath?"

"Been practicing your accent for the crowds? French or Cajun, *Capitaine*. Pick one." She advanced. "Or are you a fraud?"

He felt his balls retract and danced away from her approach. Holding up a finger, he tried an Emmy-winning smile. "Catching a chicken while costumed and running through a muddy field is quite a feat."

"A fool's feat." She rolled her sleeves. "What does that make you?"

He was doomed, but he would go down swinging. "I've always been foolish around you. I loved you in the back seat of my old car. We were eighteen. Nothing's changed!"

She snorted and pulled back a fist.

"On second thought!" Laughing and skirting her half-hearted swing, he remembered how badly he smelled and how many people watched them. He thought swinging her onto his horse would look like a boon, but if she decked him, the locals would know she had the upper hand in their relationship. He considered his options, but dropping to one knee and declaring his love might net him a broken nose. Instead, he cupped his hands as if he held something precious. "When you have a bird in your hands, you think you're dreaming. You hold on so tight, you're afraid you might collapse its lungs. It's a primitive state, chasing after your food." Opening his hands, he mimed releasing the bird. "It's a bit like kissing a woman. You should try it."

She narrowed her gaze. "Kissing a woman?"

"Going after what you want." Shifting his weight, he looped an arm around her waist, felt her tense, and clenched his ass muscles. He could feel a kick to the nuts coming as sure as he could sense spring's arrival. Oh well, nobody could blame him for trying. He puckered his lips. "Surely, your *capitaine* deserves another kiss."

She smiled sweeter than any Southern belle. "Fuck you."

The second she smiled, he knew he was in for it.

Her knee slammed into his crotch with such alacrity he marveled at her speed. Then, pain radiated through his body and echoed in his stomach. He dropped to his knees, groaned, and struggled to catch his breath. He'd been wrong about her physique. At some point, she had abandoned tumbling classes and honed her strength into a lethal asset.

He would clap, but he could hardly breathe. A

man's balls took wear, but direct hits were painfully acute. He stuffed his family jewels into skinny jeans for photo-shoots, let them bounce around on commando days, and slapped them against skin during sex, but he'd never willingly sacrificed his boys to let a woman get a leg up on him…literally. Whooshing out his breath, recovery seemed a long way off.

Good thing he had Evie. Ann's aim probably crushed possibility of future Charlet offspring. Planting his hands on the cool, green grass, he breathed deeply. "I deserved that blow."

She dropped to her knee beside him, gripped his hair, and pulled back his head. "You deserve a hell of a lot more than getting your balls busted."

Meeting her gaze, he smiled. She was still as fierce as the day she'd thrown her pom-poms so Sam could play football. Last night, by the firepit, he glimpsed the innate tenderness and lingering hurt she kept hidden. Her ferocity left room for compassion. He'd always admired how she took life's knocks and moved on, but he'd never appreciated the costs. He'd go to his grave repenting his mistakes, but he could spend his remaining time easing her way. "So, no kiss?"

She knocked him onto his side, stood, shook her head, and dusted her hands. "I went along with your shenanigans for Paps' benefit, but he's not here."

"Nope." He swallowed, rolled to sitting, and looped his arms around his knees. Given another few minutes and a cold beer, he would consider standing. "Go get you some gumbo."

"I'm not hungry."

"Sure you are." He raised an eyebrow. Everyone in town was hungry. Making gumbo for five hundred people required more than Grandma's aluminum stew pots. Rice steamed in foil-wrapped trays. Hemlock's finest stirred wooden paddles in industrial-sized vats perched on iron stands. Propane flames provided heat and steady hiss. The chicken, sausage, and okra stew wouldn't be as good as the dark, rich mix Maw-Maw Thibodeaux-Landry made, but tired, chilled, and half-drunk Mardi Gras revelers thought the gumbo tasted great.

The community center's floodlights blinked on, and the intense light cast Ann's long shadow over him. He cocked his head and glanced toward her shadowed face. "How is Paps?"

"Get up." Blowing out her breath, she offered a hand. "I don't have time to babysit you, and I'm not leaving you there."

If he stood, he would probably limp. He'd wanted to give her leverage, not ruin his pride. Asking for acetaminophen and a cold compress would probably push her past her limits. Planting his hands behind him, he leaned on his palms. "Don't go soft. Someone probably uploaded a video of your takedown and alerted their networks how you brought me to my knees"—he frowned—"or my ass. Don't ruin their moment!"

"Whatever." Lowering her hand, she cocked her head. "I was doing fine avoiding you. Whatever you're doing, drop it. Pretend we're still eighteen, and you've altered my life."

"But I'm almost forty."

"So am I!" She drew a measured breath. "I don't need you to sweep me off my feet or to redeem my reputation. In fact, I don't need you at all."

129

If she weren't raised to be a lady, she might have spat. He inclined his head. "Okay, then. Be a hard-ass."

"A hard-ass?" She huffed. "I'm tired of people walking away. Paps is the only person who stuck by my side my entire life, and now he's dying. He deserves my attention. You deserve civility. That's it!"

"Civility?" He rubbed his chin and refrained from mentioning his aching balls. "Well, thank you. ma'am. I know where I stand."

"Good. Stay out of my way." Shaking her head, she left.

Watching her, he appreciated her muscled, hardheaded curves. She'd warned him not to mess with her again, but she'd meant not to get too close, and that distinction kindled hope. Walking the line was an art form. She let him get away with declaring he missed her, but she attributed his declaration to his whiskey-fueled sentimentality. At least, he refrained from mentioning he loved her. That confession would send her running faster than a skittish kitten. He respected her reasons. Every person had regrets about their pasts.

A partygoer raised a duck call and let loose a Cajun Squeal. The call simulated feeding ducks. Hemlock's crowd hooted, clapped, and queued for supper. By midnight, the rowdy crowd would disperse to begin Ash Wednesday's fasting interlude.

He hoped Jeanne stumbled home, too, but he would help Ann's investigation.

Judge Callaway was tougher than an ironwood tree. How did southwestern Louisiana raise such fiercely independent women? Did every generation examine their circumstances and fend for themselves? Listen to their mamas' stories and realize their ancestors mucked up history? Modern women made the best of what they had, but they also made it better. He pushing to his heels and slowly rose to standing.

Living in the Bayou State could be heartbreaking, but people stayed for family ties and comforting traditions. When Ann's grandfather passed, she would leave town. The ache and the swelling in his balls would dissipate, but his memories of Ann would persist.

Life's disappointments could be so painful that they changed a person's outlook on life. The cheerful, determined teenager he fell in love with matured into a decisive, hotheaded woman who shielded her emotions. By cheating on her, he struck her a painful blow, but combative women rarely tumbled from the womb ready to fight. She bore scars from her mother's abandonment and her father's death. She was also right. He was an asshole who laid his courtship on too thick.

She deserved to be well-loved. He would do better.

Then again, he would also be smart to wear an athletic cup in her presence.

Chapter Thirteen

Lacing her running shoes, Ann prepared for an early morning run. The day after Mardi Gras usually brought headaches, but the tension in her shoulder blades came from encountering Nathan. To loosen her muscles, she stomped around the cottage.

Lindsey winced and checked Paps' vitals.

Hitting a person was the basest pleasure. While sparring, she hit until she garnered a reaction that satisfied her. Understanding why she fought led her to therapy. Over the years, she built aggression and anger. Hitting a person as hard as she could released those feelings. The trouble was, the moment her heart rate slowed, regret swamped her endorphins. Just once, she wanted to beat the crap out of someone and know they deserved it.

Bringing Nathan to his knees briefly felt good, but her reaction faded. She would apologize, but her muscles still twitched. She needed a release... Just not the release he offered. Instead of popping muscle relaxers, she would sweat him out of her system.

She chugged a water bottle, refilled it, and stretched. Single women weren't lonely. Friendship, dating apps, and battery-powered devices kept life fresh and pleasurable. Hemlock was a like a stale sock with a lace rim.

What did Nathan want her to do? Settle down,

follow his lead, and abdicate her career? Sure, she wanted a kid or two, but if she had to choose between adoption and functioning as a man's appendage, she would happily bow out of a formal relationship. If a knee to his balls failed to convey her message, she would up her ante. He missed her? She snorted. He knew as much about loving women as she knew about wallpaper.

"Duckling, where's your shirt?" Paps refilled his coffee cup and stirred in cream. "It's too early in the morning for that sports bra. You'll scare the wildlife."

She bit back a smile. His double standards were charmingly retro as long as no living, breathing women experienced them. She kissed his cheek and pulled back. "I'm going out for a run. Want to join me?"

He huffed.

She raised her eyebrows. "You can set the pace."

"Watch out for cars." He sipped his coffee. "And put on sunscreen."

She winked. "Eat your granola."

"Ha! I'll give dem oats to the tree rats." He shuffled toward the back porch where he kept a pellet gun to defend his vegetable garden. "Given the number of acorns layin' about, even the squirrels won't eat it."

She slipped her water bottle and her cell phone into her runner's belt and adjusted the cinch. Her heart rate monitor on her wrist would notify her of incoming calls and allow her to control her music. Opening the front door, she gasped.

Nathan wore a messenger bag over one shoulder and stood near a yellow bicycle. He held a manila folder. "Mornin'."

She widened her gaze. "What are you doing here?"

He scratched his temple. "Delivering my copy of the Valor report."

She jogged down the porch's front steps. "Haven't you heard of email?"

"This copy has my notes." He offered it. "I also added what the investigator said in passing but refused to commit to paper."

"I have the investigator on speed dial! You think my coworker will hide things?" She stretched her calf. "What's wrong? Your hotel's business office doesn't have a scanner?"

"Right. I could have scanned it."

She switched legs and stretched the second calf. "Or sent your assistant."

He cleared his throat. "Lisette *was* my assistant."

"Right." Embarrassment warmed her cheeks. Taking the report, she avoided brushing his fingertips and flipped through pages detailing interviews, cell phone records, and receipts. The annotations were more thorough than she expected. Sliding the bound papers under a rocking chair cushion, she put her wireless headphones in place. "Thanks. I'll copy the report and return the original."

"Or just, like, scan it, email it, and keep the printout."

Her headphones chirped to confirm battery power and connectivity.

"That way, you won't have to see me again." He raised his voice. "I'm sorry for pulling you into the saddle and kissing you."

Her music remained paused, but she decided not to mention the silence. Let him shout until his voice went hoarse. Softening her approach toward him had been a mistake. The brief thrill of his kisses lingered, but if she let her body rule her responses, she would forget history's painful lessons. "Apology accepted. You're riding a bike, so your balls must have recovered."

He blanched and adjusted the messenger bag. "Barely."

She jogged past him and turned up her music. Pounding club beats would set her pace and drive her toward the runner's high she craved.

"Wait!"

She turned down the music. Bike tires crunched oak leaves against gravel.

"I'm glad you're still running. When you weren't cheering, you were lightning on the track field."

"I'm not that fast anymore." She raised a hand to adjust her music and drown him out. "Now, let me run."

"Is that why you got a tattoo?" He slowly pedaled. "It looks fresh."

She glanced over her right shoulder at the compass rose tattoo. The fine-line design wasn't fresh so much as touched-up. Focusing on her breathing, she settled into her pace and left him to his own devices. "Everyone needs a compass rose. I run jobs, but my moral compass orients me. I don't need sacred religions, geopolitical boundaries, or entrenched grudges to tell me the difference between right and wrong."

He kept pace on his bike. "No ashes on the forehead?"

"Only if they're part of my fancy face soap." Talking while running at her preferred pace was a challenge. She could slack off, ignore him, or knock him into a roadside ditch and pretend his fall had been an accident. She glanced over. "Why aren't you wearing a helmet?"

He ran a hand through his hair. "I like to feel the wind."

"Says the future quadriplegic."

"Well, at least I'd have my memories." He rang the bike's handlebar bell. "This is Flannery's cruiser. I'm maintaining the bike for Evie."

She kept her gaze on the road. News of Flannery's death reached her in Colorado. Cheering the woman's demise felt petty, so Ann settled for silence.

"I'm not much of a mechanic, but once a month, I check bolts, lubricate components, and take the bike out for a spin. If something goes haywire with the spokes or the cables, I know which bike mechanic Flannery trusted. Someday, Evie might want to ride. Flannery taught her."

Ann increased her pace. She doubted Evie would get on a bike in the near future. The ghost bike in Hemlock was a poignant reminder that Flannery's death left a daughter without a mother. Ann knew how painful losing a mother could be. Even if she returned, she wasn't around when Ann needed her. Death in absentia stung, but vehicular manslaughter was brutal. Two miles later, she stopped for water.

He did figure eights in the rural intersection.

She ignored him and headed north. He was an annoying gnat on a yellow bicycle two sizes too small for his frame. If he wanted to maintain Flannery's bike, he had to realize he was fighting a lost cause. Maturity sharpened her instincts, endurance kept her lean, and age widened her perspective. His gesture was sweet, but only Evie could process her mother's death.

Rising a glance, she found him staring and averted her gaze. Sweet wasn't the right word. Achingly stubborn was a better descriptor. He could have gone to college and glimpsed the world beyond Hemlock, but his loyalty was like a lead weight. After suffering his betrayal, she bailed faster than a midshipman on leave. Based on his professional success and his creative daughter, he'd done just fine without her. She'd done fine, too. As long as she avoided kissing him, she could do her job.

A truck passed.

He raised a hand in greeting.

The truck's driver honked.

Loyalty be damned. Spitting into the grass, she broke into a sprint. At the four-mile mark, she braced her hands on her knees and breathed deeply. She could complete the loop and return home or run until her legs gave out. Exhaustion might be the safest option. Raising her head, she glanced over her shoulder.

Nathan waved and rang the bike bell.

Chest heaving, she considered him was as persistent and annoying as an early-morning mosquito.

"I've been thinking." He pedaled the bike to the roadside and leaned on a foot. "Why do you risk your life for Valor?"

"The same reason I stayed in the Navy. Someone has to do it, and I'm good."

"I can imagine you doing whatever you set your mind to."

Reading too much into his statements was a risky proposition. He claimed he missed her, but he probably missed her body and his chance at atonement. If he said she hung the moon, he probably wanted her to suck his dick. Men were tricky like that.

He glanced at her bare, toned stomach.

She shook her head. They were right back where they started, and that's exactly where they would stay.

The message indicator on her heart rate monitor blinked.

She pulled her cell phone from her belt. "Get lost, or I'll slash your tires and leave you in a ditch."

He rubbed the back of his neck. "That's an option?"

"Yes." Scrolling through notifications, she spied a missed call from Baptiste. If he called her instead of Jeanne, then the authorities hadn't found their missing person. Ann pressed the screen to return his call. "Shit."

Nathan peered at her phone. "Shit, what?"

She lifted a finger and listened to the rings.

"Hello?" Baptiste asked.

"Hey! It's Ann Storey form the plant society. I called you about Jeanne. Did you get my message?"

"Yeah, uh." Baptiste cleared his throat. "I had a rough weekend."

Nathan pressed closer.

She held her ground and put the phone on speaker to avoid repeating the conversation. It's not like she could go into a conference room and lock the door. She ignored Nathan's crisp aftershave and focused on Baptiste's scratchy voice. "What happened?"

"After the car drop-off, Jeanne and I got into a fight. She left me at my house. I went out drinking with some friends, and we cut up too much. Got thrown in the drunk tank for the weekend."

She frowned. "The whole weekend?"

"Ma'am, the police don't have time to process people over Mardi Gras."

She exhaled. During carnival season, New Orleans police arrested hundreds of people for minor offenses, public intoxication, indecent exposure, disorderly conduct, and reckless operation. Beer and anonymity were ready ingredients for reckless behavior. She didn't have time to let bad decisions derail her investigation. If Baptiste committed a petty crime, he should have found himself out on bail within a day. The kid got into mischief, but that was five days ago. If the police kept him jailed that long, he'd had a rough go. "Are you okay?"

"I've been"—he coughed—"better. Don't have much of a taste for booze, anymore, if you know what I mean."

"I bet," Nathan muttered. "I've heard of other people getting stuck in jail until Ash Wednesday. It's like the ultimate penance for pissing on a lamppost. When I was a kid, I thought my grandmother just wanted to scare me into good behavior. I don't envy you, man."

"Who's that?" Baptiste asked.

"My running partner." She elbowed Nathan and raised a finger to her lips.

"What?" He shrugged. "I'm empathizing."

"*You're interfering.*" She focused on the call. Mardi Gras's famous laissez-faire attitude had a downside. Law enforcement monitored parades, costumes, and marching bands to maintain order and public safety. Many people spent a disproportionate amount of time in Orleans Parish Prison for relatively minor offenses, but Baptiste's family would have called an experienced defense attorney and quickly gotten a bond set. "Your family should have sprung you."

"Well, my family left me there." Baptiste cleared his throat. "They didn't have the cash."

She exhaled. Processing might have taken a little longer than normal, but letting Baptiste marinate in the city drunk tank was totally unnecessary. "Paps would have helped your family post the bond. He appreciates how much you've done for the society."

"Didn't have that many calls. I'm out now, aren't I?"

Baptiste's gruff response terminated the discussion. She circled back to the reason she called. "So, have you heard from Jeanne since you got your phone back?"

"Nah, but I heard from Judge Callaway." He whistled. "Damn, she's fierce."

Dropping back her head, she stared at the cloudless, blue sky and considered what do to next. Jeanne had to be safe. The holidays were a chance to let loose and have fun. Maybe she needed a break from Baptiste, her studies, or her overbearing mother. Righting her head, she walked toward Paps' house. "Tell me about the fight."

Nathan walked the yellow bike.

"Just the usual stuff." Baptiste cleared his throat. "I wanted to meet her family and stuff, but she wasn't ready. I get that. I mean, it's a lot, but Jeanne was a lot, too, you know? Like, she just had this way about her. Even the bugs loved her."

"I'm sure they still do."

Baptiste cleared his throat. "Grad school is expensive. Entomologists don't get fat, juicy grants. Jeanne had to pay for most stuff out of pocket. She emceed at campus parties and mixed vintage vinyl and digital files, but the money wasn't enough."

Mardi Gras could have pulled Jeanne into a thousand unsavory situations, but she seemed bright and capable. "You didn't want her to take a gig?"

"No, I wanted her to take more. She, uh, said the hours were too rough. Her family had a house full of antique silver she only used for holidays. Not the plated stuff. The heavy, sterling silver. Judge Calloway would never miss it."

She slowed her walk and traded glances with Nathan.

He raised his eyebrows.

Southern silver was not to be trifled with. Judge Calloway would have a fit and skin Jeanne alive. If Nathan had stolen his family's silver and fenced it, then Valerie would have flayed him. Her descendants saved their silver from Civil War looters. Never mind how they treated the slaves who made the silver possible. The silver's value wasn't so much in its weight as in its symbolism.

Judge Calloway thought she'd reached a place in her life where her wealth and her status safeguarded her family, but assets could be attractive nuisances, too. Ann expanded her approach to the case. "Jeanne did this? Sold little odds and ends?"

"I mean, just once." Baptiste shouted a greeting to someone off the call. "Sorry about that. Right, some Hemlock broad saw a set of silver teaspoons in her purse and bought them. Jeanne thought making the sale was hilarious. I mean, who needs silver teaspoons?"

Ann knew exactly who needed silver teaspoons.

Nathan let the bike fall. The frame bounced and

clattered on the asphalt.

"What's that?" Baptiste asked.

"My friend dropped his bike." She cleared her throat and left Nathan to right the bicycle. "Baptiste, did you tell Judge Calloway about the teaspoons?"

"Yeah. She didn't believe me, but she would inventory her silver chest. I don't think little, old Cajun ladies are a threat, but what if Jeanne tangled with someone who took advantage? Judge Callaway has some nice stuff, but nothing's worth endangering Jeanne's life."

"As far as we know, she's just missing in action." Ann drummed her fingers. "She might be sunning in Florida, feeling sheepish, and dumping hot sauce on loaded fries."

"I doubt it." Baptiste coughed. "If I had the money, I would have given her cash. Now, I'm just"—his voice cracked—"someone needs to find Jeanne."

Ann itched to break into a run. "Take it easy, Baptiste. You haven't done anything wrong. Humor the police. My company specializes in cases like this one. We'll find her."

"Yeah, I just…" He cleared his throat. "Thanks."

"I'll see you soon, okay? We'll have another burn. You and Jeanne can fight over the heavy machinery."

"Yeah, if you say so." He ended the call.

She slipped the phone into her belt, confirmed Nathan hadn't busted the bike's chain, and sprinted home to get Paps' truck and discover why Nanette kept quiet when Judge Calloway showed up.

"Wait." Nathan pedaled up. "Let me help."

Keeping her gaze focused on the horizon, she ignored him. He meant well, but civilians with good intentions often got shot. She had enough on her hands.

Chapter Fourteen

Nathan rode into town with Ann and debated how to proceed. Orders waited on his approval, but she was ready to charge across the street in running shorts, a sports bra, and dried sweat to confront Nanette. Accompanying her would provide a front-row seat for town gossip, but staying by her side would also allow him to protect her.

Not that she needed his protection.

A credit to the training that taught her to control her emotions, Ann hadn't said a word since she put away her phone, sprinted into her grandfather's yard, grabbed the keys, and started the truck. He had ten seconds to throw Flannery's bike into the truck bed and climbed into the passenger seat before she peeled out.

He considered Nanette's Tea Room and its shaded front porch. Ladies sat on the edge of mint-green caneback chairs surrounding round bistro tables. They picked at chicken salad sandwiches and small pastries while overhead fans kept their conversation free, easy, and clear of bugs. The tea in their elaborate, painted services looked untouched, but empty flutes waited for more champagne.

Ann turned off the ignition. "Out you go."

"You know"—he cleared his throat—"I'm peckish."

She blinked. "Peckish?"

He opened the passenger door and climbed down. Bracing his hands on the roof, he shrugged. "What else can you be at a place like the Tea Room? It's certainly not the type that sticks to your ribs."

"That's the point." Her right eye twitched. Reaching behind the driver's seat, she pulled out a worn long-sleeved shirt, slipped the article over her head, and climbed down. Slamming the driver's side door, she rounded the truck's hood. "Suit yourself. Eat a croissant."

Show runners went to bat for their work with similarly determined expressions. Ann looked as resolute to solve this case as Judge Calloway was to find Jeanne. Whoever located Jeanne might enjoy chatting and roasting Hemlock's citizens, but they solved a crime. He hoped they raised their glasses instead of sharpening their spits. Falling into step behind her, he shoved his hands in his pockets and whistled.

Ann climbed the steps. "I don't need you."

The ladies at lunch fell silent.

He cleared his throat. "Noted."

Ann turned and nodded toward the truck. "What about the bicycle?"

He shrugged. "We have a saying in Hemlock. If you don't lock your bike"—he winked—"it might get stolen."

An older woman laughed.

Ann rolled her eyes. The man was more cavalier than a... *cavalier*.

"I'm sure these lovelies will keep an eye on the bike." He tipped his head toward the women on the porch. "Afternoon, ladies. Holler if anyone looks interested in my banana mobile. It's subtle, right?"

The group waved toward the restaurant. "Off with you, then."

Ann opened the screen door and walked into the cottage.

Catching the door before the wooden frame slammed his face, he stepped into the brightly lit Tea Room. The decorating wasn't half bad. Mint-green walls, gold pulls, coral-painted banquettes, and marble four-tops anchored the dining area. Floral couches clustered around a glass and wicker coffee table, and fresh flowers filled milk-glass vases sitting on a painted mantle. A swirl of funky, vintage plates decorated the wall where an oil landscape might have hung.

The space offered more than the faded Acadian flag suggested. Nanette's mash-up of French Bistro, Farm Chic, and Estate Sale Treasures flowed. Customers had plenty of light-filled room to enjoy their fussy sandwiches, bland salads, and low-carb snacks while they planned their days. A market room offered household goods and grab-and-go items on cypress shelving. The tiny shop's offerings probably kept Nanette's business solvent.

From a sunlit corner shelf sporting a bronze replica of Buckingham Palace, Kiki yawned.

He knew exactly who had pulled together this room for Nanette, and a pang of longing for Lisette's easy laugh echoed in his heart.

The kitchen door swung open.

Wearing a floral shirtdress and a fabric belt that cinched her waist, Nanette dried her hands on a waffle towel, dropped the towel in the bussing area, and scanned Ann's ensemble. "Well, look what the cat dragged in! I see you dressed for lunch."

Ann cupped Nanette's elbow and pulled her toward the marketplace. "*Tante Nanette,* a word, please."

Nanette raised her free hand to her porch customers. "The Tea Room has *such* a homey feel. Everyone loves to pop in for a chat or camp out for the afternoon. If it ain't broke, don't fix it, right, ladies?"

A Merrymaker tapped her teaspoon against her cup. "Here, here!"

He winced at the garish, ringing sound and hoped the utensil wasn't one of Jeanne's spoons.

Holding a smile, Nanette accompanied Ann into the old bedroom hosting the marketplace. Mardi Gras bunting festooned the eves. Porcelain masks and bagged candies were inexpensive gifts. As soon as Nanette cleared the door casing, she pulled free of Ann's grasp and stalled before a display of linen tea towels, boxed hand soaps, and aromatic soy candles. "What is going on?"

"Is this how you keep the tea room afloat?" Ann jerked her head toward the tea low-priced gimmicks. "Overseas shit? Smart people don't want cheap, plastic stuff. We have local artisans. *Krewes* are emphasizing reusable items. How many people in this town sell home goods? Should we talk about supply and demand?"

"Economics might be more palatable than your behavior." Nanette raised her eyebrows. "Who taught you your manners?"

He cleared his throat. "Ladies…"

"You did." A paper price tag hung from a linen napkin embroidered with a fleur-de-lis. Ann flicked the tag. "Nanette, I appreciate your intentions, but you're not the arbiter of what's valuable. You hid information." Exhaling, she shook her head. "I came to ask you pointed questions. Don't even think about offering me tea."

"Ann," Nanette hissed. "What is going on?"

Narrowing her gaze, Ann crossed her arms over her chest. "You tell me. Jeanne Calloway is missing. Judge Calloway came looking for Jeanne. You acted like you'd never met her. Turns out, you bought her silver teaspoons."

"So?" Nanette scratched the side of her lip. "They were pretty."

Ann tilted her head. "Is that all that matters?"

Nanette raised her chin.

Rolling her lips, Ann waited.

He worked his jaw and wondered if he'd overreacted to the tension between the women. They had a long, storied history as complex as any mother-daughter relationship. Lifting a set of resin salad tongs, he tested their heft, flipped over the price tag, and rolled his eyes. Sixty-five dollars was big money for plastic utensils. No wonder Nanette courted culture. If she wanted to sell finery, she had to look like she knew her business.

"So"—Ann mimicked Nanette's indignant posture—"I don't believe in coincidences."

"I barely knew her."

"What about Lisette? She's dead. She watched your cat. Should the police start asking you about any other missing persons?"

He replaced the salad tongs and moved to Ann's side.

"Oh, is that all? Pfft." Nanette smoothed her

shirtdress. "Honey, if you twist together two lengths of string, you still don't have a rope."

He stared at the beadboard ceiling and wondered about hanging himself. As much as he loved Hemlock, absenting himself from the town had nurtured an impatience for drawn-out, Southern confrontations. Ann had the right approach. A swift blow to the nuts carried efficiency. What would Nanette say if Ann knocked her one? He grinned and tamped down his enthusiasm for a matronly cage fight.

Then, he remembered Ann's threat to send him into the ditch. When had he developed such an appreciation for stubborn, violent women?

Ann raised her chin. "Be that as it may—"

Nanette raised a hand. "I'm not responsible for every little brown girl who falls on hard times. I'm sorry your friend is missing, but I didn't hurt her. If anything, I helped her."

Nathan scratched the back of his head and exhaled. Nanette was one step from calling Jeanne "uppity." Ann would probably deck her or whack her with the salad tongs. She had a righteous sense of right and wrong, but judging by their recent encounters, she also had a temper. He cleared his throat to intervene.

Ann shifted and blocked his line of sight. "Tell me the last time you saw Jeanne."

The sound of grinding teeth made him want to hurl. He wasn't above throwing her over his shoulder to avoid losing his lunch or shedding Nanette's blood. He threw back his shoulders.

"Oh"—Nanette looked out the window—"a few months ago. Guidry has better records of his volunteers than I do."

Ann tilted her head. "Humor me."

The controlled tension in her tone stayed his impulse to intervene.

Nanette sighed. "Jeanne came into the Tea Room for lunch. She showed me the teaspoons in her purse, and I offered to buy them without asking too many questions. Her other silver pieces were too fancy. I don't have that kind of money."

"And then?" Ann prompted.

"And then"—Nanette raised her chin—"I introduced an antiques resale app. Lisette made me an account and helped me source decorations. Louisiana has money hidden in its cedar closets and bachelor chests, but the state also has eccentric, old ladies who need retirement income."

He shoved his hands in his pockets. "Don't forget the ghost stories."

Both women turned and scowled.

"What?" He shrugged. "They're great for publicity."

Nanette rubbed her chin.

Ann lifted a linen towel, checked the price tag, and frowned. "What's the app's name?"

"Uh"—Nanette withdrew her phone from her shirtdress pocket—"Polished and Hammered." She displayed the phone screen. "The icon is a monogram of the app's two initials. Cute, huh?"

He'd prefer to spend his day polished and hammered, but his hotel and media empire kept him going. If the women refrained from tearing out each other's hair, then he should return to work. Instead, he pulled his phone from his pocket and downloaded the app. Listings ranged from a $95,000 sterling silver dinner and lunch set to $300 silver sugar tongs. Suddenly, Nanette's resin grabbers looked like downright bargains. He glanced up. "What's Jeanne's user name?"

"No idea." Nanette shrugged.

"Do you remember which pieces she pitched?" Ann asked.

"A water pitcher, a soup tureen, and an epergne." Nanette straightened the linen napkins Ann disturbed. "She must come from money."

He came from money, but he had no idea what an epergne entailed. The app listed thirteen water pitchers and six soup tureens. Soup didn't get enough respect. Hoping for a match to connect Jeanne and Judge Callaway's pieces, he tried epergnes. Three listings popped up. Apparently, the ornamental centerpieces held fruit or flowers, and the most elaborate specimen had a $35,000 price tag. The piece looked like a bitch to polish. Perhaps people with epergnes, who came from *real* money, employed maids to polish their silver. His hotel staff would walk out. He offered the phone to Ann. "Do any of those seller profiles ring a bell?"

"SilverFox1949, SilveradoNOLA, and 504SilverStar could be anyone." Ann exhaled. "Why couldn't Jeanne pick something obvious?"

"She stole those pieces from her mama." Nanette planted her hands on her hips. "Would you want to get caught?"

Ann furrowed her brow. "Knowing their provenance, why did you buy them?"

Provenance? Nathan suppressed his grin. The longer Ann and Nanette went head-to-head, the more Ann sounded like a local. Did she work with a diction coach to erase Hemlock from her speech patterns? While kissing her and listening to her threats, he hadn't noticed the absence.

A Merrymaker popped her head into the room. "Could I trouble you for more coffee?"

"Of course!" Nanette adopted a bright smile and passed close to Ann. "Jeanne never said the teaspoons were stolen," she hissed. "I took her at her word, and a lady's word is final. I'm not culpable."

"Ah, now she's a lady?" Ann tilted her head. "I thought she was just a—"

Nanette narrowed her gaze. "I am a woman of her word."

Ann blinked and smiled. "You are."

Nanette flounced from the room. She might pass a lie detector test, but if a Southern woman whispered her story to enough people, she turned conviction into truth. His right eye twitched, and he debated how to proceed. He could make offers on three epergnes and flush out the sellers, but investing a hundred grand in antiques sounded like more involvement than he wanted. "She's a piece of work."

"Always has been." Ann's relaxed her shoulders. "She's so cheerful and supportive in public and so cutting in private. Guessing which person I'll encounter wears me out."

He rubbed her shoulder. "Then why did you tolerate her?"

She tipped back her head and exhaled. "Besides Sam and Paps, she was the only person I had."

You had me. The claim sat on the tip of his tongue, but he couldn't bring himself to utter his confession when he clearly let her down. Instead of talking, he pulled her into an embrace and rested his chin on her head. "I'm sorry. She's a bitch."

Ann laughed and rested her head against his chest. "As long as she's still talking, you have room to maneuver. If she starts pursing her lips and looking away, then you're screwed." She pushed against his hold. "I'm fine."

Feeling her tense, he wondered how long he could savor her strength and her sweat before she realized how much her presence affected him. In a room that smelled sweeter than a florist's shop, she was the only thing real and rugged enough to survive. "Is that why you're so worried about Jeanne? You remember being lost?"

"Vince okayed the job, but yeah." She traced a finger along his chest's shirt-clad contours. "I remember trying so hard to excel and always falling short. When my mom left, and my dad killed himself"—she pulled back and pressed her palm into her eye—"I just remember feeling like everyone I loved had left me. I don't want Jeanne to feel that way. What if she's out there, wondering if someone will find her? None of my missions have ever felt this personal. It's dangerous."

He stroked Ann's back. When her dad died, she called the loss the result of a long disease. Everyone knew about Drake's cirrhosis, but they let the euphemism slide. They had also poured Drake drinks and sold him cheap bottles of whiskey, so maybe they felt culpable, too.

Nathan felt responsible for Hemlock. Given Jeanne's work with the habitat society, Jeanne was an honorary citizen. He wouldn't let her disappearance slide, but he wouldn't endanger his Ann, either. "Judge Calloway is a formidable woman. The police will investigate the app."

"And do what? Get a warrant? Subpoena records? The formal process will take days." She pushed against his hold and straightened. "Valor's resources are faster. Now that I have a lead, I can take action."

He cupped her face before her professionalism shut him out. "We got off to a rocky start"—his balls tightened in defense—"but I'm here."

"I noticed." She tilted her head.

"If you want to blow off steam, then I'll avoid judging you. I can listen to you unload." He dropped his hand from her face and missed the connection. "Sharing frustrations makes you human."

She twisted her limp ponytail into a bun and held the hair on top of her head. "Paps would always die before I was ready. Now, that day's here. Returning to Hemlock raises so many bad memories and so many could-have-beens. I should let circumstances tangle with my feelings for you."

Feelings were a good start. He opened his mouth to respond.

"Instead of staying, I ran away. Who does that?" She dropped her hair and huffed out a breath. "I should have stayed in town and toiled like everyone else. Perseverance yields bragging rights, even if you're pushing a rock up a hill."

He laughed. "Hemlock isn't all that bad. You've just been away awhile."

She grabbed the linen napkin from the shelf and shook the fabric in his face. "One hundred and ten dollars for genteel crap. She called Jeanne a little brown girl. If Nanette hadn't half-raised me, she would call me white trash. Assimilation is the only way to win."

He pulled the napkin from her grasp and set the linen on the cypress shelving. "You're wonderful. You've already won."

"Platitudes." Ann shook her head. "If Paps can spare the truck, then I'll drive over to New Orleans, show Judge Calloway the app, and compare the listed pieces against her missing pieces. If I can find Jeanne's username, I can find who contacted her."

"You think someone robbed her?"

"Maybe she refused to lower her prices. Selling soup tureens isn't like selling pressure cookers. The buyer in the parking lot has a $30,000 incentive to screw you."

He rocked back on his heels. Ann probably carried a gun. Would she shoot first and ask questions later? He barely knew the woman she became, but he ached to find out. "I have business in New Orleans, so we might as well carpool."

She raised an eyebrow. "What kind of business?"

"I promised a reporter I would come into town for press photos. I still have my first home goods store. Surprise appearances keep my staff on their toes. A few acquaintances want their projects featured on my television show. I'd rather suss out their entertainment value over dinner than video calls. Streaming audiences want more than rippling biceps and clever quips."

She looked out the window. "They'd enjoy seeing you crash and burn."

"Well, that's always the appeal, isn't it?"

"Maybe." She swallowed.

He could hear her weighing the pros and cons of

accompanying him or leaving Guidry without a vehicle. Ambling toward the doorway, he avoided applying too much pressure. She could see Judge Calloway by herself, but with her partner abroad, he'd rather be with her than wonder how the meeting went.

"A ride would be great."

He jangled the keys in his pocket. "Give me an hour."

"This is not a date or a favor. This is a mutual convenience." She cleared her throat. "I'll fill your gas tank."

Looking over his right shoulder, he winked. "It's electric."

She frowned. "I'll buy dinner."

"That's not how I operate." Living on society's fringe left a bitter taste in Ann's mouth. Every favor was a transaction. He merely wanted to keep an eye on the stubborn, willful woman he loved. Used to love. Shit, she was driving him mad. He was tagging along to keep her safe and maybe steal another kiss. "Get changed."

"There's nothing wrong with my outfit."

He scanned her running gear and avoided lingering on her exposed curves. "I'm a fan, but some restaurants still have dress codes. Do you want to scarf po'boys on a back deck while I eat Oysters Rockefeller, or do you want to run up my business expenses?"

"One hour." She blew past him. "I've developed expensive tastes in meat. The oysters are an appetizer."

He laughed and followed in her wake. "I'm counting on it."

Chapter Fifteen

Ann held her fingers in her lap, but Nathan's
electric sedan had lush interiors that begged for
admiration. She followed the seams along her supple,
leather seat and glossed a thumb over polished, wood
door panels. "Recycled tires would be more eco-
friendly seat coverings."

He laughed and adjusted the radio volume. "I don't
recall that option."

Paps' old truck did its job. Refueling the gas tank
felt like a ritual indulgence. She emptied trash from the
truck's door pockets and wiped clean the truck's
windshield like she'd done her whole life. Sitting on her
hands, she considered rifling through her purse or firing
off emails. "I'm just sayin'."

"This car's fun to drive, too."

She could channel her fidgeting nervousness into
something productive. "Let me drive."

He glanced over.

"I know these roads as well as you do." She tilted
her head and waited for his excuses. His car had an
astronomical price tag, and he kept the vehicle looked
spotless. Given her track record with vehicles, he'd be a
fool to turn over the keys, but he knew little about the
collateral damage she'd caused in the past twenty years.

"No problem." He pulled onto the shoulder, opened
the driver's side door, and rounded the sedan's front.

She gaped. Maybe he had great insurance. She considered climbing over the console, but she chose a dress to meet Judge Calloway, and flashing her lacey underwear would give Nathan the wrong idea about its presence. Opening the passenger side door, she shook out her arms and then offered him a high-five.

He returned the high-five and moved toward the passenger seat.

She dropped into the driver's seat and surveyed the controls. "Is this your baby?"

"Evie's my baby. This is a car." He buckled his seatbelt. "Have fun."

She should probably stop threatening him with bodily harm.

He moved her purse to accommodate his frame.

She considered warning him about the bag's contents. Lip balm and hand moisturizer might not surprise him, but her gun would. As long as he kept his hands off it, they would both be fine. "Just, mind where you put my purse. I brought along my gun. It's unloaded, but I don't want you to look for peppermints and find it."

He edged her purse deeper into the footwall.

"I always carry it." She cleared her throat. "Habit."

"Thanks for the warning. I'll stay in line."

She laughed. "You do that." Rolling her lips, she stopped worrying about him, gripped the steering wheel, and punched the accelerator.

The car shot forward.

She eased off the accelerator before she added a speeding ticket to her driving record. "No wonder you wanted to drive."

"Yep."

Following the road's gentle curves, she played with the car's settings and wondered what an economy version would cost. Colorado had winding, backcountry roads. She wondered why she never explored them. Probably because none of her coworkers had patience for mindless activities. If they wanted to let off steam, they went to the firing range.

The highway leading from Hemlock toward New Orleans thinned into sparse houses on big acreage, long stretches of swampy forest, and occasional intersections with flashing yellow caution lights.

"Your phone's ringing." Nathan turned from his view. "You want it?"

She blinked. "Come again?"

He lifted her purse from the foot well. "Do you want me to answer?"

Since learning about Paps' diagnosis, she answered every call but preferred to field conversations in private settings. Valor colleagues also swapped favors. Wondering how much Nathan would overhear, she worked her jaw. "Who is it?"

"Doesn't say."

She slowed the sedan. "Answer it."

Nathan accepted the call. "Hello?"

"Hello?" a woman responded. "Is Ann there?"

The caller's voice sounded familiar, but the unknown number kept her alert. "Put it on speaker." She eyed a roundabout intersection and watched a truck approach from the other direction. The controlled chaos of multiple yield signs offered cheap thrills, but tracks through the grass median indicated the locals disdained the traffic circle and plowed through it in protest. "This is Ann."

"Ann!" The woman cleared her throat. "It's Jeanne."

Startled, Ann missed the roundabout entrance and rammed the sedan's tire into the central median's curb. Faced with an impact, the sedan shuddered and skidded off the neutral ground. She slammed on the brakes and risked glancing at Nathan.

Jaw tight, he raised an eyebrow.

She reversed and navigated the circle. Her heart thudded like a drum, but she kept two hands on the wheels and focused on the call that derailed her easy driving. "Jeanne, where have you been?"

"Out of town."

Ann snorted. Free of the traffic circle, she pulled over on the roadside and lifted the phone. Given she'd just ruined the car's alignment, she might as well let Nathan listen to the call. "Your mom's looking for you."

"Is she?" Jeanne hesitated. "I'll see her soon."

"Do you need something?" She met Nathan's gaze and mouthed her apology for the roundabout incident.

He shrugged.

"Actually, I do need something. Can you l-loan me five thousand dollars?" Jeanne rushed through her request. "It's for school. As soon as my loans come through, I'll pay you back. I just don't want to miss out on the spring semester or my, like, course scheduling."

Ann knew a lie when she heard it. She looked out the window at the green buds turning winter's barren branches into a bright-green garden. The spring semester began in January. She couldn't recall the specifics of her fee bill, but she doubted the university would let Jeanne carry a balance this far into the semester. "Do I send the money to the university?"

"Um, not exactly. I, uh, have to transfer the money from my account…so the university credits my fee bill. It would be kind of, um, funny, if you paid someone else's tab, right?"

Funny wasn't the word she would use to describe the tremor in Jeanne's voice, but fear could make any saint a sinner.

"I, uh, called Baptiste, but he's broke. I hate asking you to do this, but Guidry wasn't answering, and I can't get my mom involved. She'd be devastated. I'm supposed to be the responsible one, right? This is so embarrassing."

Jeanne might be an excellent entomologist, a fierce emcee, and a burgeoning thief, but she was a bad liar. Ann dragged a hand over her face. "Can we meet over grilled burgers and loaded fries? I'm still curious about the ghost pepper hot sauce you think I can't stand." She expected a laugh.

Jeanne sighed. "I'd really like that. Soon, okay? I just need the cash."

Turning her head, she met Nathan's gaze. Deep lines furrowed his brow. She muted the phone. "Something's off."

"I know." He frowned. "Will you help her?"

Wariness would keep his heroic impulses under control and buy her time to locate Jeanne from this phone call. "Maybe."

"Ann?" Jeanne asked. "I, uh, don't have much time."

She unmuted the phone. "Where can I meet you?"

"I'll send an app link for the cash," Jeanne said. "Don't worry, I'll repay you."

Scrambling for a way to stay in touch, Ann wondered who put the nerves into Jeanne's request. She forced a cough. "What's the name of that restaurant you recommended? The one whose wings came in so hot, you thought you might lose it. I need a fix."

"Oh, uh, that place is somewhere you wouldn't feel welcome. Everyone's Black. Just wait for me to come home." The connection wavered. "We'll go together, and it'll be fine. Send the cash, okay? I'll take it from here. Check your phone."

"These 504 numbers?"

A voice echoed over an intercom.

Ann struggled to decipher the announcement. She thought she heard port before the line went dead. Wanting to scream, she tossed the phone on the dash. "Crap. Judge Calloway was right to hire me."

Nathan rolled his shirtsleeves. "You don't believe her?"

"I believe she needs the money." Ann draped her arms over the steering wheel and rested her head. "I don't know why."

He opened the car door.

She raised her head. "What are you doing?"

"Checking the tire."

Remembering the thud, she opened the driver's side door and stared at the left front wheel. Scuffmarks marred the tire, and abrasions ruined the wheel's visual appeal. "I can change it."

He rounded the car front, stood near the tire, and cocked his head. "It's my car."

"I hit the curb. Don't you have roadside assistance or something?"

Shaking his head, he popped open the car's front

storage and lifted a jack and a spare from the front trunk.

She crouched and felt the tire. "It'll hold."

He traced the scuff. "You think?"

"We need to find Jeanne."

"Okay." He offered a hand and lifted her to her feet. "Let's go."

A car raced past, and the driver honked.

She returned the driver's casual greeting with a raised hand and watched the car disappear against the horizon. Despite standing by an electric sedan, she could be anyone in the last hundred years who stopped on the roadside to evaluate a tire.

The armed forces made her practical. Everyone from the most junior enlisted E-1 sailor to the E-9 master chief petty officer knew his or her role. Officers were no different. They were managers and leaders, but they were also interchangeable.

Focusing on what was important, she settled into the buttery soft seat and wished the leather didn't plaster her dress to her thighs. Instead of complaining, she buckled her seatbelt and turned the air vent to bathe her face.

Putting the car in Drive, Nathan punched the accelerator.

Pulled forward, she grinned. "Nice."

"You inspired me. Maybe I should start calling you Captain."

He wouldn't be the first man to turn her rank into a nickname. Captains were the senior-most commissioned officers below flag officers like admirals. Captains with sea commands generally commanded cruisers or larger, but the work she did was equally important to the Navy. She kicked out her feet. "I wouldn't object."

"Would the operatives at Valor?"

She turned her head. "Now, you have questions?"

He kept his gaze focused on the road. "You get a problem like Jeanne, and you own it. I never understood how you landed in the armed services. I was proud of you, but I just couldn't imagine how you'd made the leap."

"Paps was in the Navy."

He nodded.

His silence gave her the freedom to speak. Looking away from his handsome profile, she watched the trees blur into an anonymous green pattern. "I needed an escape, and the Navy offered it. I learned how to judge people and how to stick to my word. That kind of reputation follows a person. Vince approached me about making a career change." She glanced over. "It's his company."

He met her gaze and raised his eyebrows.

People expected hidden messages and cyanide pills from her line of work, but they were only half right. Revealing details of her career would change his impression of her. She palmed the phone and considered calling Ricco.

"If you don't want to tell me, then I'll stop asking."

"It's not that I don't want to tell you, it's that I can't."

He took an exit ramp toward the outskirts of New Orleans. The building density and the advertising load had increased. "Big security problem?"

More like a big interpersonal problem. As soon as she sketched out her career with Valor, he would recast her to fit his expectations. Media created certain prejudices. She leaned into them, but her cases remained confidential. "The specifics differ, but the themes remained constant."

"Okay…"

"Okay." She cleared her throat. "Before big data, people relied on their sixth senses to tell them when something felt wrong. Quick suspicion with common sense saved lives. Artificial intelligence has streamlined the process. Data narrows the number of people who concern Valor, but determining whether a lead is loyal agent or a foreign lead considering a regime change requires intuition. That's me. I'm the human touch."

"I figured you just beat people or shoved money in their accounts."

"There are a million ways to get rich. Some people schlep antiques." She waited for his self-deprecating laugh to die off. The sound grounded her. "I appealed to people's sense of history, their patriotism, their tolerance for injustice, and their family ties. Most times, the process worked. I was very good at my work, but the missions exhausted me."

"Ukraine? Russia? Latin America?" He glanced over. "You won't tell me any stories."

"For your own good." She held her breath and waited for his arguments. *He would keep her secrets and repeat not a word. They had history. She could trust him.* She almost snorted. He was as trustworthy as a rusty watering can.

He put on his blinker and changed lanes. "Okay, so what do your gut and training tell you about Jeanne?"

His simple acceptance settled around her like a weighted blanket. Comfort allowed her to relax her muscles. She dropped her phone into her lap. "I need more data. Modern smartphones have GPS technology and precise location tracking. My Valor colleagues can use technology in conjunction with mobile network data to pinpoint her exact location. I just have to make the call."

"Why aren't you?" he asked. "Judge Calloway paid you to find Jeanne.

"What if she doesn't want to be found?" Exhaling, she replayed the phone call. Jeanne hadn't asked for help. She'd asked for money. Five thousand dollars was more than most people traded for hot sauce tips and remixes. The ask was more than Judge Calloway turned over for a fee bill or Baptiste posted for bond. Someone besides Jeanne formulated the number. Someone who sold family silver on Polished and Hammered or had rich friends and greedy relatives. Maybe Jeanne needed to protect Judge Calloway. She considered other angles. "Did Lisette ever ask you for extra money?"

"No, I paid her well enough." Nathan traversed the business district and turned on a side street. Colorful, historic townhouses filled the city block, and shady oak trees dropped brown leaves into manicured flowerbeds. Soon, a light-green dusting of pollen would cover the sedan and everything else in the Crescent City.

She itched to find Jeanne, but what if Jeanne was just an entomology grad student with a petty theft problem and an overdue bill? She wrinkled her nose. What if Jeanne needed real help?

Nathan tapped an app on his phone screen and opened a two-hundred-year-old townhome's renovated garage.

She downplayed the impressive juxtaposition. Art

and technology coexisted. A person could examine imagery from advanced satellites, listen to recorded conversations, or read emails, but they relied on instinct to unite the details. Somehow, she recognized Nathan's ability to unite details, too. No wonder he'd become famous.

Her phone pinged with the transfer link.

She stared at the message. If Jeanne was in trouble, paying ransom was a terrible idea. She had no guarantee the money would accomplish her goal. Listening to her gut, she resisted transferring the money. Judge Calloway hired her for a reason. As soon as Ann found space to make the call to Valor, she would locate Jeanne and decide what to do next.

Chapter Sixteen

Nathan disarmed the security system and plugged in the sedan. The townhouse's spacious carriageway had an electric gate and secure parking for two cars, but when he bought the 1830s Creole townhouse, he added the electric vehicle charging plug and other modern conveniences. Authentic, old-world French Quarter living was nice, but cracked plaster and scampering geckos held limited appeal. Smart appliances, robust security systems, and easy entertainment features went a long way toward upgrading his living space. The geckos probably appreciated their improved digs, too.

"Is this the French Quarter?" Ann peered from the carriageway window and scanned the street. "It's quieter than I expected."

Her interest in the townhouse's location told him everything he needed to know about her priorities. To her, the townhouse was a utility. Pointing out the original plaster crown molding in the foyer, the intact fireplaces with cast-iron gates in the parlor, and the reproduction wallpaper in the dining room would earn him polite nods. He could ask her opinion on chandeliers, fifteen-foot parlor ceilings, artisan-crafted rosettes, and modern furniture selections, but she would probably shrug off the juxtapositions and ask for his Wi-Fi password. So much for the sleek console and the jute rug. What was the point of his success if she didn't notice it?

She stared into the garden shadows. "You have a cat?"

"The tiny, black panther belongs to my neighbor and fancies lizards. Geckos. Skinks. Anoles. The beast's not picky."

Laughing, she pulled back from the window.

Her easy sound soothed him. Despite her disinterest in his design work, she was spending time with him, and that's what mattered. "This is the Lower Quarter, across from *Le Richelieu* Hotel, and a few blocks from Jackson Square and the Mississippi River. Fewer lost tourists and traffic snags keep the neighborhood quiet, but living here remains a labor of love."

She turned from the carriageway window. "You live in Hemlock."

He wet his lips. Half the time, he thought he lived on the road. "That house is for Evie. It's more casual. I do much of my work here."

"Doesn't Evie live in New Orleans?" She tilted her head. "What *are* you doing in Hemlock?"

"Maintaining my familial obligations?" Checking the damaged tire's pressure with a manual gauge, he replayed his sleepless nights finessing Hemlock's revitalization. Every decision he made maximized tourism revenue. Genteel nostalgia and whitewashed prosperity led to revenue, but they also deepened his worry lines. Standing, he stretched his back. "Flannery loved that town. It's a nice place to raise a family."

"I couldn't wait to leave." She scratched the back of her neck and examined bikes mounted on the carriageway wall. A teenager's pink cruiser stood propped against the painted walls. "You started so young."

He started without her. The air in the closed space felt stale. Opening the courtyard door, he admitted a breeze and eased the tightness in his chest. "Come on, I'll show you the rest. It's a scattershot of Greek Revival, Italianate, and Hurricane Katrina renovations, but it's charming."

Slipping into his professional voice, he showed off the renovated floors like a real estate agent pitching a prospective client. "The main house has three levels of living space, front balconies on the second and third floors, and a first floor guest suite with a kitchenette." He opened the door to the guest suite. "You can sleep here."

"Neither of us brought luggage." She hesitated at the door and turned. "Aren't we driving back to Hemlock after meeting Judge Calloway?"

He ran a hand through his hair and wondered why he assumed her purse held a change of clothes. Moving between his houses felt as easy as changing conference rooms. He had full wardrobes in every location, but what could he offer her? "Dinner might go long."

Glancing at the bed, she turned her back on the guest suite. "I'll be your designated driver."

He laughed. "Remind me to put on the spare tire."

Elbowing him in the ribs, she stepped into the narrow hallway.

He left the guestroom open to breathe, led her into the formal foyer, and jerked a thumb toward the elevator. "Unless you're desperate, skip the shuddering elevator."

"Noted."

Gripping the polished wooden handrail, he bounded up the townhouse's gorgeous stairway and entered the second-floor entertaining area. The double-parlor living room and dining room had high ceilings, original crown molding, and plaster medallions, but he'd picked out the elaborate light fixtures and brought the townhouse's majesty to eye level. Floor-to-ceiling windows in the dining room and the galley kitchen opened to a balcony over Chartres Street. Pushing a button, he opened the room's drapes, flooded the space with natural light, and waited for her reaction.

She stopped on the landing and whistled. "Fancy."

Laughing, he hung his head. "Thanks."

"You want a write-up? Call the reporters at your lifestyle magazine. They're better at judging this stuff." She dropped into an upholstered wingback chair, rested her head on the back, and looked toward the ceiling. "I do like the lights. You throw parties?"

"Here? Nope."

"Host book clubs?"

He sat opposite her and laced his hands over his stomach. "My neighbors aren't book club people."

"Figures. She lifted a crystal paperweight and caught the sunlight. "Mine, either."

The prism in her hand cast rainbows around the room. When Evie was eight, she bought the piece at an Arts Market and thought the tchotchke was fancy enough for the front room. He wanted Evie to know her opinion mattered and left the piece in place. Ann wasn't a child, but could he make room for her opinion, too?

"Did you kill an alligator to make these lamps?"

He ran his tongue over his front teeth and considered how to respond. The cast resin, steel, and wood composite table lamps from Greenwood, Mississippi, featured a faux crocodile leather column, a gilt crème finish, and brass accents. "I've always had a thing for white gators. "

"Since when?"

"I grew used to seeing the brutes smashed along the highways. Reptiles, especially alligators and snakes, don't receive positive press. All of a sudden"—he snapped his fingers—"someone finds a white gator in the swamp, and people pay attention."

She rubbed her temples.

He wondered what she thought about him, his life, and the twenty years they spent apart. Exceeding her expectations felt like his new goal.

"They're albino?"

"Leucistic. Splotchy pigment. Terrible for lampshades."

"Lucky gators." She smiled. "Sometimes, sticking out is the key to survival. I need to make a few calls to locate Jeanne through cell data. Should I go downstairs?"

Like the while gators, she might be ethereal, but she was real and being evasive. Instead of thinking about her in his quiet, lux townhouse, he should remember the reason she accompanied him to New Orleans. "Trying to ditch me?"

She stroked a finger along the lamp column's textured, white leather. "These animals would die in the wild. They're not really fit for this life, are they? An accident of birth."

"Predation takes its course "

She dropped her hand. "Not while I'm in charge."

He kicked out his booted foot and wondered if she

cared for ostriches, too. "You can use Evie's bedroom on this floor. Mine is on the third floor. I do most of my work there, and the room has amazing Quarter views, a spacious sitting room, and a connected study."

She cleared his throat. "What about the attached building off the side courtyard? The space would be more private. I can camp there."

His cheeks heated. "It's full of furniture I can't bear to sell."

"Really?" She replaced the paperweight and grinned. "Hoarder."

He dipped his head. "If only you knew. My home goods store is a front for historical preservation. I rehome antiques and hope they survive another hundred years. Making fun of relics made be famous, but I appreciate them more than anyone knows."

She pulled out her phone and tapped the screen. "You've always had a soft spot for vulnerable things."

He cleared his throat. He had a soft spot for her, but she was the least vulnerable woman he'd ever encountered. No matter how many times he attempted to help her, he failed. She could take down international operatives. He could rehome antique armoires. Loving her was the only feasible approach. He cocked his head. "What are you doing?"

"Warning my Valor buddies I'm about to call."

"Is that normal?" He barely understood her world. No wonder she had little interest in the townhouse's medallions. Was a spy satellite orbiting above his head? Standing, he walked toward the bar cart and poured himself a whiskey. The liquor burned his throat, but he was too restless to add ice. He swirled the drink. "Can security forces track a person's every move through their cell phone?"

Her thumbs flew across the screen. "Yes and no. If you have a cellphone, and someone from the Central Intelligence Agency has your phone's unique International Mobile Equipment Identity number, the agency can pinpoint your phone's location and follow your movements using cell phone towers. Getting the IMEI doesn't take much more than a subpoena, a search warrant, or a provision of the US Patriot Act. Unfortunately, we don't know who's making Jeanne nervous. If her disappearance and Lisette's death involve the app, criminals are targeting young-adult women."

The thought nauseated him. He threw back his drink. "Lisette wasn't that young."

"No, she wasn't." She pocketed her phone and rubbed her arms. "The agency can also use the phone's International Mobile Subscriber Identity. Changing out the IMSI is as easy as changing out the Subscriber Identity Module card, and SIM cards are going away. Again, we're stuck with limited information."

"I like hearing you go high-tech. It's kind of sexy." He winked. "Captain."

She rolled her eyes and stood.

Her blatant rejection made him grin. Arriving with wine and roses would yield the same reaction.

"Fuck this." She ran a hand through her hair. "When a phone sends a beacon and connects to a cell tower, the device broadcasts its IMSI number. Anyone with the right equipment can intercept and read that IMSI number. We have the text, but we don't know who's sending the messages. Instead of waiting on official tracking methods, I should just move."

"Because you have the location."

"Kind of." She examined a framed photograph of Evie. "I need more."

Watching her fidget with his bric-a-brac was more alarming than listening to her nonchalantly describe the US government's ability to monitor citizens. No wonder the feds subsidized cell coverage. Ann, on the other hand, displayed the uneasy interest of a driver considering a wrong turn. What *was* down that dark, wet alley?

Having her in his townhouse jarred him. Why hadn't he done more entertaining? With New Orleans culture at his fingertips, he never saw the point of putting on a show. The townhouse became his family's base for nights on the town, ticketed galas, and theatre trips. It held so many memories and so much remaining potential. Evie's scuffmarks littered the hallways, and Flannery's design contributions stood out like reluctant additions, but the house absorbed everything life threw at it. He wondered what Ann would bring to the table.

She tapped her phone. "No need to call in. My colleague says the call came from a location on Erato Street, but the signal's moving." She looked up. "That's nearby, isn't it?"

"It's a walk, but that area's a warren." He refilled his drink and focused on the burn. Erato Street was a jumble of buildings supporting New Orleans' modern cruise terminals and bustling cargo bays. Tourist attractions, shopping, dining, and hotels drew crowds, and nearby parking lots had space for thousands of cars. "Can your buddy give you a specific address?"

"They're monitoring the location. By triangulating the towers, they can narrow the location, but they can't pinpoint it. New Orleans isn't New York. In urban areas, we can narrow location to within fifty meters. Here? More like two hundred and fifty." Lowering her phone, she blew out her breath. "I should just send Jeanne the money, shouldn't I?"

He opened his mouth to respond.

"She demanded digital, but I could make the funds contingent on meeting her in person. I can risk five grand." She shrugged. "Everyone gets in over his or her head. She's just a kid."

He closed his mouth. Evie was just a kid. Ann was a conflicted adult. The first time he spoke to her in twenty years, and she didn't spit in his face, he latched onto the possibility of rekindling their friendship. Trading sore balls for a kiss was a decent promotion. He was way past being in over his head. Frankly, he would dog paddle if it meant he could spend more time with Ann. Watching an old man walk a dog along the sidewalk, he held his breath. "What does your gut say?"

"I wish we had access to a stingray."

Starting, he turned from the window. "Come again?"

"It's a compact, mobile cell tower. I can use the device to eavesdrop."

He shuddered. "Remind me not to use my cell for phone sex."

"Prude?"

"No." He lowered his brow. "If I imagine NOPD's finest chuckling over my exploits, the thought is enough to tank my ship."

She shrugged. "Make sure you're putting on a good show."

"Challenge accepted." He rubbed his jaw and

tipped his hand. "You in?"

For a second, her gaze widened.

Laughing, he stored away her brief, startled expression. Whether her response channeled curiosity, interest, or surprise remained to be seen. For the moment, her existence was enough. They were both figuring out how to be friends.

She walked the room's perimeter.

He was a quiet observer. His business ventures cast him as a community pillar, but his appearances were curated vignettes designed to sell an aspirational lifestyle. Who had time to mix cocktails on the verandah when they had reels to plan and shipments to oversee?

Letting her think, he lifted balcony door lock and opened the door to admit the fresh, spring breeze blowing off the river. In two months, summer heat and humidity would make the days too intense for casual ease.

Ann stopped beside him. "Why did she call me?"

He kept his gaze fixed on the horizon. "You think she needs to be saved?"

"I don't have any proof."

He turned from the window. The late afternoon sun gilded her hair. He jammed his hands in his pockets to stop himself from touching her. "Ask her to meet you for dinner."

"Assuming she's fine"—she rubbed her temples—"Judge Calloway should see her first."

He shrugged. "Invite them both to dinner."

She pulled back her chin. "Both?"

He inventoried the people he invited for dinner. He, Ann, Evie, Huanlong, and two friends angling for free promotion would have a lively meal. Adding Judge Calloway and Jeanne was as easy as making a call for a bigger reservation. "We'll get a private room to avoid shouting across the table."

She bumped his shoulder. "A private room? Life's that easy?"

"And tracking cell phones isn't?"

Laughing, she dipped her head. "Heard."

He banked her laughter. The sound was richer than he remembered. The car ride's forced intimacy tormented him. He wanted her to feel comfortable, but he also wanted a hot shower, a quick release, and an easy life. He had no doubt she would be good in the shower, but rekindling their relationship would be neither quick nor easy.

Then again, life hadn't been easy since puberty hit. He missed Ann and wanted to see her flourish. Maybe she would be better off without him.

"What are you thinking?"

His collar felt too right. She'd always been a part of his life, even when she wasn't there. He pivoted before he confessed missing her was the same thing as loving her. "Annie, life can be as easy as you want. Just say the word."

She raised her eyebrows.

"About dinner." Setting the glass on the bar cart, he flexed his fingertips at his sides. He ached to touch her. "What if Jeanne doesn't show?"

She rubbed a hand along her upper arm. "If I invite Judge Calloway to dinner, I won't mention talking to Jeanne. Rousing the judge's hopes would be cruel. As far as she's concerned, you're a business owner who might donate to her election campaign."

"Using me for my money?" Ducking his head, he glanced at her cheek and considered steeling a kiss from the blush rising on her tanned skin. "I get it."

Raising a hand, she short-circuited his thoughts. "I'm not using you for your money. I'm using you for your hospitality. This is how friendship works, right? You're helping me. I'd do the same for you."

"Yes, friendship." Instead of taking the kiss he wanted, he lifted her hand and pressed a soft kiss to her knuckles. Her skin, soft against his lips, smelled faintly of grease, and remembering the roundabout brought a smile to his lips. She was so capable she barely needed him, but success gave him an advantage. He dropped her hand and stepped back to give her space. "I'll give Jeanne the money. She's in a tight spot. We've all been there. Spend your savings on your grandfather's medical care. It's the least I can do."

She rubbed a hand over her mouth. "I can't do that."

Had she imagined his kiss landing somewhere softer? He considered the upholstered, cream sofa and wished she chose seating where he could lounge at her side and watch dust motes cast a halo around her golden hair.

Blessed with a bottle of good whiskey, he could linger on the couch all afternoon and find ways to divert her attention from Jeanne's plight. What kind of man did that make him? Jamming his hands in his pockets, he cleared his throat and wondered if he should stop taking his whiskey neat. "Forward me Jeanne's text message for the mobile payment. What's the risk?"

She blinked and looked around her. "I…"

"While you were off serving your country, I served

my self-interests. It's not much money. Let me pay her. Doing things is my love language."

She considered the paperweight. "Except we're just friends."

Her burn shattered his sunlit fantasies. He counted himself lucky she hadn't chucked the paperweight at his head for daring to make the offer. Every inch of relationship he claimed would have to be chiseled into their lives with stone-cold sobriety and rational business decisions. "Once upon a time, I loved you, and I made your life hell. I'm in your debt. Let me pay it. Five thousand is a drop in the bucket."

Letting her shoulders sink, she pulled out her phone. "Thank you."

She avoided his gaze, and he understood why. Remembering the past was painful. He had to stop relying on history to bring them together. "Your dress looks lovely, but if you want to raid Evie's closet, make yourself at home."

"Thanks." She scratched the back of her neck. "I might grab a shower."

The townhouse's tankless water heaters were a brilliant investment. He would empty half the river thinking of her standing naked under the guest bath's massaging showerhead. Sweeping past her, he strode toward the staircase to the third floor. "Go for it."

"Nathan?"

He paused and considered her standing in the cased opening separating the living room from the carpeted main hall. Backlit by a beam of bright sunlight, she looked road-weary but utterly beautiful. "What do you need?"

She tucked her hair behind her ear. "Thank you for

what you're doing. Thank you for including Jeanne and Judge Calloway in your plans. You've always been generous, but you've never been easy. I still have a scar from falling off the rope swing."

The sunlit river memory lightened his misgivings. He dipped his head. "When the water warms up, we'll have to go back to the railway bridge and jump."

She smiled. "I'd like that."

Grinning, he took the stairs two at a time and hoped she would stick around long enough for him to determine what else made her happy. A second chance felt within reach, but if he reached for the brass ring and missed it, he'd have more than a scar to remind him of what he lost.

Chapter Seventeen

Standing on the sidewalk with Judge Calloway and Nathan, Ann felt the French Quarter's lively pulse. Broad, flat Belgian paving stones covered the street. Granite curbs held back pedestrian traffic, and gas lanterns flickered beneath wrought iron balconies.

Evie, Huanlong, and Nathan's guests were late, but the restaurant would hold the room. She rubbed the chill from her arms and considered *Le Château d'Orleans'* elaborate facade. Through the first-floor windows, gilt-framed mirrors hung from a picture rail and interrupted an elaborate stretch of blue, silk wallpaper. The mirrors also reflected flickering candlelight, pristine linens, and hand-painted china. They made the intimate room seem larger, like a snapshot taken with a wide-angle lens. An aproned server refilled wine glasses. The smell of Cajun spices, fresh-baked bread, and melted butter emanated from the building.

"Should we go inside?" Nathan asked.

"Let's wait a minute. If your other guests arrive, go ahead."

Judge Calloway smoothed a hand over her pristine, black hair. She wore a cream suit and a glittering brooch. Her quilted purse hung from her shoulder. "As much as I appreciate this meal, I don't think its coincidence you invited me to dinner tonight."

Nathan cast the judge a slight smile.

Judge Calloway adjusted her pearl earring. "From what I understand, you're more of a spymaster than a political networker." She tilted her head. "Have you heard anything from Jeanne?"

Ann chewed the inside of her cheek. Deflection would be a safe bet, but shirking her involvement would also be a lie. "I spoke to her this afternoon. I hoped she would join us for dinner."

Judge Calloway narrowed her gaze. "Actual words? Not texts?"

"Yes, ma'am."

Judge Calloway closed her eyes and exhaled. Shaking off her relief, she adjusted her purse. "When I thought something bad happened, I panicked, but contemplating death helps people define what makes them happy. Most people don't know what makes them happy, but I do. Having Jeanne back in my life will make me very happy. Thank you for anything you've done to facilitate this reunion. I can't wait to see her."

Ann glanced at Nathan. The judge's buoyancy was too much. Usually, Ann dropped her recoveries at the hospital and let someone else deal with their families' emotional fallout.

He furrowed his brow and scanned the street.

She could see him thinking, but she couldn't read his thoughts. She considered ways to stall until Jeanne arrived. "My grandfather says happiness follows a U-shaped curve. Children can be brilliantly happy, young adults can toil in angst, and seniors can have crises."

Judge Calloway raised her eyebrows. "I've always been the life of the party."

Ann held her tongue.

"And your grandfather"—Judge Calloway leaned in—"is he happy?"

"No, ma'am." Ann rubbed the evening chill from her arms. "Well, yes and no. He has pancreatic cancer, but he's happy I'm home. I'm glad you're looking forward to seeing Jeanne. Family is a wonderful gift."

Nathan wrapped an arm around her shoulders and squeezed.

"It is, and yet, you're single."

Oh, here we go. She thought she left this type of matronly advice in Hemlock with Nanette's pursed lips.

"Ms. Storey, you have a decade to make big choices. When you hit fifty, bones and joints will creak. Skin will dimple and sag. Your visits to the doctor will become more frequent and more pressing. Death might be a long way off, but its visibility will seep into your daily activities. Make sure you're ready."

Ann leaned against Nathan's weight. She smelled the heady whiskey on his breath and let his ease soothe her. She imagined sipping a drink, but she'd survived this long without indulging. Nobody, including herself, knew what would happen if she started. Her mother ran off, and her father drank himself to death. She insisted on being present, but she wasn't sure where to stand. "Seeing Paps ill shook me. I'm not sure he'll get better."

Judge Calloway smoothed her skirt. "Family can surprise us. Jeanne lifted my silver. If I knew she needed money, then I would have provided it. She's always been a proud girl. Where has that pride gotten her? Mixing records at clubs when she should be in bed." Judge Calloway shook her head. "When will she grow up?"

Ann wondered if Judge Calloway's small denials paved the way for her strained relationship with Jeanne. Feeling like a person who never measured up was downright exhausting.

"I hope she joins me at church." Judge Calloway fixed her necklace. "Connecting with people we love, finding meaning in life, and performing social services are reliable routes to happiness. That's why I ran for my position, to help people. I hope she realizes how much I love her."

Ann saw echoes of Nanette in Judge Calloway's approach toward life. As freewheeling as Jeanne appeared, she balanced a heavy load. "I'm sure she does."

Rolling her lips, Judge Calloway nodded.

A patrol car pulled up.

Ann straightened off Nathan's shoulder and held her breath. Judge Calloway's official role required access to twenty-four-hour security. The police could be at the restaurant for any number of reasons.

Two police officers stepped from the vehicle, their expressions grave. A tall, broad-shouldered man with buzzed, blond hair, weathered skin, and kind eyes took the lead. His partner had bushy eyebrows, black hair, and the dark skin of someone whose family still resided in the tropics. Tourists skirted them, and the flashing blue-and-red police lights shattering the city's throwback romanticism.

"Ma'am, I'm Detective Marcus Goetz, and this is Detective Penny Sultan. Will you come with us to discuss your daughter's case?"

"No!" Looking at the night sky, Ann swore. She squared her shoulders and cupped Judge Calloway's elbow. "Let me come with you."

"I'll be fine."

The judge's determination was a sharply drawn breath. Pulled through her nose with the precision of a commander disciplining a sailor, the judge conveyed her disdain for whatever fate had befallen Jeanne. If only Jeanne and every other millennial would follow their elders' footsteps, nothing bad would ever happen. Their lives would be easy, regimented, purposeful successes. Two kids. Church on Sunday. Retirement at sixty-five.

Life didn't work that way. Jeanne was a brilliant and creative person who was desperate to find her way through life's conflicting demands. Ann rubbed her fingers over her brows and replayed her mistakes. Instead of stalling, she should have followed every lead. The only connections Jeanne and Lisette shared were ties to Hemlock and postings on a resell app. Ann's gut told her not to send Jeanne money. If Jeanne were dead, why hadn't the killers gone after Nanette or the myriads of other people who posted on Polished and Hammered?

She should have followed Jeanne's moving cell phone signal until she put eyes on the woman. Anything would have been better than relaxing into Nathan's Southern hospitality and thinking about giving him a second chance.

"This isn't your fault." Judge Calloway's voice faltered, but she slipped from Ann's hold and anchored her right hand over her purse strap. "Jeanne's my daughter. If she needed money, she should have come to *me*." She turned to the officers and then lifted her chin. "Tell me what you have to say."

The judge's defensive posture almost undid Ann. The woman's armor must have supported her throughout her life. Ann longed to offer her a shoulder and dry her tears, but Judge Calloway stood ramrod-straight.

Detective Goetz cleared his throat. "Jeanne's alive, but barely."

Judge Calloway clenched the officer's forearm. "What happened?"

"She's in critical condition in the ICU. Someone shot her in the head. Neighbors reported the sound of gunfire about 6:15 p.m. on the 3600 block of Erato Street near South Tonti Street. Responding officers found a woman inside an SUV in the B.W. Cooper area. Her ID identified her as Jeanne Calloway, reported missing earlier this week." The officer exchanged a look with his partner. "I can show you a photograph to confirm her identity."

Judge Calloway dropped his forearm. "Please."

Ann struggled. Judge Calloway might have presided over a thousand criminal cases during her career, but none of them involved her daughter. ICU meant critical trauma, and the photograph of Jeanne might be the last one Judge Calloway saw. Ann stepped forward. "Wait. The last memories I have of my father are tangled with his hospice care. I can't lose those images. Do you want this photo of Jeanne to stay with you, too? Go to the hospital and lay eyes on her yourself."

"What if it's not her?" Judge Calloway's voice shook. "What if she's dead? She's everything. I can't get my hopes up."

"You won't be alone. She has Baptiste and her

professors. She has me. You have me, too. You don't have to see that picture. I don't know how badly she's hurt, but if things go poorly, don't let that crime scene photograph be the last image you have. She's a brilliant, cheerful woman. She's so much more than her circumstances."

Judge Calloway swallowed and looked away from the uniformed duo. "Officers, show Ms. Storey the photograph."

The lead officer extended his phone.

Ann stepped around Judge Calloway and took the phone from the officer's hand. His grip had warmed the phone's plastic case, but Jeanne might be stone-cold dead. A spotlight cast her features into stark relief and highlighted the blood splattering the SUV's fabric upholstery. Her head lolled to the side, and her red braids hung over one side of her shoulder. If Ann could reach through the photograph, she would cradle Jeanne.

Instead, she handed back the phone. "That's Jeanne." Her words tasted as bitter as bile. She wiped a hand over her mouth. "Judge Calloway, you need to go to the hospital." She swallowed. "Quickly."

Judge Calloway reached a hand toward the restaurant's plastered wall. Her eyes rolled back, and she slumped against the building.

Ann caught the unconscious woman under her arms.

Detective Sultan eased Judge Calloway from her grasp and checked her vitals.

"We've got a fainter." Detective Goetz radioed for an ambulance.

The derision in his voice grated on Ann's nerves. He might mean well, but his indignation stung. Jeanne and her mother were more than case I.D.s and crime scene photographs. Hand clasped at her sides, she wanted to scream out her frustration and swipe the man's radio from his grasp. Instead, she breathed through her nose and watched the taller officer support Judge Calloway. When she felt like she could trust the ass-hat not to drop the judge, she turned her head and met Detective Goetz's gaze. "What if it hadn't been Jeanne?"

The man shrugged.

"You have kids?" She pushed into his personal space. "Siblings?"

He tugged his ear. "Two brothers, Frankie and Dickie, but they're no good. Look just like me, but we barely talk. 'Good riddance,' Pappy said."

At some point, her parents wrote her off, too. Fragments of Dad singing along with Springsteen's "Highway Patrolman" played through her mind. Dad loved *Nebraska*. For so long, she loved him, too. Then he drowned his sorrows instead of being present when she needed him. Alcoholism was a disease, but the habit wasn't an incurable diagnosis. Dad's need to drink away his feelings had a cure, but he wasn't brave enough to swallow it. Even when he was drunk and happy, while she sat beside him and organized his towering CD rack, she hoped his spell would be his last. It never was.

She planted her hands on her hips. "Well, Jeanne *is* good, and Judge Calloway *loves* her. She chased leads to find her missing daughter. While the city grappled with Mardi Gras and drunken tourists, that tiny, indomitable woman fought off fears and pieced together Jeanne's last-known whereabouts."

Detective Goetz adjusted his belt. "I know."

"So, if I had a kid or a sibling who I loved and almost lost, I might faint, too."

"Yeah." Detective Goetz looked away. "I guess."

She jabbed a finger into his chest. "Take Judge Calloway to Jeanne's bedside."

"Yes, ma'am."

She turned toward the restaurant. Nathan hovered near the entrance, his brow furrowed, and his hands jammed in his pockets like he wanted to help but had no clue how to proceed. Her rage, frustration, and fear for Judge Calloway, and grief collided in a searing burst of energy. She kicked a glass bottle from the gutter. The vessel skidded along the pavers and released a muffled *pop* as it shattered against a wall. "Someone shot her!"

Stepping forward, he wrapped his arms around her, buried his face in her hair, and held her while sobs wracked her body.

"She's just a kid!"

"I know." He stroked her hair. "I know."

Leaning into his stance, she shuddered. "I have to go to the hospital with Judge Calloway. I have to tell the police about the earlier call. I have to—"

He tipped her chin. "Annie, the paramedics have Judge Calloway. Jeanne's in the Intensive Care Unit. Let me take care of you. I have plenty of bottles for you to throw. We can make it rain glass, baby. Just let me take you home."

His steady, calming idiocy soothed her rage.

The sound of sirens overwhelmed the officer handing Ann his business card. Paramedics burst from an ambulance and tended to Judge Calloway. Their urgent voices cut through the scene's lantern-lit loneliness. Medical efficiency satisfied lingering tourists and peering restaurant patrons. Everything would be okay. The authorities were on scene. Ann clutched the NOPD card and wondered how a scrap of cardstock could hold so much weight.

Letting Nathan lead her toward the valet stand, Ann watched paramedics load Judge Calloway onto a stretcher. The professionals would tend to her physical ailments, but they had nothing that would ease her grief. Ann had seen sailors, family members, and dreams die. Every loss hurt. A person could fight their feelings or flee them, but during the night's darkest hour, fears returned. Judge Calloway could find a way to deal with her near-miss, but she would never be the same.

Chapter Eighteen

Nathan parked the sedan in the townhouse carriageway and climbed from the vehicle. Since leaving the restaurant, Ann had silently stared out the car window while the French Quarter and the city's guests had the time of their lives. He remembered the numbness he felt after Flannery's passing.

Giving Ann space to process her emotions was the polite response, but they shared too much history for politeness. He'd never met Jeanne, but her assault affected Ann, and Ann's pain affected him. He opened the door to the courtyard and waited for her to choose solitude in the guest suite or his company in the courtyard.

Slowly, she emerged from the passenger side and walked past him into the open space where glimpses of stars, gurgling fountains, and wisteria's climbing, purple flowers could witness her emotions.

"The guest suite has a kitchenette." He leaned against a plaster wall. "You can sleep here or take a guest room upstairs."

"So you said." She sat on a chaise lounge with striped, green-and-white cushions, doubled over, and hung her head between her knees.

Putting a hand on her back might earn him more than tender gonads. He needed to tread carefully and consider what she needed. "Do you want to drive back to Hemlock tonight? I can cancel my morning meetings."

"No." She straightened and flopped back on the lounger. Staring toward the sky, she flung a hand over her forehead and let her hair pool on the dusty pavers. "I need to meet with the police tomorrow. Two dead women connected to Hemlock aren't coincidental. If the police don't know about the app, they need to."

He sat near her legs and rested a hand on a calf. The simple comfort of human touch might ground her. Mixing business with pleasure led to heartache and life-altering consequences. Some consequences, like Evie, were beautiful blessings. Some of them, like getting too close to Lisette and mourning her death, were heartaches he preferred to skip. Ann's practical, government-issued approach toward life had its merits, but he doubted either of them had figured out the secrets to happiness. "You don't want a drink."

"No." She turned her head and glanced over. "Sorry about your dinner party."

"If only Jeanne were there." He sighed. "Do you want to talk?"

"Not really. Talking never helps. It's either fight or flight. The hospital staff does everything they can. I want to run until my muscles ache, double-back, and do it again."

The defenses Ann built were tall enough to keep away casual observers, but he'd known her when she still thought putting toothpaste on a zit would fade it. He was nearly family, and family didn't desert. He leaned back on his palms. "After Flannery died, I realized I was a shit husband."

Ann straightened and scrunched her fingers in her

hair. "I believe you. You were a shit prom date, too."

Laughing, he stood and walked toward the outside bar. Pulling a beer from the fridge, he opened it and let condensation bead on the green glass. After so many decades, he wasn't sure what loving a person entailed. He spoiled Evie and guessed what everyone needed. Occasionally, he failed. Raising the beer to his lips, he drank.

Didn't his intentions matter? He provided for his family, delighted in his kid, and worked until exhaustion subdued his misgivings. Had Flannery enjoyed their life? He'd never asked. She made meals, looked after Evie, and filled her days with the social exchanges women treated like currency. Most times, he felt superfluous. Maybe he was.

Leaning a shoulder against a painted, black iron pole, he examined the underside of a second-floor interior balcony. Mildew crept along the paint. He should call the pressure washers. He wiped a finger along the wall and felt the feathery softness of accumulated dust. Building the hotel in Hemlock had kept him away from the townhouse for long so that neglect had set in.

The neighbor's black cat wound around his ankles.

A gecko scampered out of reach.

He sipped his beer. "Flannery was always disappearing on these long, random bike rides. When we didn't have family plans, she was on the road by herself or with her cycling friends. I got to thinking she couldn't stand the quiet space between us, but I was too scared to ask what she needed. What if the answer hadn't been me? What if I wasn't enough? I mean, maybe I always knew. She could take Evie and start fresh without me. I couldn't risk the questions."

"Maybe she liked to cycle." Ann stood. The iron lounger scraped against the flagstones. "Maybe she needed fresh air and confirmation she still breathed. It's not always about you, Nathan. This shit with Jeanne and Lisette is heavy, but it's not about you. I failed Jeanne. I should have extracted her."

He hooked Ann's arm before she could storm from the courtyard and muffle her great, heaving sobs beneath a pillow. "How?"

She seethed.

Finishing the beer, he lowered his hand and relaxed his grip on Ann's arm. "How exactly were you supposed to find Jeanne and keep an attempted killer from putting a bullet in her head? She put herself at risk. She made bad decisions. You don't have to repeat them."

Ann leaned close. "You think you failed Flannery because she didn't fawn over you every day of her damn life? You're so successful that you don't recognize need. Jeanne *needed* help. She called me." She jammed a finger against her chest.

"For money."

Pulling back, she shrugged off his hand. "Money is the only currency some friendships need. Baptiste was locked up and paying his own way. Maybe she should have leveled with Judge Calloway, but things weren't right. I don't know why Jeanne called me, but she shouldn't have had to resort to selling silver on some app and meeting a creep in a parking lot to pay her university bills."

"What will you do?" He tucked a piece of hair behind her ear.

She flinched. "I don't know."

Pushing Ann to admit her limits might be the thing that saved her. She might not want human contact, or his touch in particular, but she needed a reality check like Jeanne needed stranger danger and common sense.

He could weather a few more assaults, but burying Ann would break him. He crossed his arms over his chest. "Chasing Jeanne's mistakes will lead to more suffering. You're a badass, but you're not a one-woman army. Whatever's going through your head, quell it. You can't avenge her assault."

Ann yanked the bottle from his hand and hurled the vessel against the weathered courtyard wall. Glass shattered and fell into the iron plants with muffled sighs. Her shoulders shook, and tears glistened in her eyes. "She was so young! This assault shouldn't have happened. She should have been safe."

"I know." He pulled Ann against his chest and wrapped his arms around her shaking frame. "Lisette should have been safe, too. There won't be a third woman, Annie. I'll help you any way I can. Tomorrow, we'll go to the police. You can call everyone you know at the Valor, but please"—he pulled back and met her gaze—"don't go rogue."

Nodding, she swallowed.

He eased back and opened the French doors leading to the guest suite.

Wordlessly, she followed him into the room, turned, and sank onto the bed.

Standing at the threshold, he cocked his head and drew a deep breath. If she wanted to break things, then he could find crockery, but she looked exhausted enough to sleep. Walking inside the suite, he cupped the sides of her face, his thumbs on her cheeks, and kissed her soft, perfumed hair. The smell gave the courtyard wisteria a run for its money, but she needed someone to care of her, not compliment her hair. "Get some sleep."

She gripped his wrist and yanked.

He stumbled forward, off-guard and unprepared. If he thought she had the body of a studio junkie, he was mistaken. Her strength was as honed and effective as her training.

"Kiss me." She raised her chin. "Make me forget."

He defiant gaze challenged him. Swallowing, he shook his head and braced his arms on either side of her. Their foreheads touched, and the slightest shift would send him tumbling into bed. "Ah, I don't think that's a good idea."

"But grinding your cock into my heat on horseback is a good idea? You want to know what women want? Ask them. Tell them they can have anything their heart desires, and you'll provide. Then, listen." She closed her eyes and breathed deeply. Finally, she looked into his eyes. "I'm not asking you to marry me. I'm asking you to fuck me. I'm asking you to help me stop thinking about Jeanne and everything wrong in my life." Tilting her head, she kissed him hard and pulled back. "Can you do that?"

He was only a man. Absorbing her kiss, he closed his eyes and waited for her fury to burn out.

She knocked him sideways and straddled him on the bed.

His defiant cock short-circuited the commands from his brain. He ached for her heat and the old, thrilling connection they shared, but twenty years had passed. She'd put him in his place so many times she'd left ruts. Just because she felt hurt and lashed out didn't meant he should give her release. As soon as their sweaty skin cooled, she would flee toward the anonymity she knew best. No matter how far she roamed, he would miss her. He planted a hand against her chest.

"I won't ask again." She raised her head. "I need you."

The sincerity in her gaze toppled his remaining restraint. He cupped her face and used a thumb to wipe away a tear. "Can I call you Captain?"

"Always." She claimed his lips. Pulling his shirt over his head, she spread her fingers against his pecs. "Call me whatever you want. Call me yours."

He tugged her dress over her head and revealed her lace bra and panty set. Another night, he would lean back and admire her curves, but this wasn't a slow, easy prelude to good sex. This was desperation. Meeting her need, he matched the aggressiveness in her kiss and stroked her tongue, his lips hungry and brutal to find the pace she needed.

She sucked in a desperate breath.

He gripped her hips and groaned. If she changed her mind now, then he would need a surgeon's care to ease the pressure building in his dick.

Changing her angle, she sucked on his lower lip and dug her teeth into his lip with a fierce nip.

The pain warned him how close she hovered near desperation and fear. Knowing Jeanne was in the ICU was a painful reminder of death's proximity. He would help her feel alive. If she needed angry sex to feel her heart beat, then he would provide it. Flipping her on her back, he reversed their positions and cupped her breasts. Their weight felt familiar and luscious. He could suck her nipples into his mouth and lavish her skin until she moaned his name. He dipped his head toward her right breast.

She thrust her hips.

Grinning, he raised his head. "No?"

Pushing him back, she stood, backed him into the corner, and unbuckled his belt.

His shoulder grazed a shelf, but he didn't care about the bruise or the consequences of giving Ann what she needed and what he craved. He stripped off his pants, socks, and shoes. She watched him undress, her chest rising and falling. He wanted to bury his face between her breasts. Standing in his briefs, he caught her hips and then cupped her ass cheeks.

She draped her arms around his neck. "You don't have to do this."

He choked out a hoarse laugh and squeezed her ass cheeks. "Oh, trust me, I want to do this. I want to do you. Just don't beat me to a pulp in the morning." Short-circuiting her defensiveness and her tendency to threaten him, he slammed her back against an antique armoire and braced a hand above her head.

Moaning, she cupped him through his briefs and bit her lower lip.

Her lips glistened and transfixed him. He ground his cock against her hand and tested her resilience.

She tightened her grip.

He used his teeth on her earlobe, this time biting harder than her lip until she winced and turned away. He pulled her back. Knowing she felt both pleasure and pain, that she would tell him what she needed and wanted, mattered as much as the smell of sex rising between them. He could surrender to his base needs, but he needed her along for the ride.

"I always wondered what you would feel like." He ghosted his lips along the column of her throat, his thoughts circling to draw out her response. What part of their high school make-out sessions had she enjoyed the most? How much of their last make-out session was a thrilling ride, and how much was him?

He slipped a hand beneath the seam of her underwear and found her drenched. His objectives wavered. Finesse could wait. Ripping off her lace and sinking into her pussy would relieve them both. "Are you sure you want me to know what you feel like? What if I can't get enough?"

She gripped him. "I can handle you and your needs."

He thumbed her clit, rubbing small circles where pressure would steal her reason. "I know you can." He softened his touch and sighed into her mouth. She tasted of salty tears and the sweet, smoky aroma drifting from the restaurant. The taste was as sinfully delicious and unapologetically decadent as hard candy. He would drop to his knees and bury his face in her folds, sucking her clit until she cried out his name.

Her fingers threaded through his too-long hair and twisted it, her hips grinding against him.

Her feedback was loud and clear. She was too impatient for foreplay. He grabbed the back of her thighs and hiked her legs to circle his waist, aligning his cock with her groin and the heat he craved. He could be impatient, too.

A decorative accent fell to the floor and shattered.

The loss sounded too much like Ann's broken bottles. He held Ann in his arms, the woman he disappointed twenty years ago. She was strong, but she told him how much his betrayal hurt. If he hurt her again, he would bear the shame of another betrayal. Twenty years after his first mistake, maybe he should know better.

Giving her what she wanted might harm her, and the realization cooled his ardor. He should set her on her feet and redirect her frustration into another outlet. City Park had miles of trails. If she wanted to run herself into oblivion, then he would chase her through the midnight trails and scare off the users. When she fell to her knees, her tears mingling with the spring mud, he would carry her back to the townhouse and tuck her into bed. His approach was much more responsible than a quick, mind-numbing fuck. He loosened his hold on her ass.

She pulled back and narrowed her gaze. "What the hell are you doing?"

"Trying to be an adult. If you regret this choice in the morning, then I'll feel like shit. You'll never forgive me. It's not worth it."

She gripped his chin. "I forgive you. You were eighteen. You drank and made a bad decision. That decision hurt me and made me wonder how long you'd thought about other women. I wasn't enough for you at eighteen, but I swear to God, if you ghost me, forty will be the year that kills me. I will never speak to you again."

Silence would be better than regret. He'd told her he loved her, but he hadn't known the term's meaning. Infatuation ruled his life. Lust upended it. He couldn't let that mistake happen again. Unwinding her legs from his waist, he ducked out of her grip and drew in deep breaths.

She slapped him.

The sting felt good. He would hold the line for both of them.

Feet on the ground, she planted her hands on her hips. "You're trying to be noble? Fuck noble. If I wanted a prince, I wouldn't be hanging around with your spit-shined ass. I know exactly what I'm asking for. Fuck me, no strings attached."

He rubbed a palm against his eyebrow. She'd always been fierce, but the United States government had honed her edge.

"You don't want me?" She tilted her head. "Are you too polite to say it? Damn. That's it, isn't it? I basically attacked you."

Her wavering question undid him. He reached forward, hooked an arm around her waist, and pulled her close. "I've always wanted you." He gripped her soft blonde hair in his fist, pulled hard, and forced her to look up. "You're more than enough. Any man would be lucky to have you."

She blinked. "But I want *you*."

His body tingled. He'd never felt so focused. He released her hair. "Okay."

"Okay?"

The minute he heard her ask for him, he'd already lost the battle, but he'd mounted a good fight. Tomorrow morning, she could redraw the lines of their friendship and tell him where he stood. He would live within her boundaries because being her friend was better than missing her. He laid her on the queen bed and hesitated.

She wet her lips.

He could imagine a thousand better scenarios, but he would take advantage of this gift and deal with the fallout tomorrow morning. Rolling his hips against her, he pushed his erection into her thigh. "Look at me."

Closing her eyes, she hooked an arm around his neck and fiercely kissed him.

Ann Storey went after what she wanted. Fresh out of high school, she wanted distance, but fate dragged her back into his arms. He would use her forthrightness to his advantage and do his best to give her everything she needed. Breaking the kiss, he cocked his head. "You'll tell me what you want, Ann. I'm no good at guessing what you need. If you don't tell me, you won't get it."

She fisted his shirtfront. "I want you to fuck me, Nathan. I don't want to hold a thought in my pretty, little head. Years from now, when you're upstairs, thrusting over your boring, missionary-loving second wife, you'll remember letting go in the guest suite. You'll remember how good we were, and you'll miss me." She released his shirt and flopped back on the bed with a grin. "So sorry."

He laughed, unhooked her bra, and freed her breasts. Admiring her lean torso and generous tits, he rubbed her nipple between his fingers. "You're so full of it. It's sex. Tell me what feels good"—he winked— "Captain."

Nestling her knee below his balls, she urged him forward. "Will do. Touch me. Make me so wet and tight that I'm begging for release before you slide into me. Don't you dare tease me with oral. I want it fast and hard. Make me shatter."

So, he wouldn't be dropping to his knees. He grazed his teeth along her nipple and raised his head. "Oh, is that all?"

She laughed and pulled him into a kiss.

Pleasing her felt so easy. He broke the kiss, skimmed his lips along her flushed neck, and found her underwear damp with desire. He slid a thumb along the lacey fabric and explored her responses until she gasped. Her reaction told him where to pleasure her, and her wetness told him she wanted him, but he would make her beg. Missionary-loving second wife? He couldn't imagine anyone under him but Ann. Chasing kisses along her skin, he increased his pace and worked her swollen clit.

She gripped his hair and pulled his lips to hers. Riding his hand, she moaned.

He slipped his hand past the lace barrier, grazed her sensitive skin, and slipped two fingers inside her. Her muscles clenched around his fingers. He dragged out a breath. She was so eager and so wet he could almost forget the stakes.

Biting his chin, she thrust against his hand and nudged him into action. "You're thinking about this too much. We're not making love."

He stilled his fingers and raised his head. "If I fuck you like you're asking, then the tourists will hear your screams."

"Promises." She dug her heels into his ass. "Do it."

"Christ." He ripped off her underwear and braced himself over her. "The minute it—"

She raked her fingers along his back.

Her searing marks felt good. He understood her

tendency to deal in base responses. Hard-hitting releases were so clean and easy that they eclipsed subtleties, doubts, and misgivings. Flipping her to her stomach, he lifted her hips and stroked her pussy. Her wetness coated his fingertips.

Open and exposed, she flexed her hips.

Coating himself, he rolled on a condom, slapped her ass, and watched his mark spread across her skin. Finding her clit, he teased her and reveled in her throaty moans. "Yes, Ann. I'll bring you close and carry you over the edge."

She looked over her shoulder. "You promise?"

"Yes." He held her gaze and slid inside her. "You're so beautiful."

She opened her mouth to argue before accepting his compliment and closing her eyes. "More, Nathan."

In and out, he thrust, flesh slapping flesh as he worked her clit and pounded her slick seam from behind. She canted her hips and dipped her head, changing the angle and letting him watch his cock as he slid into her heat.

His control wavered. If he kept moving, if he kept savoring her exquisite tightness, if he kept meeting her punishing needs, he would explode. Breathing deeply, he stilled his thrusts and pulled her back against his chest. Her skin, sweat-slicked and heated, melted against his. He tightened his grip and struggled to catch his breath.

She moaned. "Nathan."

Hearing his name on her lips shattered his control. The minute she'd asked for a release, subtlety had flown out the window. Tonight was about giving her what she needed. He'd be damned if he didn't deliver.

Sinking to his heels, he positioned her over his cock, her legs splayed wide, and buried himself to the hilt. Shuddering, he felt his control slip another notch. "Touch yourself."

She shifted her hips. "This is good."

Sweat dripped down his back. He caught her hand, wrapped an arm around her waist, and pressed her fingers between her thighs. "I said, touch yourself."

Shuddering, she set their entwined hands in a rhythm against her swollen clit.

He felt the rhythm in his bones and thrust up, surging his thighs and rocking his dick into her heat until she tensed. All the muscles in her back and ass were tight against his chest and quivering. He could stay here forever.

She screamed, contracted around his dick, and dropped her head against his shoulder.

Holding back was no longer an option. He thrust into her maddening clutch and pistoned her hips onto his shaft. His release raced through his body, and he shouted her name as he clutched her.

Chest heaving, he braced a hand against the bed frame to stop himself from tumbling her to the rug. The awkwardness would come when he dispatched the condom and made a show of inviting her to sleep upstairs.

Instead of rehearsing his lines, he pulled out, dropped the condom to the floor, and stood, lifting her in his arms. The guest suite's bed was perfectly good. If he'd done his job, then she would fall asleep before satisfaction eased into reality.

She raised her head from his shoulder. "Nathan..."

"Shh." He pressed a kiss to her hair, dropped onto

the guest bed, and tucked her against his chest. His heart beat in his chest, and his dick lay at half-mast against his thigh, but satisfaction made him selfish. "Give me a minute to regroup. If you want more action, then I'll fuck you until dawn."

She laughed and tucked her face into the dip between his shoulder and his neck.

Exhaustion pulled his head against the upholstered headboard. He swore he heard her whisper a vague "Thank you," but no matter how many times he swallowed and eased the dryness in his throat, he couldn't find the right words to respond.

She felt so good in his arms that instead of fighting sleep, he relaxed into holding her and admitting the secret he'd carried through his marriage. He treasured his daughter and his prosperity, but Ann inspired him.

Her fierce demands and heady determination fired a spark in his soul he barely recognized. If he hadn't been such a high school fuck-up, he might have stood a chance of loving her and maturing into a man he admired. Instead, he was a whitewashed success story crafted to take care of other people. He'd stumbled with Ann, failed with Lisette, and wasted too many hours on mass-marketed smiles.

Ann was right. She'd move on, and he'd miss her for the rest of his life. The thing she'd overlooked, the thing that would eat into his soul, was he'd been so conscious of protecting her he'd failed to protect himself. No matter how peacefully she slept at his side, the comfort was temporary. His success felt empty. He could have led a better life. He could have been a better man.

Evie had everything he could provide, but in

fulfilling his obligations, he'd pushed away his dreams. Maybe self-sacrifice was the definition of parenthood, but love and bitterness were uneasy cousins. If he let his regrets out of their tiny, well-guarded box, they might grind his veneer until one day, he would crack. Anyone who knew him would know what a fool he'd been to keep everything he felt locked inside.

Chapter Nineteen

Ann rolled over in Nathan's bed. She could curl into Nathan's heat, but the unfamiliar surroundings stole her early morning languor. Turning her back, she matched his breathing and watched leafy shadows move over the townhouse walls. Outside, neighborhood cats meowed their injustices, and rumbling sanitation workers dragged heavy cans along rough streets. Hissing garbage truck hydraulics popped and faded away. The lower quarter's quiet, morning hum would soon turn into a gridlocked circus.

Wrapping a heavy arm across her abdomen, Nathan pressed a kiss to her shoulder. "You're awake early."

She could answer him in so many ways. Cathartic, exhausting sex had beat back her nightmares, but his familiar, reassuring scent anchored her throughout the night. She'd known he would stay, just as she'd known her strength would get her through the meaningless fantasy of waking in his arms. The hurt and betrayal stemming from his high school behavior were rooted in love. As long as she viewed last night's hookup as an exercise between two consenting adults, she could compartmentalize her life and move on.

Jeanne would have a longer recovery getting over her ordeal.

Rolling toward Nathan, Ann propped herself on her

forearm and brushed his sleek, black hair off his forehead. "Thank you for taking care of me last night. I owe you."

He flopped onto his back and stared at the ceiling. "You don't owe me anything."

"Good to know." She climbed from bed and stretched her hands over her head. Letting him brush off the debt was too easy, but she had to prioritize her time. Untangling her feelings toward him sat at the list's bottom. "I told Jeanne I finish what I start."

He planted an elbow and rested his head on his palm. "Meaning?"

She lowered her arms and exhaled. "Meaning, I invited her to burn a pine stand. She never came home. She was in my life, and she mattered. I don't care why she fenced Judge Calloway's antiques. She was my responsibility, and I will help the NOPD determine who shot her. If that means camping out in the precinct office, I'll do it."

"I would call the tip line." He yawned. "That's what the news articles always say. Authorities ask anyone with information to contact authorities."

"Right, so my message can spend a few days filtering through official channels. Or"—she raised her eyebrows—"I can visit the officer who gave me his card at his office on Royal St."

Nodding, he dragged a palm over his eyebrow. "I'll come with you."

"That's not necessary." His generous offer made sense, but she needed him involved like she needed Baptiste to start knocking on doors. Good intentions got people killed. She walked toward the pile of clothes on the floor, bent, and retrieved yesterday's stale clothes.

Slipping on her underwear, she organized her thoughts.

The crime scene photograph from Jeanne's discovery would stay with her for a very long time. Keeping that image from Judge Calloway was a small victory. Keeping Nathan from the investigation was imperative.

He was fit and charming, but he was more accustomed to green rooms than interrogation rooms. No matter his willingness to come to rescue her with a mind-blowing orgasm, she drew the line at putting him in danger. Evie, bless her heart, needed him alive more than Ann needed him by her side.

"Will you call the officer first?" Nathan asked.

She slipped on her dress. "Yes. I'll make an appointment."

"Good." He stood and padded toward the bedroom door. "I'll make coffee."

Watching him walk from the room, she wondered if he would retrieve his clothes or if he had a maid who did his laundry. She toed his discarded slacks and shrugged. Whatever she'd instigated by stripping naked and using him for sex, the outcome wasn't an offer of domestic bliss.

Ten minutes later, she followed the mellow rock and the smell of coffee to find the kitchen on the second floor. Nathan, unshaven and wearing jeans and a button-down shirt, leaned against a cabinet while music gently thrummed through the room. A potted orchid bloomed from a glazed pot sitting on the marble island.

He jerked his chin toward a mug holding a splash of cream. "You need help using that machine?"

She eyed the black, plastic coffeemaker. A touch screen offered sliders for size, strength, and milk foam.

If Nathan were coffee, he would be large, potent, and cheerfully decadent. She had the bandwidth to choose between espresso and cold brew, but the rest of her situation required distance and a blistering hot shower. A night spent in New Orleans, a city of shadowed promises, almost guaranteed sore thighs. The townhouse stairs weren't the culprit.

"I can order breakfast."

She shook her head, offered him an appreciative smile, and lifted the mug. "This is great. I can decipher the machine."

"Do you need more?"

Did she? She chewed the inside of her lip and wondered if marrying her high school sweetheart had downsides she had never considered. What if he'd skipped that party and ignored Flannery's interest? This townhouse might belong to Ann.

Nathan would lovingly fix her coffee, her tires, and her life. Even if she worked, her professional ambitions would take a back burner while she raised her kids. When they went to college, who would she be? An older woman anticipating grandchildren? Potted plants scattered around her garden would be the only things to tide her over. She pressed the screen, kept her back to Nathan, and listened to the machine grind beans. "I know what I'm doing."

The song switched to *Shallow*, the love ballad between Lady Gaga and Bradley Cooper. Ann hummed along with the lyrics. *Ain't it hard keepin' it so hardcore?* Then, she snorted. Cocaine would keep life interesting, but instead of following a line, she sipped her coffee. The potent brew would chase away her lassitude and misgivings about last night, but she needed time before the caffeine coursed through her system.

"There's sugar in the cabinet."

She chewed her bottom lip and clutched her drug of choice. Behind her, a handsome man with impressive bedroom agility waited for her to address their tryst. She couldn't do it. Turning and meeting his gaze was too much to ask.

His house, a mix of cold plaster and warm leather, was an achievement many women craved. Did they know what came next? Southern woman didn't start out loving potted plants. They had big dreams and global curiosities, but one day, someone arrived with a potted plant and thrust the plant into a woman's arms. *Here, love this. Nurture this. By the time you retire into an independent living community, expect to have fifty pots lining your walkway.*

Shuddering, Ann felt the townhouse closing in. She loved plants. Brilliant, vibrant, unique plants thrived in the ecosystems where they belonged. Inside the city, natives lingered in cheap, black plastic pots. Larger containers and better soil gave them a chance, but they couldn't control their fates.

If she'd followed the path so many of her peers chased, would her world shrink until she saw an orchid and wondered if she could coax it to flower? Would curating friendships, planning dinner parties, and entertaining kids become her entire existence?

"Ann?"

She eyed the orchid, suppressed her stifling panic, and met Nathan's gaze. "I called Detective Goetz. He's not available until three."

Nathan toyed with a shirt button. "Okay, I have a

confession."

Tilting her head, she narrowed her gaze. He'd sworn he had nothing to do with Lisette's disappearance. If he knew anything outside of his private investigator's report, he was days late reporting his information. She would rat him out to the NOPD as quickly as she could.

"I forgot to plug in the sedan." He ran a hand through his hair. "We'll have to walk or take the streetcar. I think there's a bus system." He widened his eyes. "Oh, wait. A car service!"

She huffed out a laugh. The precious, handsome man who'd fucked her senseless last night was now worried about how he would escort her around town. He had just remembered the existence of rideshare apps. *Sweet baby*. At least, he hadn't suggested a horse-drawn carriage. She set her mug on the countertop. "I want to meet with NOPD solo. We can"—she shrugged—"grab brunch in the meantime. You can do your business stuff while I meet with the officers. This doesn't have to be a team effort."

"So, you'd prefer to ditch me and handle this on your own?" He rubbed a hand over his stubble. "The sooner, the better? Won't even go for lunch?"

Her cheeks warmed, but she nodded. "Precisely."

He winked. "Won't happen, Buttercup. Detective Goetz gave me a card, too. My appointment's at two-thirty. He's very interested in my report."

Her nose twitched.

An hour later, she sat in a red streetcar and felt her stomach rumble. The line traveled between the Aquarium and the French Market. A person visiting New Orleans couldn't find a more touristy gimmick than the lumbering trolley. In the time required for the car to rumble between stops, anyone with full mobility could walk to their destination.

Nathan leaned back in his seat, closed his eyes, and absorbed the sun. "I love spring. Give the weather a few more months, and we'll sweat through breakfast."

The wind played with his hair.

Sweating with him was the only thing she had figured out, and full-throttle sex revved her appetite. Eating breakfast might have been smarter and quelled her hunger pains. She looked toward the muddy Mississippi, watched barge traffic, and wondered why her time in Colorado had been as dry as a meditation garden.

"We can grab a muffaletta at Central Grocery, or Sidney's Wine Cellar has a grab-and-go cooler. I'm not sure if Johnny's or Manolito are open this early, but I could definitely go for a Cuban sandwich and a fresh fruit daiquiri."

Her polished lover rambled adorably. She checked the time on her phone. "It's early."

"Instead of Bloody Marys, I can think of better ways to pass the morning." Grabbing her elbow, he pulled her against his side and kissed her hair. "Just say the word. Or, um, strip."

She laughed. Refusing to raid Evie's closet, she went for a shower and a full refresh. He smelled like fresh oregano and headstrong male. His spicy-sweet, familiar scent calmed her edginess. Being annoyed with him felt like a fruitless effort. He hadn't mentioned last night. She hadn't, either. Relaxing against his side, she savored the sunshine and the breeze. She could think of worse ways to spend her mornings.

"We should talk about—"

"Cubans?" She turned her head and met his gaze. Talking about hot-pressed bread with mojo pork, ham, Swiss cheese, and house-made pickles had to be safer territory than sex. "Too much salt."

"All righty, then." He cleared his throat. "Muffalettas?"

What was it with this town and sandwiches? Next, he'd offer *banh mi*. She liked the *Dong Phuong* Bakery as much as the next person, but these doses of salty, savory goodness held the potential for long-term complications. So did her life. He didn't want to talk about turning foreign agents or advancing national agendas. She didn't want to talk about antique chests or central casting snafus. If food was their common ground, then picking brunch was a roundabout way of discussing sex. Her appetites were clear. "I can enjoy a good sandwich, but I don't make a habit of it."

He straightened his slouch. "Nobody is asking you to live off muffulettas, but they're not so bad, are they?"

She slipped away from his arm and tucked a piece of hair behind her ear. "At the time, they seem like a good idea, but an aftertaste lingers."

"Aftertaste?" He rolled his eyes. "How much can you ask from a…sandwich?"

A lot.

The streetcar lurched to a halt before the shops on Canal Street.

She stood.

A few years ago, the big-name hotel under construction at the corner of Canal and N. Rampart Street collapsed and blocked the streetcar line. While hotel developers, overpaid lawyers, and sheepish builders managed the fallout, the city rerouted the Route 49 streetcar line.

Maybe she should be at the Union Passenger Terminal, asking after Jeanne and antique resale shops. The terminal was Amtrak's major southern terminus hub, and three long-distance trains, the *City of New Orleans*, the *Crescent*, and the *Sunset Limited,* unloaded passengers at the UPT. Some unhoused people lingering around the terminal could turn stolen items into quick cash. They might know what happened to Jeanne or who she crossed.

Walking the streetcar aisle, Ann lifted a hand to thank the driver and disembarked. She would eat a sandwich with Nathan, meet Detective Goetz at his office, and decide between stopping at the port and making her way toward the terminal. Tracking a missing woman through a city of four hundred thousand people was a hell of a job. She understood why the NOPD struggled to find her during Mardi Gras, but the party had ended.

Nathan slipped the streetcar driver a tip and disembarked to stand beside her.

She held a hand over her eyes to block the sunlight and scanned her options. "Look, there's a fried chicken place."

"Fried chicken?" He rocked back on his heels. "Really?"

Dropping her hand, she faced him. Cars and trucks weaved through lanes of traffic. Exhaust fumes mingled with stale grease. This city section, close to the historic districts but not quite in them, catered to casinos, bars, and lingering transients. "Fried chicken's quick and delicious."

"And that's all you want?"

Slowly, she nodded and put her goals ahead of her feelings.

The CIA's motto was "The Work of a Nation. The Center of Intelligence," but its unofficial motto quoted Christian scripture, John 8:32. "And you shall know the truth and the truth shall make you free." Valor took a page from the spy agency's playbook.

She needed to streamline her activities and focus on her goals. As the war in Ukraine began, her Valor missions intensified. The Eastern European conflict created a once-in-a-generation opening to torment Russia. Mortality loosened loyalties. She needed to find the person who witnessed Jeanne's assault, lived with the horror, and wanted to turn on them.

Nathan had come to her rescue, but she was in no position to offer him more than a quick release. "I appreciate getting the job done. A person's hungry, they eat. You ever offer a famished stranger food and have them turn you down?"

"Yes, it's called dietary preferences. It's also called good manners, and the courtesy works both ways. I've choked down more quiche than I care to admit." He grabbed her hand and tugged her close enough to create a pocket of intimacy on a busy street corner. "This is neither the time nor the place for this conversation, but I suspect you're about to bolt."

She swallowed her denial.

"We should have stayed at the townhouse and sorted out what happened last night. I sidestepped getting attached, but I failed."

She stared at his hand holding hers. "I failed, too,

but I can't deal with my feelings right now." She raised her head. Fucking him might have been a mistake, but waking in his arms was a disaster. His past betrayal broke her heart and scarred her. "I felt it, too. Later, okay?"

"Later?" He raised his eyebrows. "Every time I said I missed you, I meant I loved you. I don't care if you want a five-gallon bucket of chicken for lunch, but don't brush me off. Mistakes shouldn't haunt a person for the rest of his or her life. We were so good together. We could be better. Just tell me you've forgiven me. Tell me there's a chance to start over."

Pulling free her hand, she cupped his face. "You broke my heart—"

He gripped her forearm. "I know."

"—but not my spirit. I've spent twenty years healing, but I've also spent twenty years looking over my shoulder and feeling relieved. Heartbreak was the kick in the pants, but I needed it. Rejection chased me out of Hemlock, and I've rarely looked back."

His identity and success were so tied to Hemlock that her rejection felt like a double-slap. He scrubbed a palm against his brow. "Is the town so bad?"

"It's stifling."

Dropping the hand, he nodded.

"I wanted to fit in, but I never belonged. Maybe I understand my mother's flight more than I thought I did." She chewed a thumbnail. "High school relationships rarely work out. Loving each other doesn't guarantee happiness."

He wanted to reach for her but held himself in check. "You make life work out."

She laughed and dropped the hand. "You keep

telling me you're a doer, but you can't force fate. We might have fallen apart in college or taken jobs in different cities."

"Or, we could have chosen each other."

"But that's not what happened." Stepping back, she tilted her head. "I would always leave, and you would always stay. If one person sacrifices their happiness for the other person's dreams, how could they be happy?"

He crossed his arms. "I woke pretty damn happy."

"I woke up"—she considered her words—"happy, too, but that's not my townhouse or my life. They both belonged to Flannery. I can't call her a bitch because she's dead, but I can't step into her shoes, either."

Running a hand through his hair, he looked toward the river.

She watched his thoughts play across his face. The gray buildings and urban traffic stole the sparkle from his green eyes. She wished she could be an easier person, grateful for the people who came into her life and offered love, but she was someone who doubted how long that love would last.

After she solved Jeanne's case and tended Paps, she would return to Colorado and determine her next steps. Nathan had his businesses. When she dreamed of him, she would picture him windswept and smiling, riding along a country road without a care.

He shoved his hands in his pockets and turned. "Fine, let's get chicken."

"But no more"—she made air quotes—"chicken, right? I shouldn't have put you in that position. If the tables had been turned, you would have never asked me for sex."

"I dunno." He rocked back on his heels. "If

therapeutic sex if the only thing I can get, it felt pretty damn good."

...until the sex wasn't enough. She wondered how much the effort cost for him to wrap himself in glossy bravado. Mature adults could talk about their sex lives and their feelings without reverting to innuendo, but she and Nathan were like two high school kids stumbling through life. She took his hand and pulled him into motion. "Let's just eat, ok? I'm starving."

He raised an eyebrow. "Worked up a good appetite?"

She slapped his chest.

Grinning, he let the innuendo stand.

Her phone rang. Pulling the device from her dress pocket, she answered the call. "Hello?"

"Hi, this is Dr. Caroline Smith from East Acadiana Parish Hospital. Is this Ann Storey?"

Ann gripped Nathan's arm and stayed him. "Yes."

"Ma'am, we've admitted Guidry Storey. He fell last night, and Lindsey called an ambulance."

"Okay." Ann took a deep breath. "How bad is it?"

"He broke his hip, but the scans revealed additional cancers."

The doctor's cold, clinical statement triggered alarm bells. During the late postoperative period, recurrent cancer was the most common cause of death in pancreaticoduodenectomy patients. She'd read so many medical journal articles she could spell the word backwards. "But I thought you got all the cancer. I thought the chemo…" She swallowed the urge to fight and argue. The doctors and surgeons had done everything in their power. She exhaled. "Thank you for calling. I'll be there this afternoon."

"Okay, then."

Ann ended the call.

Nathan cocked his head. "I'm sorry."

"Me, too." She opened a rideshare app and summoned a car. Letting Nathan take care of her felt nice, but she was more than capable of taking care of herself.

"What about Detective Goetz?" Nathan asked.

She raised her gaze from the app. "Stay here and tell him everything. He can call me. As soon as I learn Paps is stable, I'll return and finish tracking leads. I'll put him in touch with Hemlock's Detective Sullivan." She swiped between apps. "I'll send Judge Calloway flowers. I'll…"

Nathan stepped forward and wrapped his arms around her.

Shuddering, she leaned against him. Sunlight, oregano, and exhaust fumes swirled into a heavy fog that clogged her throat and summoned tears. Wiping the snot from her nose, she kept her head hidden against his chest until she could control herself and breathe deeply enough to form words.

He smoothed her hair away from her face. "Losing the people we love hurts."

Raising her head, she made eye contact before looking away. "Trust me, I know."

Chapter Twenty

Nathan walked through the hospital doors and found Sam sitting in the waiting room on the third floor. Her colorful outfit outshone the room's dull, practical colors. If dusty-maroon and light-pink signage conveyed health, Sam's red braids shone with vitality. He dropped into the fake leather seat beside her chair and cleared his throat. "How is he?"

She set aside her phone. "Visiting hours end at eight."

"That's not what I asked."

"And that's not why we're all here. He's dying, Nathan. What else did you expect?"

Bitterness stole politeness from her voice. He exposed his palm, waited for her to take his hand, and squeezed her hand in solidarity. "How's Ann?"

"She's been in there since she arrived from New Orleans. I came out here to answer emails and give them time alone. The news must have shaken him, Nathan. I've never seen a man go downhill so quickly."

"He's in pain."

Sam cleared her throat and retracted her hand. "So is Ann."

He kicked out his legs. "She can handle it."

"And yet, you're here."

He stared at the ceiling acoustic tiles. The hospital system paged a doctor. An orderly pushed a cart through double doors. The cart's wheels squeaked. The doors swung. Life went on. "I am."

"Then go on in there. They'll both be glad to see you."

Will they? Instead of voicing his question, he stood and walked toward Guidry's room. A few hours earlier, Nathan had walked into Detective Goetz's office and laid out what he knew about Lisette's death and the app tying together the two homicides. Both the precinct office and the hospital had the same antiseptic smell, as if urine and blood were facts of life. Doctors and detectives performed miracles for some victims, but life moved on.

He opened the door to Guidry's room and pushed back the curtain. Guidry slept with IV needles taped to his skin. Someone had neatly combed his hair.

Ann sat in a bedside chair and leaned her arms on the bed railing. She repeated local duck names like a Cajun lullaby. *"Canard francais, Sarcelle d' été, Canard branchu, Poule d'eau..."*

Leaning against a bare wall, he remembered the first time he set his sights on an American Coot. He'd been five years old and excited to sit in the blind with his dad, his maternal grandfather, and an uncle. The waterfowl pecking in the marsh were the size of small chickens and swam beside mallards, but they were closer related to cranes. He didn't care about their family tree. He wanted a glossy duck mounted on his wall and flavorful meat in the gumbo pot. Buckshot, be damned. He would pick out the scrap. He raised his gun.

His grandfather, who begrudgingly spoke English, laid a hand on Nathan's gunstock, gently lowered it, and asked him to hold his shot.

"But they're right there!" Nathan gestured toward the cold water and the milling coots. "Six of 'em!"

"And what are they?"

"Coots!" he shouted.

A bird flapped its wings and took flight.

In the cramped, wooden cabin on stilts, Nathan's relatives exchanged glances.

"Das a water chicken. *Poule d'eau*. If you can't name 'em, you can't eat 'em." Grandfather listed the French names for the waterfowl overwintering in Louisiana. His ploy bought relative silence and time for a bigger flock to gather.

Nathan still itched to pull the trigger, but he obediently repeated the names.

Before Grandfather finally let Nathan take aim, he warned him not to worry about missing his target. Hunters across Acadia, St. Landry Parish, and Vermillion Parish used different names, but they all patiently kept their eyes on the prize.

Nathan's stuffed and mounted coot still hung on his wall, but *Pépé's* lesson hadn't sunk in. Nathan couldn't pin down Ann's personality. She was alternately fierce and soft. Her fluctuations baffled him, but spending time with her was a hell of a ride.

He wondered when she learned the local names. Guidry or Drake might have taken her hunting, but he'd never thought to ask. He was pretty sure he'd missed his shot to ask her benign questions, but he walked to her side to offer her and Guidry whatever support he could provide.

She leaned against his thigh.

Exhaling, he placed a hand on her back and let his

presence convey his empathy. Monitors beeped and screens displayed Guidry's vitals. Robed in a thin cotton gown and a waffle blanket, Guidry looked slighter than the vital man Nathan remembered cheering from the sidelines.

"He's sleeping so much." Ann cleared her throat. "Even when he's awake, he's barely cognizant. The pain medicine helps, but I can't tell how bad off he is. I'm not sure I want to know."

He dropped a hand from her back, lifted a chair, and sat beside her. Sitting at bed level, he could see Guidry's chest rise and fall. The visual offered more comfort than the continuous machines.

"My grandfather on Dad's side died when I was young. On Mom's side, he lived to be ninety. Listening to you recite duck names, I thought about the first time he took me hunting. I could barely hold the gun." He frowned. "I never took Evie."

"There's still time." She took his left hand and squeezed it. "Although I don't know if she'd go."

He forced a laugh. "Huanlong might."

"Maybe."

Keeping their entwined hands on his thigh, he leaned back into the chair. Even though their hookup left an aftertaste she'd rather forget—he was pretty sure they weren't just talking about sandwiches—here he was, putting himself in a situation where Ann might use him and walk away. He'd been so conscious of protecting her he'd left himself vulnerable. If he threw another chain around his heart, he could pretend neighborly obligations were reason enough to call during visiting hours. He wouldn't crack.

"Is your grandmother still well?" Ann asked.

"Grandma Nancy? She's as fit as a horse. Mentally?" He sighed and leaned back his head. "I don't know if I want to get that old. Reaching my age and still having a living grandmother is an awesome gift, but she's not all there."

Ann squeezed his hand.

He maintained the contact and held her hand. "Grandma Nancy's generation had incomparable women. They knew as much about the stock market as they did about Gorham and Reed and Barton. So many of them have passed, but the ones remaining seem like they're barely with us. The things that come out of her mouth." He whistled. "She lives in another world."

Ann turned her head. "I never heard her say an unkind word about anyone."

"Except politicians."

She smiled and squeezed his hand.

He debated between lightening his tone and confessing his complex relationship with his grandmother. In the antiseptic hospital room, pretenses felt vain. "Granny loves her family, the Lord, and her silver collection. She's impeccably dressed and incredibly over-jeweled, but every time I visit, I feel like I'm putting on a show. She sees her little grandbaby, not a grown man. I don't visit as much as I should."

"Paps sees me." Ann pulled free her hand and rested her left arm on the bedrail. "He's always been my hero."

"I know. He happily wore the tie-dye shirts you made him. My folks were like that with Evie. People need a certain level of self-assuredness to set aside their pretenses and savor your lives. One day, I hope I get there."

"You'd be an awesome grandpa."

"Lawd." He made a show of standing and backing from the room. "Not yet."

She caught his hand and tugged him into the chair.

Finding peace in the room's quiet intimacy, he sat.

"My mother left. My father couldn't get his shit together long enough to be a parent. Without Paps, I would have self-destructed a long time ago. He taught me those duck names. He bolstered my ego and told me I could run faster than my peers, cheer harder than my competitors, and fight as well as any man. Every time my self-confidence slipped, or my jaw quivered, I felt his steady hand. Eventually, I didn't need to hear his words of encouragement. I felt better knowing someone in the world believed in me."

A tear rolled down her cheek.

He wanted to wipe away her grief, but he held still. Until she invited him, she would fight her battles on her terms.

"I want to help Paps fight his cancer, but returning to Hemlock brought back so many memories. Some memories are good, but there aren't enough good ones to wash away the bad ones. And then we found Lisette, and someone shot Jeanne." Her shoulders shook. "It sucks. Nobody should be afraid to live their life."

Her indignation brought a smile to his lips. For a moment, they were back on the high school bleachers, complaining about exams.

"When you're a caregiver, you spend all your time fighting other peoples' battles. Paps used to tell me that if you fought a good fight, you could find nobility in your defeat. Screw that. I don't want to be noble. I want

Paps to stick around another two decades so he can be old and senile like your granny."

"I know, Ann. I want that, too." Leaning forward, he scooped her into his arms and settled her against his chest. Waiting for her to tuck her head against his shoulder, he sighed. If sex rocked his world, intimacy would knock him out.

He'd told her that doing things was his love language, but listening to her extol Guidry's virtues, Nathan understood Ann needed painful, rehearsed lines that required more forethought than lust. She needed to hear them out loud and hear them often. When you loved someone, you value his or her needs as much as yours.

Having so many people walk out on her—her mom, her dad, and then him—left her defensive. When she suffered Guidry's passing, she would lose her biggest fan. Collapse wasn't an option, but she would do the same thing she'd done after high school. She would run.

He wasn't surprised when she joined the Navy and worked for Valor. Patriotic callings required her to be noble and fierce, skills that came naturally. Over the last few days, he'd also glimpsed the tenderness she kept hidden beneath her beautiful exterior. Maybe that tenderness was what had drawn him so many years ago. When she threw her pom-poms for Sam, she put her high school career on the line for a friend.

He thought he could throw around money and time to ease her return to Hemlock, but he couldn't insulate her from Guidry's death. He couldn't save Lisette or Jeanne. So far, the only things he excelled at were being present, making money, and making Ann come. His nose twitched. His resume wasn't half bad, but if he wanted more from Ann than a litany of regrets, he would have to do better. Since hospital confessions weren't exactly romantic hallmarks, he held his tongue.

"You don't have to be here, you know." She lifted her head. "Sam will bring me home. Or maybe I'll sleep on the convertible chair."

He eyed the hospital furniture and shifted her weight to get more comfortable. Loving his daughter came naturally. Loving Ann was a whole 'nother ballgame. He wouldn't want either of them to sleep in that chair, but telling Ann to find another bed was tantamount to challenging her to sleep in the chair. He cleared his throat. "You can stay at the hotel. Just tell them to comp you a room. It's walking distance."

"That's kind, but unnecessary. Is that what you did? You walked?"

He swallowed. "The paramedics brought Flannery to the hospital with serious injuries. She nearly survived. I spent days taking care of Evie and nights sitting here."

"I'm sure that was hard." She dropped her head back to his shoulder. "Sorry about what I said about your townhouse. You built a nice life with Flannery. I'm sorry you and Evie lost her."

Accepting her condolences would table the conversation, but the deflection would also gloss over a part of his life he struggled to accept. "I wasn't a great husband. I tried, and maybe that's all that counts." He cleared his throat and kept going before he lost his nerve. "Evie loved Flannery. She was a great mom. At her hospital bedside, I thanked her for Evie and everything she did for our family. I don't know if she heard me, but I hope so."

"I hope she did, too." Ann stood. "I'll tell the nurse I'm leaving. Will you sit with him?"

Watching Guidry's chest rise and fall, he nodded.

Ann left the room.

Guidry coughed, opened his yes, and turned his head. "You."

"Yes, sir." He rubbed his sweaty palms on his pants.

"I should have known." Guidry audibly exhaled. "All these years, you lingered at the conversation's edge and listened to stories about her exploits. Maybe you thought nobody noticed, but I did. You might have a second chance with her, but don't mess up. Only fools hang their hat on lucky breaks."

"Yes, sir." Nathan moved a hand toward the bed controls. "Would you like to sit up?"

"Can't hardly find the strength." Guidry's eyes fluttered closed. "I thought I'd beat the cancer, but something else was wrong."

Nathan rested his chin on a palm. "Why didn't you tell her how you felt?"

"What good would it do? She still has to bury me. We made good memories. She's strong" A cough rattled in his chest. "That's all she needed."

He begged to differ and opened his mouth.

"She's always been worth the fight."

Nathan had more to say about what Ann needed, but keeping Guidry comfortable trumped his opinions. "Yes, sir."

Five minutes later, the old man fitfully slept.

Ann laid a hand on Nathan's shoulder. "How is he?"

Looking up, he swallowed. "He stirred and said you were worth the fight."

Tears welled in her eyes and slipped down her cheeks.

He caught her hand on his shoulder. "He'll wake again. He's strong."

"I know." She swallowed, pulled free her hand, and reclaimed the adjacent chair. "Thanks."

Sitting at Guidry's bedside felt like a quiet privilege. He maintained his silence, but he took Ann's hand.

She squeezed his in return.

Sam slid open the curtain. "Hello?"

He tightened his hold on Ann's hand, sure she would bolt.

Ann lifted her other hand and covered a yawn. "Is it already eight?"

Furrowing his brow, Nathan resisted taking charge.

"Sure is. Thought I would check on you before the nurses made their rounds." She eyed the whiteboard with medical notes and phone numbers. "Or are you planning to spend the night? I heard they make a mean omelet."

The effort to keep his mouth shut hurt his jaw.

Ann slipped from his grip and stood. "I'll sleep at your house, if that's okay?"

Sam adjusted her purse. "Of course."

Standing, he jammed his hands in his pockets and resisted pointing out the hotel at her disposal or the guest room in his house. Either would do fine, but he preferred her in his bed.

"What did Detective Goetz say about the app?" Ann kept her voice low.

Sam gathered Ann's things. "He wants to carry out an undercover operation and plant tagged antiques. If the detectives can follow the tagged good to a warehouse, they can get a warrant and search for evidence to tie the buyers to the homicides. I have a feeling a young, female NOPD rookie is about to receive a crash course in undercover operations." She rolled her eyes. "Nothing like posing as fine-ass bait to advance a woman's career."

Butting a shoulder against Sam, Ann took her stuff. "It's New Orleans. Who know what kind of bait they'll use?"

Sam laughed.

A nurse paused outside the door and cleared her throat.

He checked the time on his watch. Visiting hours ended five minutes ago. Instead of ushering them out the door, he jammed his hands in his pockets and rocked back on his heels. "I let the detectives pick out a few items from my New Orleans shop. With any luck, we'll have news on the investigation within the week."

Sam and Ann stared.

Ann blinked. "Thank you. You didn't have to do that."

"I hope it works." He pulled his hands from his pockets and shrugged. "All right, I'm heading out. Night, ladies."

Catching his hand, Ann stopped him. "Hey, thanks for dropping by, and Jeanne, and"—she cleared her throat—"everything. I don't know how well Paps can hear with all the pain meds in his system, but he surely recognizes your voice. If he doesn't remember you stopping by, then I'll tell him."

He wet his lips, glanced at Guidry, and pressed a tender kiss to Ann's cheek. "I didn't stay for him, Annie. I stayed for you."

She squeezed his hand. "Thank you."

"Duckling...." Guidry coughed.

Nathan released her hand.

Turning, Ann crouched near Guidry's side and gripped his hand. "I'm here."

Nathan exchanged glances with Sam, whispered his thanks, and slipped from the hospital room. He'd done all he could.

Chapter Twenty-One

Ann threw a hand over her eyes and blocked out the sunlight streaming through Sam's living room curtains. The old, brown leather couch beneath her had come from Sam's parents' house. White creases lined the aged leather like roots searching for water in smooth, brandy soil. Ann remained sober, but she would happily rot on the couch, establish roots, and become one with the leather. The other option, facing the day and planning Paps' funeral, hurt too much to bear.

Over the preceding week, Paps had refused treatment for his secondary cancer and passed away.

The doctors respected his wishes and provided hospice care.

Taking no action caused Ann's stomach to ulcerate and her legs to twitch, but she had tabled her counterarguments. Exhausted and brokenhearted at the thought of losing Paps, she savored their last days. She thought she stayed in Hemlock to fight on his behalf, but she'd been wrong about his needs.

He fought long and hard for the things he loved. Shipping her to her maternal grandparents on the West Coast was an option, but he suspended his retirement and loved her with wholesome oatmeal, Cajun lore, and tenacious grit. Even as he neared death, he squeezed her hand and reminded her of her strength.

No wonder she'd learned to be strong. He'd imbued her tenacity and gumption. When sleep apnea stole his breaths and weariness slowed his heart rate, she honored his final wishes. She held his hand and let him go.

Today, she had to get off this damn couch. Sitting, she swung her legs over the couch's side, planted her feet on the carpeted floor, and pushed herself to standing. The room swayed. Drawing a deep breath, she waited until the living room steadied and took a stiff step toward the kitchen.

A flower arrangement from Nathan sat on the kitchen table. Sam's coffeemaker gurgled and hissed. Ann bypassed the hydrangeas and lumbered toward the caffeine fix.

"Looking good, Storey." Sam raised a mug to her lips. "*Night of the Living Dead* suits you. Don't worry about your stank. Skipping showers keeps my water bill low."

Flipping her the bird, Ann filled a mug with coffee and clutched it. "Who elected you mayor?"

"Not your Colorado ass."

"Humph." Ann closed her eyes and savored the coffee mixed with half-and-half. "I'm heading to church this morning to make arrangements for Paps' service."

"Good luck."

Expecting consolation, Ann peeked open one eye and found Sam flipping through a catalog.

After humoring Ann's grief immediately following Paps' passing, Sam's coping mechanism took a hard, right turn toward nonchalance. The mayor spent a good portion of her week overseeing events, and Paps' last rites might be another check-the-box activity.

Ann cleared her throat and set the coffee mug on the countertop. "Thanks for letting me stay. I'll be out of your hair tonight. I'm sure you want your space."

Sam tossed the catalog in the recycling bin and wrapped her arms around Ann. "Stay as long as you want, you idiot."

In Sam's arms, breathing seemed like an overrated bodily function. Ann considered pulling free, but she relaxed into Sam's hold and closed her eyes. Same, stupid, wonderful perfume. Same rock-steady presence that went beyond a pair of broad shoulders and a deep chest. Even the pot on the back porch couldn't explain Sam's unflappable staying power. Hemlock might burn to the ground, but Sam would persevere and comfort the survivors. Ann wondered who would comfort her.

Ann would do whatever she could to honor Sam's emotions, too, albeit with a tad less force. She should be an old hat at saying goodbye after losing her mom, her dad, and both her paternal grandparents, but every time she lost someone, her world shrank. She didn't care if Sam doused her in Love's Baby Soft. As long as she could count on her friend, she would take whatever comfort Sam dished out.

Sam released the hold and clapped a hand on Ann's back. "You want me to go with you? The priest can be a little"—Sam wrinkled her nose—"persnickety."

"Nah, Nanette's coming. She's planned more funerals than the town mortician." She peeled a banana and took a bite. The sweet, familiar fruit calmed her anxieties. When Dad died, his physical absence matched his vacancy from her day-to-day activities. For so long, he'd just been...gone. Paps' death felt like a stunning blow. A memory-numbing concussion would be a small mercy, but sharp twinges of grief and regret remained raw. Losing him unleashed a whirlwind of grief and frustration. She'd fought so hard, and her efforts hadn't been enough. She had to honor his last wishes.

His written instructions requested cremation. She would ask the church to inter half his ashes in the church columbarium. Then, she would scatter half his ashes among the longleaf pines. He would finally be at peace.

The split, to Paps' way of mind, was symbolic. When Ann's time came, she wanted a natural burial. The cremains of Drake Storey, her father and Paps' son, sat in the family niche. Paps had found a way to stay with both of them.

He didn't need a committal service or a fancy headstone, but the Acadian flag outside the town hall would fly at half-mast. Sam would see to it.

All Ann had to do was exchange niceties with the local priest.

Nanette picked her up from Sam's house. "You ready for this?"

Ann fastened her seatbelt and flipped the car visor. She checked the makeup that hid her under-eye circles and brushed a stray hair from her nose. "As ready as I'll ever be."

Nanette patted her leg. "Don't you worry. The pastoral staff has done this so many times they don't even need their notes. All you have to do is decide between a Catholic Mass or Liturgy of the Word."

Ann wondered if a third option existed. Paps' instructions hadn't specified how to enact his wishes.

Were the decisions so obvious she should know better? While she chewed her thumb, she watched Hemlock's tall, white, brick church come into view. Union gunboats heavily damaged the 1860 structure during the Civil War. Repairs gave the building a fresh façade, a new roof, and two hundred years of unquestioned authority. The church presided over the town, but the townspeople defied the swamp and defended Hemlock's historical significance. In recent decades, both entities had mixed results.

If her meeting with the priest summoned too much grief, she would dart through the town's ox lots and shady alleys until she found somewhere to regroup. The Tea Room would give Nanette too many opportunities to pry, but Ann could browse the used bookstore or duck into Nathan's hotel for lunch among the tourists.

Her nose twitched. In the swirl of activities following Paps' hospitalization and subsequent death, she had barely had time to think of Nathan, Jeannie, or Lisette, a stranger whose death still bothered her. Nathan knew her, and Ann felt his grief by proxy. If she carried his burdens, she might share his joys, too. Evie's wedding was a bright spot. Spring brought new beginnings. Despite Ann's temporary presence in Hemlock, she would find a way to drag herself from winter's tragedies and move forward.

"I think you should go with a full mass." Nanette toyed with her necklace. "It's proper."

Ann started and looked toward Nanette's stately profile behind the steering wheel. She was twenty years older but just as refined and made-up as she'd always been. A healthy dose of moisturizer helped, but so did her determination. Small business entrepreneurs owed half their sales to their social network. No wonder the town's *Duchesse* did well. She mapped Hemlock's social interactions with the precision of a general. Her dress, light-gray with a teal-and-white collar, conjured respect and the Virgin Mary's respectful, maternal influence. And lest anyone doubted her credentials, her teal, pearl-encrusted headband was gaudy enough to inspire respect. Ann ran a hand over her face. "What if nobody comes?"

Nanette waved off the question. "Everyone loved Guidry. Didn't you see the flower arrangements?"

Ann watched Hemlock's buildings blur into one another. She barely had the energy to shower, much less read the cards and bouquets delivered to the farmhouse. As soon as she left Sam's protective enclave, she would receive the town's condolences, prayers, and funeral casseroles. She couldn't do it.

Burying herself in work held a familiar appeal. She could finished the prescribed burn and file the society's quarterly reports. The NOPD might have questions about her interactions with Jeanne and Judge Calloway. Perhaps her Valor network could identify pattern in the call logs. Knowing where to direct her energies, she straightened in the passenger seat. She would confirm Paps' eternal resting places, settle his estate, and return to her life in Colorado.

Nanette parked the car.

Ann opened the passenger door and stepped into the muted sunshine. She considered the church bell tower and scanned the steps like she was the one who'd suffered two bouts of cancer. Listed on the National Register of Historic Places, the church radiated gravitas. She hadn't set foot in the building in twenty years, but she suspected the 1860s organ still boomed, the endowed stained glass windows still admitted drafts, and the polished pews were still hard to leave bruises.

Paps loved hearing "Old Rusty" reverberate through the church during Sunday Mass. While he was ill, Ann gave him grief about his attendance.

"I have a Bible and can hear the music just fine." He mimed playing the organ's keys. "They don't need me taking up room in their pews. The Lord and I are square."

His faith comforted her. Now, he needed peace and quiet. She would ensure he had it. Squaring her shoulders, she turned toward Nanette. "I've got this. Can you wait outside?"

Nanette wrinkled her nose. "Are you sure?"

Lifting a palm, Ann nodded.

Two hours later, Ann slammed closed the church office's wooden door and considered spitting on the cracked, brick sidewalk.

The priest had gently pushed back on Paps' burial plans.

When she used the term *gently*, she meant he refrained from looking her in the eye and telling her she was a heathen idiot.

Spending an hour in the priest's dusty office, where filing cabinets held records of first rites, and the secretary sat like a smiling, placid cow, Ann fought tears as she picked apart the priest's theological arguments. Doing things the *right way* and honoring Paps' wishes felt like a tightrope walk. At any minute, she would lose her balance and tumble into the abyss. Before she walked into the church office, she had no idea if Paps' wishes bucked norms or flagrantly disregarded community practices, but she had her orders. Well, the priest had set her straight, hadn't he?

Snaking through carpeted hallways with low-hung ceilings and flickering lights, she rubbed together her fingers and wiped her palm on her skirt. The church's front, aged and impressive, inspired parishioners. The rear, secretarial and seeped in mildew-tinged, conditioned forced air, made her want to scream. Blinking at the bright sunlight, she exited the church.

Nanette waited in her heated car.

Ann climbed into the passenger seat, slammed the door, and crossed her arms over her chest. "The priest said a proper burial is the way to go. Paps' request left out details, but 'our bodies, made in the image and likeness of God, will one day be raised up in the same way that Christ was raised incorruptible.' I should honor Paps with a full mass and a burial." Banging her head against the seat rest, she relayed the priest's remaining theology lesson.

"He's right." Nanette patted her thigh. "Let's keep things simple."

Shirking her loyalties and siding with authority had always been Nanette's backup plan. Ann couldn't toss her pom-poms and have an ideological tantrum at mid-field, but the impulse to throw something simmered like restless energy. Unfortunately, lashing out would earn her a pamphlet on anger management issues. Trust her, she had several. Turning in her seat, she faced Nanette. "Paps' wishes were very clear. He wanted half his ashes in the family niche and half in the woods."

Nanette clutched her purse on her lap. "Guidry put you in an impossible situation. Focus on the path forward. It's for the best."

Eyes wide, Ann wondered if Nanette had picked out her funeral hymns. "Surely, if I divide up Paps' cremains, then God can still raise him up."

Nanette kept her eyes on her purse. "Who am I to say what God can do? Lay Guidry to rest."

Covering her face, Ann wanted to scream. She was so accustomed to action she'd lost the subtleties of everyday life. Who was she to question authority when she *was* the authority? She would lay Paps to rest all right...beneath the swaying pine trees where he could find his hymns in a bluebird's song.

Nanette cleared her throat. "Annie, I was thinking white lilies on the casket."

"Lilies?" Ann dropped her hands from her face. "What about irises or"—she struggled to find inspiration in the shadowed SUV—"the beautiful plants growing around Hemlock? The plants Pops put in his yard? Why do you fall back on old standards?"

"Because they work." Nanette cleared her throat. "If lilies are good enough for my father, they're good enough for Guidry."

"But"—Ann rubbed a hand over her mouth— "Guidry wasn't your father. He was *my* grandfather. Let's celebrate his life with the things he held dear, like natives. Aren't they good enough?"

"Oh, sweetie, they're fine." Nanette cupped a hand behind Ann's head. "None of us are from here. We make the best with what we have. You know that. Going with the flow is the easiest course of action."

Ann summoned a placating smile, but in the SUV's claustrophobic confines, she felt bile rose in her throat. She understood why Mom ran from expectations and why Dad drank himself to death. Neither of them could tolerate Hemlock's expectations. The town's suffocating, Southern humidity didn't run them off. Guilt and desperation did.

Conservative values, religious devotion, and humble gratitude made a person a dutiful citizen, but asking for more made them as discordant as a Mexican whistling duck. She pulled away from Nanette's gesture and grasped the door handle. Guess what? Thousands of those boisterous, whistling ducks migrated through the southeast and nested in more hospitable climates. As soon as she laid Paps to rest, she would take a page from the family playbook and migrate, too. If she remained in Hemlock, she might go cuckoo. Opening the SUV door, she admitted the cold, winter air. Even with the high humidity, the breath of fresh air felt brisk and refreshing.

"Ann?"

Pausing, she carefully chose her words. Nanette took an orphan under her wing and molded her into a feminine ideal. Ann appreciated her cheer coach's guidance but hated defending her needs against her mentor's expectations. "Nanette, thank you for looking after me all these years. When I needed someone after Paps and I grieved Dad's death, I turned to you. When I felt like Nathan's betrayal shattered my future, I followed the pathway you blazed into the Naval Academy, but I questioned whether you'd washed your hands of me. No matter your motives, you helped me succeed, but I have to honor Paps' wishes above yours. He wanted to be buried in the places that spoke to him, and I'll make it happen."

"Like a heathen!" Nanette chewed her bottom lip.

"What will people say?"

She laughed. The town's tight-lipped, asinine conventions could be as strangling as kudzu. She offered Nanette a sad smile. "The same thing they've always said. There goes Annie, bless her heart."

Nanette brushed a stray hair from her forehead. "You always were Guidry's girl."

"Thank you." Ann squeezed the hand on her leg. Slipping from the car, she raised her face to the sun and disciplined her rampaging emotions and shaking body. Standing up for her country was one thing, but standing up for herself made her want to double over and hurl. No wonder she avoided entanglements.

Pivoting from Nanette's car, she crossed the street and aimed for a cool, non-judgmental used bookstore where three dollars and a yellowed paperback would buy her enough time to control her emotions.

Nathan stepped out of a building's shadow. "Annie?"

Starting, she stopped and examined the clover-filled grass at her feet.

"Rough day?" He positioned a black, plastic trashcan in the service alley.

She raised her head and placed him in the wild confusion people called mourning and grief. His house, connected to the hotel via a walkway, sat on the far corner of the block. Smoke rose from his backyard. The wind shifted, and the alluring, heady smell of slow-cooking brisket floated upwind. He had every reason to be outside his house, but didn't hotel owners have staff members who could take out the trash and leave her to her misery? "I'm fine."

"Liar." He tilted his head.

She'd never been fine, but she summoned a defense to her lips.

He raised his eyebrows.

Hiding her pain from him had never been her forte. "I hate feeling like the town misfit."

He lifted a hand and dropped it. "You're not a misfit. You're whoever you want to be."

Tears pricked her eyelids. When they were two teenagers taking refuge in one another's company, life was simpler. She could allow herself a brief indulgence and put aside her grief. Taking his hand, she squeezed. "Thanks for listening."

Chapter Twenty-Two

Ann stared at his open palm. Of all the people who could witness her moment of weakness, Nathan was the last person she would pick. Her feelings toward him were so mixed she'd shoved them into the back of her mind and buried them under endless tasks and painful emotions. Drawing a deep, shaky breath, she forced a smile. "Life isn't that easy."

"Of course it is." He dropped his hand. "What are you doing out here?"

She jerked her chin toward the church. "Making arrangements."

He widened his gaze. "Oh. Right."

"Right." She swallowed. She had texted him and thanked him for sending the flowers, but she hadn't expected more than the pleasant text she received in return. He had no obligation to be there for her. At every chance, she pushed him away. Except for the night she sought comfort, she could barely call him a friend. She couldn't exactly climb his porch steps, ring the brass doorbell, and ask him to fuck away her lingering grief.

The thought had occurred.

He wiped clean his hands and walked forward. "I'm sorry for everything."

"Yeah. Thanks." She hitched her purse strap. "I should, uh, go. The flowers were lovely." She cleared her throat. "Thoughtful."

"Ann? Honey?" Nanette shouted across the street and shaded her gaze. "Come on back!"

"Shit." Lifting a hand to acknowledge Nanette's concern, she raised her voice. "We'll reconnect later!"

"But what about the—"

"Later, Nanette!" Nathan cupped Ann's elbow and pulled her toward his cottage.

She relaxed against his strength.

The cottage had a brass knocker instead of a doorbell, but despite its nostalgic charm, she shouldn't be in his house. Instead of changing course, she gratefully followed him up the cottage steps and into a cool, shadowed hallway. The long, tall passage allowed air to move through the cottage on hot, summer days. Spring's arrival urged pecan trees to leaf out, and blooming privet readied to take over the frontage road, but the hallway stood as a respite from the outside world. She leaned against a wall and let her head fall against the cool plaster. "Shut the door. I doubt she'll follow."

"She's not a vampire, is she?"

Ann snorted. "Her sunscreen's good."

He laughed, closed the door, and leaned against the brown, stained wood. "What's going on?"

She wanted more than his pity. As her childhood heroes had disappointed her, she had wondered if she had erred in placing her trust in them or if she had been the defect. She would forever be grateful for Paps' love, but he might have preferred traveling the world instead of raising her. Sure, he made the choice, but did he make a good one? His last, sweet words confirmed he had no regrets. She refused to worry about regrets, too.

She cleared her throat. "Nanette and I went to the church office to plan the funeral."

He cocked his head. "And? What? The *Duchesse* of Hemlock wants you to book the merrymakers as liturgical dancers?"

She snorted. "As if. Following his wishes is just"— she waved a hand toward the apostolic structures— "harder than I thought. I thought I knew the rules, but I was wrong. I'm not facing reality…yet."

"Sure you are." He walked past her. "Come on, I'll make you an iced tea."

She watched him cross the hallway. His stride and easy grace looked more alluring than a punishing run and a steaming bath. A door with a frosted-glass inset lent him a sunlit aura. She pulled back. "I don't need a pep talk."

"Good. I've only have tea and beer."

"I could just"—she cleared her throat—"grab lunch at the hotel and calm down. I'm not your problem."

"You've never been a problem." He disappeared through a doorway. A cabinet banged.

Her rebuttal died in her throat. Nanette might still be outside. Ann eyed the cottage's long, carpeted runner. The hallway probably ended at Nathan's charming backyard, his stupidly successful hotel, or a line of curious tourists who recognized his face and fantasized about his interior design work. If they spotted her slinking away from his cottage like an intern who couldn't keep her hands to herself, tongues would wag.

Playing chicken with a speeding cargo train sounded more appealing than maintaining appearances. When he took out his trash, Nathan probably didn't plan to shelter her from social expectations, but he would let her be herself. The last time she'd entered one of his houses, she'd woken naked in his guestroom and had worried she would never want to leave. Iced tea had to be less confusing.

Dropping her shoulders, she padded the runner and followed him into his kitchen. Like the New Orleans townhouse, the room looked like a magazine spread. Spotless white walls, exposed cypress beams, vibrant veined marble, and high-end stainless-steel appliances made the room look less like a family kitchen and more like a cooking show backdrop. She focused on the small, apple-like fruits clinging to leafy branches like shiny, gold-and-red stained cranberries. "Nice mayhaws."

"Evie picked them yesterday morning. She wants to try making jelly." He looked up. "Lemon in your tea?"

She claimed a barstool at the marble island. "Sure. Where is Evie?"

"Went back to New Orleans. She paints and helps manage the shop during the week." He set the tea before her and braced his palms on the island. "How are you?"

Sipping the tea, she savored the mellow, dark-brown brew and sucked on an ice cube. "I've been better."

"I'm sure."

She waited for him to comment on the shadows beneath her eyes or ask how she slept.

He poured himself a glass of tea and set the pitcher back in the refrigerator. Leaning against the counter opposite the island, he held his full, icy glass. "Nanette getting on your nerves?"

"Kind of." She rubbed her chin. "I thought she would support Paps' preferences, but she went along with the priest's suggestions. I should have known better."

He covered a yawn. "What did she want?"

Dragging him into a religious debate seemed as worthwhile as housing a snow shovel in south Louisiana. He couldn't change the weather, Paps' requests, or the priest's responses. "She wanted lilies."

"The horror!"

She rolled her eyes. Every time she thought she knew what her therapist would say, the expert broke out another clinical term that put her in her place. Moral injuries occurred when someone held a particular set of beliefs about the way life worked. When they went through experiences where life violated those core beliefs, they needed time to heal. Mom ran off, and Nanette stepped in, but Ann had a hard time wrapping her head around her relationship with the Duchess. She sighed. "White ones, I presume. Why does everyone do the same thing?"

He shrugged. "Get a psychology degree. That question goes beyond theology or the funeral. It's about control and defending the right ways to accomplish shit. If you deviate, you admit your peers might be wrong. Might as well fall in line."

Her Naval Academy instructors had said something along the same lines about following orders. Unlike her terrified, eighteen-year-old self, she stuck out her tongue at the concept. "Gag me."

Nathan laughed.

"What about magnolia blossoms? Magnolias are

native"

"Natives might not have the same resiliency as engineered varietals. I plucked honeysuckle and tasted its sweet nectar, but that doesn't mean the experience defines me." He shuddered. "Nor do I want that stringy weed on my casket. Imagine how fast the vine wilts."

Imagine how fast Nanette would wilt outside Hemlock. The ungrateful thought died on her lips. Nanette chose Hemlock. Ann honored her choice, but she didn't have to mimic it. She exhaled. "I'll look at what's blooming in Paps' yard. I guess I should have told the florist to pick natives for Lisette's bouquet, too. I wasn't thinking. I just wanted to send something to acknowledge your loss and stay as far away as I could."

"Trust me, I noticed. Lisette wouldn't have cared which flowers you picked. She liked bold, vibrant colors. Gilt frames. Metallics. The vase would have mattered the most."

"And did the florist send a good vase?"

He smiled. "No, but I changed out the vase."

She shifted from his appealing confidence. Air-conditioning and iced tea cooled her overheated body and gave her a chance to control her emotions. Even while on duty in the desert, a person needed rest breaks. Hemlock was nothing like Fallujah, but her life still felt like she lived on the front lines. Complaining about someone as helpful as Nanette was like complaining about water quality. Desperate people were thankful they had anything to drink at all.

Perspective didn't erase river water's subtle, silty residue. Ann searched for the familiar feeling, but the tea offered zero grit. Nathan probably had a high-performance water filter. Sighing, she traced a thumb along the marble's rounded edge. "Your houses are so different from your hotel office."

"The cottage is a blank slate. Evie can leave her mark on it."

Dropping a hand to her side, she found him watching her. "But Evie lives in New Orleans. Why would you build the house to her tastes?"

He shrugged. "She might want to come home."

"To a magazine spread?" She arched an eyebrow. "If she's coming home, she's coming home to you, not your whitewashed kitchen.

"Maybe." He finished his tea and set the glass in the spotless sink. "As long as she has choices, I'm happy. Hemlock's a great place to raise a family."

Ann stared. Sam might have coined the tagline, but the slogan made Ann groan. Hemlock was safe and nurturing, but it was also simple and restrictive. Davies, the shop manager, helped citizens shine. Ann hadn't seen him at any social events. To be fair, she hadn't received many invitations, either. If she needed a critical ally, she should drop into the shop and unionize with the outsider.

Unfortunately, conversing with Davies didn't hold the same appeal as fraternizing with Nathan. His handsomeness and familiarity beckoned her to lose herself in his arms, but she couldn't run to him every time she needed an outlet. She could ask him how he learned to design pleasing, aspirational rooms. Surely, interior design was a safe, sex-free topic.

His grandmother's plantation house had airy verandahs and four-poster beds. His parents' brick mansion had French patio doors and concrete fountains. At some point, he absorbed his family's design aesthetics and turned them to his benefit. His polished, harmless demeanor conveyed diluted grandeur, but his aesthetic felt more like a commodity than a personal preference. She tiled her head. "You're the *capitaine*, but you didn't ask for that role, did you?"

He frowned and cleared his throat. "Come again?"

"When everything went down, you didn't think you had a choice." She rounded the island and walked toward him. Gripping the front of his white, button-down, she rubbed the fine fabric between her fingers. Starched linen. She almost wanted to laugh. Who had time to iron linen?

She held his gaze. "You didn't ask for this life, did you? One silly night upended your dreams, and you scrambled to meet your obligations. Who would you have become, Nathan Charlet?" She tilted her head. "Who are you?"

He blinked. "Fuck if I know. I did what I had to do."

Laughter seemed disrespectful, but she offered him a smile. "I should apologize. In New Orleans, I took advantage of your good nature. People probably do that to you all the time. It won't happen again. I'm sorry." She stepped back. "The sex was good, but no one should be coerced into sex."

He worked his jaw. "Just good?"

"Great sex." This time, she did laugh. "But, I mean, I used you. I'm sorry."

He caught her hand. "I let you use me. You're more than a random fangirl bingeing my shows and asking for an autograph. We've been part of each other's lives for so long that sinking into you felt like coming home. When you're gone, I'll miss you something fierce, but I know better than to expect miracles."

"Do you need miracles?"

He glanced toward the staircase. "Every day, I descend those stairs because it's the right thing. Life's hard. Being with you is easy."

She rubbed her upper arms. "I'm not an easy person."

He trailed a finger along her upper arm. "Don't apologize for who you are. I knew the outcome of pursuing you. With Guidry gone, you'll head back to Colorado."

"Probably."

He wet his lips. "Probably."

"I have to settle Paps' estate. Sell the house." She pulled free her hand and traced the outline of Nathan's belt buckle. The quick jerk of his stomach muscles told her she might be on the right tack. Maybe he didn't regret New Orleans. Grazing her finger along his jeans and visible erection, she savored his twitch. He was as sensitized as she was, but she refused to point out his desire or ask for a second, mind-numbing intervention. She could handle her grief and manage life in Hemlock. If he wanted something, he knew how to go after it, too. Trouble was, the boy never knew what he wanted. Flannery had taken advantage of his good nature.

Ann wanted to get laid. She swallowed. More specifically, she wanted to strip Nathan and assure herself that no matter how wrecked she felt, some things in life were good and true. Losing herself in Nathan's arms ranked at the top of her list.

He cleared his throat. "This is a bad idea."

She pulled her shirt over her head. "Probably. Feel

free to say no."

Wetting his lips, he opened his mouth.

"No?" She dropped her shirt.

He closed his mouth.

She stepped out of her skirt and stood in her underwear. "Hell no?"

"Fuck, Annie." He ran a hand through his hair. His blood pulsed in his neck vein. A bead of sweat dripped down his temple. "This isn't a good idea for either of us."

So many people had ideas about how she should conduct her life that she wanted to scream. Instead, she scratched the skin behind her ear, unclasped her bra, and dropped her underwear to the floor. Naked, she waltzed through the cased opening separating the kitchen from the hallway and scanned the cottage's living room.

Potted plants and gilt frames balanced slipcovered sofas and a brass coffee table stacked with large-format photography books. Evie wasn't coming back to Hemlock for coffee-table books, and Ann wasn't swaying her hips to talk about interior design.

She also wasn't leaving Nathan's cottage without making a point. Her connection to Nathan had always been the strongest relationship in her life. She knew him better than he knew himself. He hurt her, but she survived and prospered.

If he could get over his ideals long enough to acknowledge how good they were together and how little location mattered, he might be willing to establish shop in one of Colorado's trust-fund outposts. They could be together every night. Evie and Huanlong could visit. Hemlock could be a memory. That prospect alone almost made her climax.

She eyed the slipcovered sofa and imagined herself as a hazy-eyed nude sprawled along the pristine, cream linen and painted with bold, black strokes and heavy oil paints. Before bedding him in New Orleans, she'd expected him to be polite about sex. If she had a gun pointed at her head and was forced her to speculate on his kinks, she would describe his bedroom style as mass-market, perfunctory precision. Life had burnished his quirks. He was so on trend, he was a polished turd. If his partners settled for subdued moans and polite directives, they made a poor choice.

She'd been wrong. He took his pleasure from her body like a shipwrecked sailor desperate for something more than rainfall and coconut water. Her body was a feast, and he was famished.

Before she could disappear into her memories, she felt him scoop her into his arms and rolled her onto the couch. Finding herself spread out on her stomach on the sectional, she looked over her shoulder and grinned.

He nudged a knee between her legs and traced the lines of her tattoo. "You should get another tattoo."

"Oh yeah? Your name?"

"Wouldn't that be nice?" He smacked her ass. "Do you still doodle my name in your notebooks?"

"Asshole." She tipped back her head. "Maybe."

"I thought so." Pressing a bruising kiss to her lips, he slipped a hand between her legs, wet his fingers between her folds, and stroked her clit.

She arched into his touch. If she could catch her breath, sassing him would be easier.

He abandoned her lips, gripped her hips, and slid in to the hilt.

Sass was no longer an option.

Bracing himself on his palms, he lowered himself and kissed her neck.

The change in position shifted the pressure of his cock and hit the right place to send her spiraling toward release. Instead of gasping, she arched her back and pressed her ass into his abdomen as if she could wrap an arm around his neck and have everything she wanted from his dick to his lips. If he maintained his thrusts, then she would come quickly, uncontrollably, and loudly. Then, who would have the upper hand?

"Stop wiggling." He slowed his thrusts and wrapped an arm around her abdomen. Holding her back to his chest, he moved inside her, long and deep.

Shuddering at the change of pace and pressure, she fisted her hands into the slipcover. "I don't need a tattoo to remember you."

"I know. I've never forgotten you, either." He pressed a soft kiss to her shoulder and cupped a breast. "You've always been with me. I blame myself for losing sight of you and failing to understand your worth. I wish I'd known better."

"You say the sweetest things about your sloppy seconds."

He pinched her nipple. "So damn stubborn."

She flexed her hips, letting her body deliver her retort.

Groaning, he slipped out and lowered her to the sofa.

The cold air chased goose bumps across her back. "What are you doing now?" She peered over her shoulder and found his steady, blue gaze. The intimacy slowed her racing heart. "Change your mind?"

He adjusted her hips and smiled. "Changed my goals."

His confession sounded strained and self-effacing. He might be generous and devoted, but he wasn't an idiot. She could picture his boyish, high school smiles...faint, warm, and trusting. His modern smiles were deep and rich, like the smiles of a man who'd assessed life's offerings and knew what he wanted.

His gaze roamed her body.

She took a deep, shuddering breath and relaxed into the piece of art he deserved...warm and luxurious, heady and smoky-sweet. "We don't have to do this. We can play guitar video games."

Laughing, he trailed his fingers down her back and pulled her closer.

The linen slipcover rubbed her sensitized skin.

He exhaled. "All those years ago, I imagined doing so many things with you, but I always went back to..."

For a few heartbeats, she heard the air-conditioning quietly hum and blocked his words. Life made her a trembling, needy overheated mess, but he anchored her. Amidst the honors of her deployments, she'd come back to memories of him. If she could keep her dignity, she might have come back to his bed.

He moved his hands between her legs and spread them.

She felt cold air on her core, and the thought of him intimately staring at her, open and exposed, felt better than obscene. She flexed her hips and luxuriated in his appraisal.

"You look amazing."

His voice was low and quiet, almost reverent. He faced her like she was a fine work of art, and his value judgment eclipsed her uncertainties. She was still seconds from asking him if anything was wrong or if he liked what he saw. She wondered if she should break the intimacy with a small, deprecating joke...confess she usually waxed but admit she'd been so busy crying out her eyes on Sam's sofa that she'd forgotten mundane concerns. *What were a few stray hairs between mourning one's biological family and cosseting her found family out of fear of breaking it?* The gravity of her questions would steal his breath and his arousal. What would he say out of politeness? Her pussy was a nine out of ten? It was a ten.

Before uncertainty stole her self-confidence, she felt him lift her hips and press his tongue, his lips, and his nose square into the heart of her wet, aching center. Inhaling sharply, she tensed before pleasure won her over. Abandoning chilled clarity for the heady luxury of his attention, she savored his careful, slow licks, the flicks of his tongue against her clit, and the strength in his arms gripping her thighs.

He pulled away. "More?"

"More." She moaned. "Definitely more."

Laughing, he resumed his feast.

The first touch of his rough jaw, shaking with amusement as he pressed a kiss against her inner thigh, concentrated her senses. Limbs shaking, she relied on his strength, abandoned herself to the waves in her tightening core, and gave into her selfish pleasure. She tumbled over the edge and rode the crashing waves until she felt like a beached surfer, limp and wrecked in the middle of the afternoon on a slipcovered couch in Nathan's cottage. "Shit."

"You wanna go again?"

Grinning, she pulled against his hold and waited for him to release her. Scrambling forward, she planted her ass and wrapped an arm around her drawn knees. "That wasn't my plan."

"What was your plan?" Cocking his head, be grabbed her ankle and pulled her forward until she sprawled along the cushions. "See how far you could push me? Forget reality. I'll tell you what, Ann. Every time we fuck, you wound me. I don't need needles and ink to mark my life choices. I have memories. Even if you ruin me, if you walk away and leave me in Hemlock like a torrid affair, I'll remember how you came apart on my face." He released her ankle. "You'll ruin me. I'll know exactly who owns me, and I'm okay with being ruined. Use me all day. Forgetting you is impossible. There won't be anyone else."

She stared and struggled to process his admissions. Benchmarking her lovers against him set impossible standards. She was never free to give herself to anyone but Nathan, but she accepted the disappointment. Now, the smooth, heady pleasure of his kisses on her lips, folds, and skin were addictive. The acceptance and love in his gaze were dangerous. They threatened to reclaim her heart. She pulled back. "You miss my body."

"I miss you."

She wet her lips. "You don't know me."

"Funny, I think you just came on my face."

"But that's not me!" She propped herself on an arm. "That's sex."

"Is that all you want? Sex?" He flipped her over, stroked her folds, slid a finger into her heat, and splayed his other hand along her lower back. Holding her in place, he pushed deep inside her and gripped her hips.

Denying the bolt of pleasure and filling stretch of his dick was useless. She was wet, safe, and drawn to the delicious friction their bodies produced. Arching her hips against the pressure of his hand, she chased the quick, fluttering contractions traveling through her body as he used his length to its full advantage.

"I can feel you coming."

She couldn't find the words to respond. Instead, she twisted her torso and met his gaze. When he pumped into her, he matched her gaze and cataloged every second of her response. With one muscled, shaking arm planted on the sofa and one hand splayed above her ass, he watched her with a steady, enthralled gleam. She wondered if he would memorize this afternoon and file away the experience for rainy days. Instead of fixating on her flushed skin and trembling flesh, he held her stare.

He was right. She was screwed. Skin-to-skin, she believed in fantasies, but she wasn't as cerebral as he was. She used her body to accomplish her goals, but her body and her mind wanted what they couldn't keep.

He fucked away her fears, and he was so generous he exposed his heart and hoped for the best. She climbed his front steps, drank his stupid tea, and sashayed into his living room as if her actions didn't matter. Her heart—scared, yet still beating heart—should have put his interests ahead of hers. She should have shied away from his acceptance and solved her own problems. He would never come to Colorado. She would never stay in Hemlock. They would end bitterly disappointed, and this pulsing, thrilling connection would haunt them both.

"You're too beautiful to resist." He increased the

rhythm of his thrusts.

"We should stop." She moaned.

He immediately paused. Arms shaking, sweat dripping from his skin, he exhaled. "Okay."

"No, I mean." She scrambled to articulate her thoughts. "Don't stop."

"But—?"

"Just…please, tell me you won't hate me."

Shaking his head, he lowered himself and pressed a kiss to her shoulder. "I could never hate you." He moved inside her, slow and easy.

The intensity and pressure of his thrusts should have been enough, but the ease and angle of his new movements stole her breath. His purposeful movements were like a love song. If only the song weren't so bittersweet. In an instant, she accepted this afternoon would mark her for life. Feeling connected to a person who knew her like he knew the back of his hand might be more painful than high school love, but she would savor the experience. "More," she ground out.

Snaking his arm around her abdomen, he lifted her hips, pressed kisses along her back, and moaned. "I might not have more. Keeping myself from slamming into you is like swimming upstream. I'm so close to coming, I can feel the current steeling my resolve."

His guttural, breathy, harsh confession tipped her over the edge. Releasing her willpower, she shouted his name and let herself go.

The sun dipped behind the trees as Ann sat in Nathan's lap, naked and sweaty. She wiped his black hair from his face and kept her thoughts and misgivings buried deep in her chest. She was furious at herself for imagining a shared life. Planning Paps' funeral and enjoying the seasons were the only things she should do, but the bell tower across the street and the green buds on the trees were too garish. Nathan's living room was cozy and satisfying. She might never leave.

He could bring her token gifts from the outside world and ply her with Southern fare. She could grow limp and useless, refuse to take custody of potted plants, and spend her life tottering around the cottage and making the same three recipes on repeat until they defined her. He would grow tired of her lassitude and make excuses to spend time at the New Orleans townhouse. She would get the hint and leave. Everything could come to a quiet, peaceful, no-fault conclusion. If only they were different people. She sighed.

"What are you thinking?" he asked.

"I'm imagining us lazy and happy… for a while."

He pressed a kiss to her hair. "We're not those people."

"I know." She burrowed her nose into the familiar, yeasty smell of his armpit. "But wouldn't it be lovely?"

Yawning, he nodded. "I should check on the brisket."

"I should go back to Sam's."

"Fine." He tightened his hold. "We'll let the brisket burn."

She laughed and raised her head. "I know you have your life. I'll just, um, shower and plan my next steps. You can drop me off at Paps' house. Hopefully, the coons haven't taken over."

"I'll go with you." He set her on the couch beside him and reached for his phone in his jean pockets on the floor. "Wily little bandits."

"We can do this again." She swallowed. "I won't bolt."

"Liar." He cleared his notifications and unlocked the phone screen. "It's your call."

Flopping against the sofa back, she closed her eyes. When she understood logistics and tradeoffs, making calls was her forte. In Nathan's dim cottage, the delicious ache between her thighs was the only bearing she had.

"Shit." His voice quivered.

She opened her eyes and looked over.

His hand holding the phone shook. He jammed a finger against the screen.

The phone's ring filled the cold, humming space between them. She straightened. "What's wrong?"

"Um." He cleared his throat. "I got a text." He swallowed and jammed his fist in his mouth.

Stroking his back, she feared the worst. Evie'd been in an accident. His parents had died. His show had gotten cancelled.

Evie's voicemail message played.

"Honey, when you get this message, call me. I love you." Nathan dialed Huanlong.

She gripped his bicep and squeezed. "What's wrong?"

"A text." He cleared his throat. *"If you'll pay five for a stranger, how much will you pay for your daughter?* It's a joke, right? Same number. Extortion. Evie's fine, right?"

"Yo, man! What's up?" Huanlong answered Nathan's call.

"Where is she?" Nathan ground out the question and dropped his head into his palm. His hair fell over his face. "When did you last speak to Evie?"

"Uh, she went to the store to meet a client. Something about a big sale. Why?"

Standing, Ann collected her clothes and tamped her fears. Cold, calculated training took over her thoughts. She withdrew her phone and called Detective Goetz. Next, she would call Valor. Nanette had lines to the White House, but Ann had lines to wire-tappers and special investigative units. If someone had taken Evie, her appearance lacked the ambiguity of Jeanne's and Lisette's disappearances. People naturally sought patterns, and labeling triads was mumbo-jumbo and hocus-pocus. People both retaliated against exes and hexed voodoo dolls. Ann didn't believe in hexes or triads. She believed in facts.

Someone in the state had a nasty pattern of preying on young, vulnerable women. If Paps and Nanette hadn't gotten Ann to the academy, she might have been a lost soul looking for connection. Evie wasn't vulnerable. She was a strong, capable young woman who'd become a sick person's target. Ann wasn't vulnerable, either. As soon as Detective Goetz answered the call, she would light a fire under his ass until every office in the NOPD focused on saving Evie and the women who might become a serial killer's next victims.

"Hello," Detective Goetz said.

She glanced at Nathan.

Compressing his lips, he blinked back tears. "Huanlong's losing it. Evie's not answering her phone. Her location signal's turned off. She's missing." He slipped into his shirt and secured the buttons. "I'll pay the ransom."

She raised a palm. "Absolutely not. You have no guarantee they'll honor the deal. As long as they want your cash, she's alive."

He ran a hand through his hair. "But—"

"Hello?" Detective Goetz asked. "What's going on?"

She tore her gaze away from Nathan's anguish. Training overpowered her impulse to wrap her arms around Nathan and comfort him. She rested a hand on his right cheek and silently held his gaze, telling him she understood how much Evie mattered. Whatever he needed, she would provide it, but her top priority had to be leveraging law enforcement's resources. She dropped her hand and focused on the detective waiting on the line. "Sir, we have a problem."

Chapter Twenty-Three

His nails bitten to the quick, Nathan sat in a nondescript port office with Ann and the NOPD officers investigating Evie's disappearance. His knees shook. He quelled the tic, but other parts of his body defied his control and tensed in response. He abandoned his knees and pressed Ann until she ignored their complicated past, took Evie's case, and leveraged Valor's resources. He refused to relinquish his daughter.

Evie's life depended on the morning's outcome. After Ann relayed the text message he received, she worked with Detective Goetz and Valor contacts to track the cell phone user who contacted Nathan. Professional courtesy stretched all the way to Hemlock because Detective Sullivan assigned a patrol officer to escort Nathan and Ann to New Orleans. Ann drove his car and gripped his left hand.

He couldn't find the words to thank her, but he hoped he would find his daughter.

"Okay, tell the person you're willing to pay the ransom." Detective Goetz crossed his arms and jerked his chin toward the phone.

Nathan placed a call.

"Make sure Valor can hear the audio, too." Jaw set, Ann kept her gaze on the technicians and their data relay.

He nodded. Valor could use voice recognition software to monitor absolutely everything in the district. They didn't have enough people to listen to community wiretaps, but they had artificial intelligence. Phone calls could be transcribed, and transcripts were easily searchable. Someone would slip.

"Yes?" a computer-generated voice answered the line.

Clanging metal and inaudible loudspeakers buzzed in the background. Nathan struggled to listen for clues. "This is Evie's father, Nathan. I'm willing to pay."

"Excellent," the caller said.

Nathan glanced at Officer Goetz.

The officer nodded.

Nathan swallowed and concentrated on the phone call. "How do I transfer the money? The amount exceeds my mobile banking limit." He followed the script the officers recommended and waited. Patience might stop his heart.

NOPD officers had used Ann's Valor estimate and the location of Jeanne's discovery to position a stingray in the port district. Intelligence agencies and law enforcement moved stingrays into neighborhoods and waited for suspect cell phones to connect to the devices. Stingrays looked and acted like cell towers. Once a cell phone connected to the cellular network, the stingray operator had access to all the calls and data leaving the phone. The compact, mobile cell tower was an eavesdropping device but couldn't track movements. The officers would have to rely on audio clues to find Evie.

"You understand what to do?" the computer-generated voice asked.

Nathan glanced at the NOPD officer. Unable to focus, Nathan hadn't understood the caller's instructions.

The office cocked his head.

"I understand." Nathan swallowed and hoped others retained the details.

The kidnapper ended the call.

Ann walked forwarded and offered a bottle of water. "Good job."

Nathan uncapped the bottle and drained it. "Thanks."

Ann watched the stingray technician separate the recorded background noise from the voice stream. She sighed. "I hate using these things. The Electronic Frontier Foundation calls them unconstitutional, all-you-can-eat data buffets, but what other choices do we have? If we do things the old ways, we'll run out of time."

"Hey, don't knock the tech." The stingray operator leaned back in his chair. "This shit costs $100,000 from electronics companies, but anyone with a bit of technical knowledge can patch together a homemade ray. It's really just an IMSI catcher with a cellular base station. Find the base stations in your area and the frequency they are operating on, and you're halfway there. 2G and 3G cellphones are a piece of cake. 4G, LTE, and 5G technologies are a little more challenging." He clucked his tongue. "Upgrade your phones, my friends."

Detective Goetz tapped the operator's head. "Less talking."

Ann smiled.

Nathan searched his soul for anything but nerves

and fear.

"Traffickers are very strategic about who they target." Detective Goetz leaned back in his chair and bridged his hands behind his hair. "They prey on vulnerable youth who don't have support systems. I hate to admit it, but traffickers are sophisticated, cunning operators. They deliberately target transient or homeless teens. These assholes are ruthless."

Nathan had spent the whole previous night pacing the townhouse and drinking himself into a stupor. Without alcohol's numbing pall, he would have spent the night imagining his sweet baby girl in the hands of sophisticated, cunning assholes who thought they could make a quick buck off her misery. "Evie's not vulnerable. She finished her BA, fell in love, and came to New Orleans to help me and to paint. She doesn't know hardship. Maybe that's my fault. I should have taught her to be warier."

"Nah." Detective Marcus stretched his hands over his head. "Don't blame yourself for this mess. Whoever took her wants cash, not people. This Polished and Hammered app's a new one, but its allure to traffickers makes sense. Easy pickings. Desperate people. Most of the time, we charge these assholes with pandering and soliciting before we get them on human trafficking."

"Or murder." Nathan ground out the words. "Sir, I don't think you get it. Something about these assaults is different. Evie *has* a family. Jeanne and Lisette *have* people who loved them. These women aren't victims looking to fulfill basic needs. They come from good families."

"And look where they are," the Stingray officer mumbled.

Drawing a sharp breath, Nathan swore. "You don't get to decide which people are worthy of your time and which aren't!"

"You know how many victims I've seen?" The officer blew out his breath. "Eight billion people in the world and half of them have no common sense."

"That's enough." Detective Goetz laid a hand on the officer's shoulder. He waited a beat before raising his eyebrows and meeting Nathan's gaze. "You're right about one thing. All leads come back to you. Your daughter, your assistant, and your girlfriend's buddy. If this is a public relations scheme with a dose of sympathy, you'll spend your life behind bars."

"Grow up." Nathan shook his head. "I don't have time for your good cop-bad cop shtick."

The stingray officer chuckled.

Detective Goetz shrugged. "You pulled strings to rally the NOPD's resources around Evie's disappearance. Judge Calloway tore me a new one over the phone. Ann's got some Valor suit breathing down my superior's neck. She knows what you're doing? Your girlfriend in on it, too?"

"Ann's not…" He stalled, caught sight of Ann's narrowed gaze, and reconsidered his objections. All leads *could* point to Ann, but she was more likely to tell off Nanette than to prime him for heartache. She was too proud for pettiness. Some women would throw a fit for what he did. She gathered the remnants of her pride and enrolled in the Naval Academy.

Instead, she assessed situations, identified goals, and marched on. Look how many times she'd overridden his better judgment and pulled him into bed. If she wanted to traumatize him, she could have started twenty years ago. Hatred might fester into malice, but Ann didn't hate him enough to play the long game. She feared repeating her mistakes. Fool me once, shame on you. Fool me twice, shame on me. He would do everything possible to avoid making that mistake. He ran his tongue over his front teeth. "You got kids, Detective?"

"Three." Detective Goetz worked his jaw. "Why?"

"Because if you have kids, you know what it's like to sacrifice. To love them so much, you'd starve before they understood hunger. If I wanted the public's sympathy"—he wished he could spit on the floor—"I would have rescued an elderly dog. Let my followers glimpse the Alzheimer's disease eating away at my grandmother's personality. Adopted a honey badger."

"Is that an option?" The technician looked up.

Detective Goetz sneered. "Not for you."

Nathan paced. He put his trust in authority and hoped the institution saved Evie from Jeanne's injuries or Lisette's fate. Maybe he should pay the ransom and trust a six-figure bait would ensure Evie's survival. Picking apart the sound files for location clues was like searching for a white crawfish in a flooded rice field...damn near impossible. He gripped his hair and pulled.

"All right, that's enough. Come on, Nathan." Ann grabbed his elbow and pulled him toward the office door. "Let's get some air."

"Sure." He cast a glance over his shoulder, locked gazes with Detective Goetz, and shook his head. If he had spent the last two decades honing his intimidation skills instead of his likeability, Detective Goetz might have wet his pants.

Ann tugged him into the hall. "Don't let him get to you. He's just pushing your limits to see how you'll react."

Nathan stopped near a water fountain separating two restrooms and pulled free of her grasp. "Is that what you do? Push people's limits until they crack?"

She rubbed her temples. "Sometimes."

He stared. Ever since the text announcing Evie's abduction, he feared he'd be the person who failed to meet his obligations, but he'd never doubted Ann. She was so capable he wished he could be her. He wished he could hold her and give her the freedom to lower her guard and lay her worries at his door. Instead, his wealth was the only thing he could offer, and he felt powerless.

Ann considered the carpet. "All that shit about human trafficking doesn't track Evie's abduction. I got you into this mess. I should have never let you pay Jeanne's request. Without that connection, they never would have targeted your wealth." She looked up. "I'm sorry."

He'd heard of trauma bonds forming between criminals and their victims. The painful bonds hindered detectives from pulling testimony from trafficking victims. Breaking trauma bonds didn't happen overnight, but the bonds could break. People could look back on their pasts and make objective judgments about the shit they'd endured. He took her right hand and squeezed. "It's not your fault."

"Maybe it is." She exhaled. "Maybe I should have set aside my pride and turned over my suspicions to law enforcement. It's just, line are blurring. Criminals don't wear black. Private-sector folks and cybercriminals are getting in on the action. Nobody has an anchor."

He stared at their joined hands and wondered if life in Hemlock created trauma bonds between its residents. Having survived hurricanes, foreclosures, substance abuse, and withered expectations, he, Ann, and their peers had little choice but to cling to each other and hope for the best.

Describing Hemlock as a great place to raise a family was like describing a dream. He wanted the hotel to anchor the town, the shop to delight residents, and the food to kindle fond memories. People could cruise through town, pause to consider Flannery's memorial, and admire the town cemetery. Life could be slow, graceful, and easy. But who had time for permanent vacation mode? He searched for the right words to absolve her doubts.

She sighed. "I wasn't front line against the foreign spies, midnight hackers, and bad seeds stealing America's secrets. China, Russia, Iran, and North Korea are the bogeymen, but they rely on their citizens to do their dirty work. I teased apart the threads of their loyalties and lured them into new allegiances. I showed our enemy's citizens that organization and respect could run a country more efficiently than chaos and threats. Some people made the leap, but many others stayed in their native countries. I don't want Evie to be a failure."

"They'll find her." He swallowed. "God, I hope so."

"Me, too." Ann smiled. "She has your eyes."

He drew in a sharp breath. "I know."

She nodded. "I'll pop into the restroom and be right out, okay?"

"Sure." He swallowed. "Thanks for getting me out of that room."

Glancing at the door, she darted forward and claimed a quick kiss. "Hang in there, Nathan. We'll find her."

He watched Ann walk into the women's restroom and felt his right eye twitch. *I know*, he wanted to say. Fear was the best emotion he could summon. *I hope so. God, let us find her.* If he could bring Evie home and tell her how much he loved her, he would be the luckiest man in the world. His little girl, with rose-gold hair and pouty lips, thought he could deliver the world. He couldn't, and fate had little tolerance for sentimental fools.

A tall, broad-shouldered man with shoulder-length blond hair, smooth skin, and hard eyes walked the hallway wearing plain clothes. Nathan wondered whether the police academy screened applicants for certain appearances. This man's confidence belied his boyish demeanor, and yet, he looked familiar enough to blend into a crowd.

"Long day?" the man asked.

Nathan dipped his head toward the water fountain.

"Nah, don't drink the river water. Here, let me give you this bottle." He held out a liter of water. "Haven't opened it."

Raising his head, Nathan took the bottle and twisted off the cap. The plastic seal's quick click confirmed the man's claims. Nathan raised the bottle to his lips. "Thanks, man."

"Don't mention it." The man raised his left hand, a scoop of white powder nestled in his palm, and blew the powder into Nathan's face.

Nathan coughed and sputtered. Unprepared for the fine, white cloud, he inhaled the tasteless, odorless powder and wondered what had just happened. "What the fuck?"

The man stepped back. "Don't worry, Nathan. I don't need your kid. That's Devil's Breath, and it'll bring you to your knees. Ever had a bad trip? This's worse. That shit will disorient you, incapacitate you, and give you hallucinations so frightening you'll scream for mercy. Best part is, you won't remember a fucking thing." He laughed and knocked the water bottle away from Nathan's grasp. "My Columbian buddy introduced me to *burundanga*, and now it's my gift to you, though I doubt you'll enjoy the ride."

Nathan braced a hand against the wall and sank to his knees. Shifting, incoherent thoughts pulled his gaze toward the restroom door. He hoped Ann would stay inside and never know what had happened. He hoped she would come charging through the door and cripple the blonde asshat who'd sneezed into his face. He closed his eyes and blinked away the bright lights piercing his eyes. More than anything, he hoped Evie knew how much he loved her.

"I own you, dude." He jerked Nathan to standing. "Follow me."

Like a child, Nathan did. The hallway melted around him, the scene more disturbing and disjointed than his worst nightmares. He struggled to understand whether to stay near the restrooms, listen to the blond man, or dance the hallway.

"This way, jack off." The blond tugged him around a corner. "Let's get you to a computer terminal."

Following a wavy, blurred line, Nathan shielded his eyes from bright lights and followed the man's lead.

Chapter Twenty-Four

Nathan moaned. His arms pinned behind his back felt sore and his shoulders ached. He tugged against a tape restraint and winced.

"Watch it," Ann hissed. "You'll take me down, too. I think they taped around both our wrists for good measure."

He looked over his shoulder and found her against his back. She'd been part of his life for so long that her physical presence made sense, but the exact circumstances of their date escaped him. "What the hell is going on? If this is some messed-up escape room, I'll tear this place to the ground."

She snorted. "How much do you remember after leaving the NOPD's neighborhood hideout?"

Someone bound his hands and subdued Ann. He should remember fighting, but after Detective Goetz ran his mouth, none of his memories made sense. Blinking, he sifted through patchy sensations until he constructed the bits and pieces of his memories into a broken mirror. The disturbed and disjointed mental image, like nightmarish vision, overlaid his fear for Evie. "You went to the bathroom, and Detective Goetz came into the hall to confront me?"

"Not the detective." Ann adjusted her shoulders.

He remembered wide shoulders and a familiar face. "Who?"

"Maybe one of his brothers. Definitely a family member. When I left the restroom, I saw him keep a hand on your shoulder and direct you toward the exit. I confronted him, but I don't remember much, either."

"What the hell happened?" He tried the bonds. Thick, hard plastic bit into his skin. "Did he hurt you?"

"They gave me a quick blow to the head, but they gave you scopolamine."

"I'm sorry they hurt you." He flexed his bound muscles and wondered if he would ever get his hands on the jackass who touched Ann. "I feel groggy."

"The feeling will wear off."

"Good." He peered through the darkness and stared at an exit sign's glowing red letters. A faint, oily smell and the cold concrete floor made him think of a mechanic's shop. He listened for sounds, but the slow, steady hum of distant machinery provided few clues. He worked his shoulders again. "Did they take me by surprise? Did I fight back?"

"Um." She cleared her throat. "Not really. Scopolamine interferes with your neurotransmitters. Your brain couldn't consolidate short-term memories into long-term memories. Significant memory gaps, confusion, and compliance mean"—she cleared her throat—"you didn't fight back."

"Fuck." He'd turned into a pliable, scared idiot who couldn't protect his woman. All he'd wanted to do was find Evie, protect Ann, and return to Hemlock to convince Ann to stay.

She chuckled. "There's a bright side."

He groaned. "Tell me about it."

"They sat you at a laptop and told you to log into your accounts and transfer money to their account. You couldn't remember your password or your credentials." She snickered and rested her head on his shoulder. "If you'd turned over the cash, you might have been killed on the spot."

He shifted an elbow and jabbed her. "Thanks for pointing out the bright side."

"Yep."

Adjusting his hips, he searched for a more comfortable position on the cold floor. "So, badass, what tricks do you have up your sleeve? We gonna make a bomb out of a stick of chewing gum or something?"

"How? You have some?"

He rolled his head around his shoulders. He could imagine connecting a self-inflating life jacket, a rescue boat, and a signal flare to make this old warehouse go *boom*, but he couldn't play a cable television hero with his hands tied behind his back. His life skills included fishing, shooting, and making media appearances, but those skills were useless to find Evie. Exhaling, he wondered if he should have given scouting more than the old college try. "I don't have a pocket knife or industrial tape, either."

"Letter opener? Steel file?"

He laughed and thought of all the beautiful antiques he'd sold. Dovetailed joints and polished finishes exemplified craftsmanship, but modern furniture makers had mad skills, too. Living in the past only made sense if a person was scared of living in the future. If he could get himself, Ann, and Evie out of this mess, he would happily burn all those beautiful antiques to the ground. Don't tell Valerie he traded her knowledge for social media fame and laughed as everything burnt.

"They're coming back for more cash. Hold out, and you'll live." She sighed. "Maybe we'll both live."

He turned his head and spat into the darkness. The crooks' attempts at extortion and money laundering hardly fazed him. As long as Ann and Evie escaped, the jackasses could have the cash with his blessings. "Take care of yourself."

"You might die broke."

He laughed. "Then I won't need the cash."

"Nathan…"

He needed more than humor to escape this situation. Helping Ann was his best course. He closed his eyes, exhaled, and recalled the times he sent large, international payments through global payment networks. Wire transfers were outdated. Cyber bankers used multi-rail platforms to optimize payment routing. Making large payments felt like stepping into a black hole, but he trusted that someone to control the light switch.

He usually didn't care whether bankers cycled between blockchain technologies, treasury, or third-party payment processors. Every transaction left a trail, and the money reached its destination. He just, um, had no idea what kind of password or PIN the networks needed. His drug-induced ignorance might have saved him. At least his stumbling failures bought him time. "Don't worry about the money."

"You told them you had five million in cash."

He grimaced. "At least."

She snorted.

"What? The sum doesn't matter. Even if I could remember my credentials, most of those financial services require security documentation. Their payments processing and compliance teams don't want their hands slapped for fucking up. If they don't ensure the security and expediency of customer payments, then customers stop using them. How does Valor pay off informants?"

"Not my department."

"Well, I doubt they're buying prepaid gift cards. The engineers behind the cyber banking networks know more about money laundering and fraud than whatever small-time crook who slapped a handful of powder in my face and thought he would get my cash."

She lifted her head. "Don't you sound worldly?"

He snorted. "Hardly. Did they mention Evie? At all?"

"No, I'm sorry."

He sighed. "I have so many regrets. I should have taken her fishing. Bought more of her paintings. She's the best of me."

"They have you. They might not hurt her."

"Or, they might dump her in the river." He blinked away the wetness in his eyes. Imaging his sweet daughter facedown in the mighty Mississippi was too much.

"Maybe she's okay." Ann cleared her throat. "They didn't shoot Jeanne until you paid them. Hold out as long as you can. Detective Goetz might be honest. My Valor peers know what's going on. The cavalry's coming."

Turning his head over his shoulder, he leaned his cheek against her matted hair. The visceral pleasure anchored him. He'd woken a mess of nerves, but her presence calmed him. "I doubt it." He drew in a deep breath and exhaled. "I'm sorry so many people had to leave us before we could get our heads on straight. I teased you about using me for sex, but I savored every minute. If I have to die in a dank warehouse, there's no one I'd rather be with. You're everything."

"Your adrenaline's going a mile a minute."

He laughed. "No. I'm stone-cold sober. You're so kick-ass, but so many people have left you that you're insecure. You're afraid you're not worth the trouble you cause. Trust me, you're worth it. The day you threw your pom-poms, I realized you were beautiful *and* fierce. You absorbed life's knocks and compartmentalized your tenderness and lingering hurt."

"Because I'm an adult."

"Because you're tough as nails, but you don't have to be a badass around me. If we get out of this mess, let me take care of you. Caring doesn't have to be sex. You can lower your guard and trust me. I messed up, but I also grew up. If you'll give me a chance, I'll show you how much I love you."

"Well, you have a few hours. Give it your all. Sonnets are acceptable. I remember the one you wrote senior year."

He appreciated her self-deprecating humor, but he'd known her long enough to hear the uneasiness behind her deflection. If she had free movement, she might hug him or slap him for declaring his love, but she would take action.

He'd always admired how she took life's knocks and moved on, but he'd realized how much she depended on action to stabilize her emotions. He could give her the freedom to linger in moments of uncertainty. Sure, if she wanted to fuck away her fears and frustrations, then he was game, but he wanted to be present for so much more than her heartaches.

Ann recognized beauty in nature's brilliance. He recognized beauty in her resiliency. When a person found time to draw a deep breath, life could be beautiful. He hoped they would draw their last breaths together, but he prayed slipping from this world wouldn't occur in a dark, abandoned warehouse. He cleared his throat. "You don't want me to profess my love before some wannabe commando plays out his video game fantasies?"

She snorted. "I can think of more romantic settings."

The possibility of never again seeing daylight lingered as a distinct possibility. He cleared his throat. "You know the importance of simple kindness. You treat people like your interaction with them might be the last thing you do on this earth."

"You don't really know what's going on in peoples' lives. Kindness can make a difference. It's the least I can do."

"Trust me, you could do less." He felt her chuckle but failed to hear the recognition behind her laughter. Perhaps all people should be kind, but she went out of her way to connect with strangers. Maybe she remembered how isolating loneliness could be. "You're also pretty good at empathy. I listen to clients, but you recognize a person's struggles. The way you buttered up Judge Calloway"—he whistled—"not everyone could see past her steely façade and respect her fear."

"Going through therapy brought me a new understanding of how people struggle when they have mental issues. Empathy, especially for things I don't understand, goes a long way."

If he could rub a hand over his face, he would. Deflection might not be a skill employers prioritized, but she had mastered the art of turning her behaviors into global standards. If she could blame her kindness and empathy on toeing the line, then he could point out how far over the line she stood. He swallowed and wished he had a cold glass of water or an iced beer to ease the cloistering humidity from choking his lungs. "So, your training makes you kind?"

"Right."

"And you naturally value physical fitness?"

"Is this about my ass?" She wiggled against the restraints. "If we get out of this mess, you can ogle my backside as much as you like."

"It's not about your ass." He rolled his eyes. "You take care of your body. You don't drink."

She sighed. "Dad was an alcoholic."

"You're not Drake. I think you miss feeling safe in someone's arms. Pushing yourself to stay strong is your way of ensuring you can take care of other people."

"I might have to save my life, help a family member, or rescue a stranger. If I wasn't this strong, do you think I could have lifted Paps from bed during his chemo? Hemlock's not bursting with orderlies." She exhaled. "Not that I saved him, but I just wanted to be there for him like he was there for me."

"You were." He pushed love and conviction into his words. Telling Evie he loved her art and the tender, ambitious person she'd become was straightforward. The kid was in her early twenties. Loving her was as easy as breathing.

Telling Ann he loved her battered and bruised soul

was a pressing need. If things went south, he wanted to die knowing she'd heard him profess his love. He saw her, and if nothing else, he wanted to be more than the idiot who'd cheated.

"Why are you telling me all this right now?" she asked.

I'm afraid I'll lose you, Evie, and my life. He swallowed his fear. "I appreciate your perspective. You went through a bunch of shit, and you calibrated your reactions to life's hiccups. For instance, you're not crying and losing your mind in a vile, Southern Louisiana warehouse."

"Don't sweat the small stuff."

He laughed and pressed against her for an instant. "I won't sweat it, but I want you to know something. I have a bunch of cash and pretty things, but the relationships in my life are more important. Those relationships can stop me from considering big-picture alternatives. You don't have that problem. You love people, you recognize your importance, and you maximize your impact in their lives. Even if loving them means giving them a swift kick to the ass. That's incredibly profound."

"Dad told me to live a little bit every day. He tended to *drink* a little every day, but he took his opportunities. No one knows how much time they have left. Live every day as if you stole the day from death's grip and create happiness from darkness. That's the best he could do. Sometimes, he was happy. I wish his happiness had been sustainable."

"Sometimes, you're happy."

"I've been happy with you."

He closed his eyes and savored her confession.

"I just"—she exhaled—"I don't know how to say thank you…for seeing me. For loving me the way I am. When we were kids, we weren't in the same place. Maybe we'll never be there, but I'm happier knowing you're alive in the world. Maybe you can find time to visit me."

"Maybe you can stay in Hemlock."

She laughed.

He heard the pain behind her release. Life left behind so many unseen scars. "Fine. I'll move to Colorado. I'm sure they can find more water."

"Hardly."

"But I'll be with you." He nudged his head against her head. "You were right about Evie. She's an adult. She doesn't need me anymore. Maybe you don't need me either, but I need you."

"Maybe, I need you, too." She sighed. "You're right. Hemlock's not *that* bad."

He struggled to remember anything past the minute the goon drugged him, but he had years of memories with Ann. In second grade, the teachers lent them old-time costumes, paired them up, and taught them to dance to traditional tunes. Amédé Ardoin was a French-speaking Creole music pioneer whose life ended in tragedy, but he wrote beautiful music. "Le Blues Des Voyages" sounded melodramatic until someone glimpsed love they couldn't claim. Nathan sang the song in French and hummed the familiar melody. "Oh, where will I stay?"

"With me." Ann gripped his fingers. Bound with ties, she grabbed for a connection. "Stay with me."

"I will."

Overhead lights flashed and hummed. The old

fluorescent bulbs flickered on. He scanned the pallets of rolled goods stacked to the ceiling surrounding him and Ann. He spent time exploring warehouses full of furniture, but this one smelled like decay, and now he knew why. The warehouse held aging cotton products. No wonder the air felt thicker than humidity. He would rather submit to waterboarding than slowly choke to death on dust motes. Why the hell were they in a cotton warehouse?

A door creaked open.

"Fuck." He dropped his voice. "Someone's here."

She relaxed her posture. "Ready to do the talking?"

He snorted. "I have the cash. Trade greenbacks for our lives. Or your life. Or Evie's life." He choked down his fear. "Please, save Evie."

Ann squeezed his fingers. "We'll all getting out of here."

"I hope so." Swallowing, he slipped on the neutral mask he wore at auctions. Nothing in the room frightened or intrigued him. He could be anywhere. His bravado was so thin he questioned his ability to keep a neutral expression in place. If a physician slipped a stethoscope against his skin, the quack would hear Nathan's heart beating faster than a hummingbird's wings. The damn thing was likely to pop.

He understood the stakes as readily as he felt the plastic ties binding his limbs. If he could get Ann out of this mess, he would do everything possible to save her, but her freedom might leave scars.

"Don't be a hero," Ann whispered.

He smiled. "You read my mind."

"But will you listen?"

"Probably not."

She scored her thumb along the tender skin between his fingers.

The pain, brief and intense, faded as he heard footsteps approach. "Yes, I'll listen. Do you know what else I regret?"

"Reading too few thriller novels? Blowing off stunt doubles? Stopping at green belt kung fu?"

Even as a monster approached, she found time to laugh. No wonder her peers followed her orders and trusted her. He wet his lips. "You can raise a kid in so many ways. I thought I had to marry Flannery and sacrifice my life for Evie's happiness. I was wrong, and I regret the harm I caused you and Flannery."

"I believe you."

"If I'd been braver, I would have tried a different pathway. I would have groveled for your forgiveness, and I would have supported you, Evie, and Flannery. I wouldn't have hidden from the hurt in your eyes and left you to deal with the fallout. Just because that shit worked for prior generations doesn't mean it works for us."

"I forgive you. Now, shut up." She threw her weight to the side and nudged him until they could both see the pair of broad-shouldered, slow-walking threats coming toward them with greedy smiles.

The man from the NOPD hallway swung a machete at his side and walked between the pallets like he had all the time in the world. The smaller man held a laptop and darted his gaze from side to side, as if he'd never been in a warehouse. "I love you." Nathan closed his eyes and silently prayed for Ann's and Evie's safety. If protecting them was the last thing he did, he would gladly take a bullet. Trouble was, the goons probably had guns, too.

"I love you, too." Ann ground out the declaration. "Now, please, be quiet and stop fidgeting before I slam my head into yours and knock you unconscious."

He had no doubt she would do it.

"Well, well." The broader man's yellow teeth had seen too much chewing tobacco and too few brushings. "Look who's awake."

Nathan wanted to throw out a quip, but he replayed Ann's threat. Silent and stoic, he settled for his second impulse and glared at the people who'd caused so much pain in innocent lives. Despite what he told Sam on Mardi Gras day, the man had a pattern. He doubted Lisette and Jeanne were their only victims.

Maybe the Mutt-and-Jeff duo weren't serial killers. If Shorty had an alibi, he still had to explain his presence in the warehouse. Once he tasted power, the sidekick might be the blond giant's willing accomplice.

"Cat got your tongue?" the broader man asked.

Ann cleared her throat. "Hi, Dickie." She raised her eyebrows. "Marcus said you were no good, but I dismissed his sibling rivalry. No one expects killers to be quite so buddy-buddy with the NOPD, do they?"

Dropping his chain to the cement floor, Dickie crossed his arms. "Marcus mentioned me?"

Ann shrugged. "Only in passing."

Dickie glanced at his sidekick. "It counts."

She jerked her head toward the shorter man. "This Frankie?"

"Yes, ma'am." The shorter man beamed. "Frankie Goetz."

Dickie cuffed him on the back of the head. "Idiot."

Nathan worked his jaw and put together the pieces

of information to build a narrative. Detective Goetz, Frankie, and Dickie were the sons behind Gagne & Sons, one of Louisiana's last remaining cotton farmers.

At one time, farmers and slaves grew cotton all across Louisiana, but times changed, and environmental conditions herded cotton crops toward the state's northeastern quadrant.

These days, modernized farms planted eight hundred thousand acres of cotton in the alluvial soils bordering the Mississippi and Ouachita Rivers. The crop still floated the river on barges and waited for buyers, but designers prized the resulting homegrown, made-in-the-USA textiles for local ties.

The mechanical cotton picker reduced the need for seasonal labor and kicked knuckleheads like Frankie and Dickie off the farm. Detective Goetz probably left of his own volition.

Nathan hadn't heard much about Gagne & Sons in the last few years. Rumors of code violations explained lapses in their production. Maybe Father Gagne took a look at his sons and threw up his hands.

Either way, the pallets surrounding Nathan looked like the cotton byproduct and the residual fibers left on the seed after ginning. At the product chain's bottom, comber noil and cottonseed meal were sustainable, raw feedstocks that sold for pennies on the pound. After producers removed short fibers during yarn production, the soft, high-absorbent waste product went into medical supplies, cleaning cloths, and paper manufacturing. Nathan wouldn't mind wiping his ass with Gagne & Sons toilet paper, but he preferred not to have the family's nitwits in charge of his life.

Watching the two brothers glare at each other, he

bit his tongue, tasted blood, and wondered how sibling bonds stretched into criminal pursuits. He thought of Lisette like a sister, but his relationship with her drew on shared experiences and mutual respect. Frankie acted like a pee-wee football rookie reject waiting for coach's attention, and Dickie looked like the kid who still wanted to be his team's running back. Nathan swallowed the spit collecting in his mouth and scanned both men for guns.

Dickie jerked his thumb toward his sidekick holding a laptop. "Now that the Devil's Breath has worn off, let's see if you can remember your passwords. Every time you fuck up, Annie loses a limb. I hope your memory's better when you're sober."

Sweat beaded on Nathan's skin. He kept all his passwords in a password manager app on his phone. Logging into a website from a remote laptop would never work. He could try the web's two most commonly used passwords, but Ann would bleed, and he still wouldn't get in. "That won't work. I don't know my passwords."

Raising his combat boot, Dickie kicked Nathan in the side.

Pain radiated through his core. Swallowing the misery, he understood why criminals repented and geriatrics released family secrets. Dying with a clear conscience offered sweet, unburdened relief. He wasn't any more likely to guess his passwords than to guess Me-Maw's secret recipes, but he could buy Ann time.

Shorty flipped over a pocketknife and cut Nathan's ties. "Give it a try, asshole."

"Get me"—Nathan ground out the words and flexed his hands—"my phone."

Chapter Twenty-Five

Ann kept her senses trained on her surroundings and her gaze fixed on Dickie and Frankie. The squabbling brothers couldn't stop messing with each other long enough to separate her and Nathan. Forced proximity made her claustrophobic, but Nathan had already seen her crumble. His embrace lacked judgment. She never wanted to find herself separated from him again, but she needed space to flex her muscles. Eyeing the brothers, she wondered which brother shot Jeanne and who carried a gun.

The odds of surviving this mess looked dim, but she viewed her and Nathan's predicament as a purely mechanical problem. They *would* escape this warehouse and find Evie. She repeated the affirmation until her doubts dissolved. Her mind felt detached from failure's consequences.

"C'mon, idiot. Cut him loose and give him his phone."

"Don't have it." Frankie glared at his big brother. "You told me to search them and leave their things in the office."

"Well, go get it!" Dickie rubbed his temples and pointed toward the exit sign. "We're waiting."

With a huff, Frankie placed the laptop on top of a pallet of goods, hiked his jeans, and stomped toward the warehouse door.

Dickie probably had a gun. The man gave orders. If someone balked, he would want reinforcements. She doubted he had an ankle holster. His piece probably stuck out of his waistband. If she could get close enough, she could grab it. Too bad the brothers were smart enough riggers to use tape bindings instead of rope. If she'd been faced with knotted ropes, she and Nathan would already be free.

"Antiques business wasn't profitable enough, eh?" Nathan asked.

"Stupid, sentimental fools always countered my offers with family stories and untraceable ties. Half the silver goes to the smelter, anyway. Melting the pieces for scrap is a lot easier than arguing over local history and artistic value."

"But you listened."

"Occasionally." Dickie flicked dirt from under a nail.

Nathan stretched out his legs. "An iconic sterling silver pitcher might sell for three times its scrap value, but very few people have name-brand silver. I get it."

"Do you?" Dickie narrowed his gaze. "I thought you were in this business."

"I sell dreams." Nathan cocked his head. "What's yours?"

Dickie grunted and looked away.

At least, they're no longer talking about silver! She blocked out the banter between the men. Whether Nathan wanted to understand Dickie, or he wanted to buy her time, she would let him run his congenial mouth until she had a plan.

She ignored Frankie's response and raised her gaze to the warehouse's tall, flocked ceiling. Lofty spaces regulated interior temperatures during summer months and severely reduced sheer acoustic noise, but the warehouse's lofty ceiling had utilitarian goals. The open space supported ventilation systems, created storage, and accommodated product movement.

Given the number of pallets on the floor, the warehouse operators probably had a crane, a forklift, or other lifting equipment staged nearby. Someone might have left behind the machinery's keys. She desperately wanted to chew her nail and find a way out of this mess. Impaling Frankie on forklift arms had some appeal.

"I did the same thing that makes Marcus a successful detective. I listened for details and put together clues." Dickie paced. "When somebody sells off their family assets, they're desperate."

Nathan bit his lip. Dickie's bitter statement summoned court liens, family tensions, and vulnerable people with big problems.

"Where you see smoke, there's fire." Dickie shrugged. "I'm happy to make their problems disappear."

"Permanently" Nathan cocked his head. "Is that what you mean?"

Dickie stopped pacing and shrugged. "Dead people don't give a shit what happens to their antiques, and they usually have cash on hand—twenty thousand for tuition and ten for car repairs—the details hardly matter." He shook his head. "The sum adds up, right?"

"Evie didn't have twenty thousand," Nathan whispered.

Dickie leaned close to Nathan's face. "No, but I'm banking you do."

She winced. Even though Dickie stood at her back, she could tell he needed a bath, a toothbrush, and a lobotomy.

"Where is Evie?" Nathan pulled against the tape. "Let her go."

Dickie straightened and yawned. "Not until I bleed you dry, asshole. Not so big in person, are you? I always heard television added ten pounds."

Rolling her eyes, she hoped Dickie enjoyed penal poverty. Five bucks for a cig and ten for a good night's sleep would be the metrics that kept him awake at night. Life behind bars added up. Detective Goetz's brothers needed more than their big brother's interventions to get them out of this mess.

Frankie walked back, swinging her purse. He dumped its contents on the cold, concrete floor.

Amid her lip balm, pocketknife, and dried oak leaves, she spotted her wallet, her phone, and Nathan's items. Subduing her hopes, she checked again. Her Sig Sauer P320 9mm pistol should have been in her purse. She brought the piece everywhere. Raising her gaze, she scanned the brothers' forms and suppressed a smile. An idiot had her gun.

The news thrilled and devastated her. Her gun's design flaws might be an advantage, and the brothers might be incompetent marksmen. Either way, she needed more than fumbling fingers and bad aim. Nathan's life was on the line.

She explored multiple scenarios in her mind. If a brother shot a person with her piece, the ballistics evidence could indict her. She refused to add that complication to the mix, but she might use their thievery against them.

Paps taught her to respect a gun's power. She would use her knowledge. If she got Frankie to drop the gun, its discharge might create enough confusion to enable her to overpower him. Someone might take a bullet. The odds of her and Nathan escaping this warehouse through down-home charm and affable negotiations suggested she would have to take the risk.

Luckily for her and Nathan, she doubted the brothers would kill them before draining Nathan's bank account.

Dickie kneed Nathan's side. "Okay, buddy. Time to type."

She wiggled her wrists. Without Nathan's bindings, she might have room to collapse her hands and pull free of her bindings, but she would need time. Instead, she waited until Nathan stood and made eye contact. She jerked her head toward the laptop waiting on the pallet and urged him to proceed.

The minute all three men had their backs turned, she used her slight height to her advantage. Rocking forward, she pulled her bound hands under her butt, legs, and feet. Once she had her hands before her, she raised them above her head, jerked them against her abdomen, and flexed apart her elbows. Although the tape was incredibly adhesive, the material was still vulnerable to tears. The tape split on contact and freed her hands.

Dickie turned.

She slammed into him, wrapped her arms around his waist, and searched for her gun. Feeling cold metal beneath his waistband, she gripped the gun's butt and pulled.

Dickie flung her against a stack of pallets loaded

with cotton rolls.

She bounced off the paper-wrapped textiles, planted her feet, raised her gun, and pulled the trigger.

The trigger released.

Empty. "Fuck!"

Frankie pulled a shotgun from between two pallets, primed it, and countered her threat.

Shit. She hadn't seen that coming, either. Glancing at Nathan, she jerked her head toward the exit. "Run!"

He shook his head. "Not without you!"

"Stop being so damn generous." She edged closer and dropped her voice. "When I tell you to jump, you ask how high?"

He wrapped an arm around her waist and pulled her to his side. "Cute. What will you do with an empty gun? Beam him over the head before he shoots you in the stomach? I'm not interested in looking over my shoulder and watching you die."

If she didn't formulate a quick solution, they would both die. Nathan's familiar warmth would be her last pleasurable sensation, but she could think of lonelier deaths. Whether wandering Hemlock's shaded pine forests, New Orleans' humid streets, or this warehouse's moldy shadows, she felt better in his company. His self-confidence and gregarious ambitions outshone her self-doubts. Trusting him was like permitting herself to breathe.

She edged her body to the side to shield him, held her gun in a loose grip, and watched how Frankie held his shotgun.

The man probably had more experience shooting soda bottles off fence posts than shooting moving targets. She glanced toward the exit. Maybe they would run, weave through the pallets, and take their chances on his poor aim.

Dickie walked closer and shook his head. "You thought we came to have a nice chat? Rough you up a little and let you leave? Darlin', as soon as we took you and your flyboy, you were as good as dead."

If he came within reach, she would slam her piece into his temple. The blow might not knock him unconscious, but the stun would buy her time. She raised the gun.

"Cute." Dickie rolled his eyes. "Shoot the gun from her hand."

She snorted and waited for Frankie to try. Hollywood's Old West lawmen shot weapons out of people's hands, but the feat was harder than it looked. She could move her body at will, and Frankie didn't have much of a chance of hitting his target.

People always wanted shooters to aim for an arm or a leg to disarm the bad guys, but that strategy often backfired and pissed off the people holding guns. If you wanted to stop an aggressor, you aimed for their center of mass or their head. Instead of arguing with Dickie's order, she circled her gun above her head. "Welcome to the fair! Take your best shot and win a prize!"

Nathan dropped his head to her ear. "What are you doing?"

"Finding out whether he's trigger happy."

"For the sake of argument, assume the answer's *yes*!" Nathan reached behind her and yanked her hand. "Crazy woman."

Arguing with his assessment seemed like a waste of time.

"Aren't y'all the cutest?" Dickie spat and grabbed

ahold of her other hand. "Give me the gun!"

She tensed her muscles and widened her stance.

"Let her go!" Nathan sneered and attempted to sidestep her.

He would have better luck taking a sledgehammer to a brick wall.

"And lose my leverage?" Dickie snarled. "Who should I kill first? Her or the girl?"

"Why don't you go…"

Ann zoned out and let them banter. Caught between two men, one who would love her and one who would murder her, she considered head-butting them both and making a run for it.

Frankie retained his shotgun.

Still, she might succeed.

Dickie yanked her arm. "Go piss yourself!"

Her shoulders ached, but she held firm. Escaping without regrets was never her goal. She wanted everything life offered. If she ran from this warehouse and abandoned Nathan, her life wouldn't be worth living. Twenty years ago, he betrayed her, but he regretted his decision. She refused to regret loving him. He was generous, loyal, and a riot in bed. She wanted to live by his side, but she had to rescue him from this dank, dust-filled warehouse.

She considered her surroundings and recalled field trips to parish agricultural fairs. The pallets held cotton motes, and the combustible bundles would burn as brilliantly as last year's tinder. She merely needed a spark. Too bad she'd never started smoking.

"I grew up with people like you," Nathan shouted. "You're a bully who hides behind his brother's shotgun. Too scared to take aim yourself?"

Nathan either had a death wish or knew buying her time was the best thing he could do. She watched Frankie pace. With his shoulders raised high and his chin tucked now, he looked like an anxious turtle.

"You hear that?" Dickie shouted over his shoulder. "This little shit thinks I'm a white-trash bully."

"Well, you is!" Frankie laughed nervously. "Always have been."

She wondered how much danger Frankie would tolerate before he cut and run. She didn't want him to escape, but overpowering one brother would be much easier than overpowering two. If he bolted, she would hunt him down. He and his brother were greed-fueled, opportunistic killers. Left unchecked, they would choke out the brilliant, vulnerable people who made south Louisiana unique. She wouldn't let that happen.

Tilting her head, she weighed her options. She wouldn't risk Nathan's life to save hers, but she had to trust him enough to use him wisely. "Enough!"

The men fell silent.

Pulling her elbow toward her chest, she yanked Dickie off balance and knocked Nathan's feet out from under him.

Nathan hit the floor and grunted.

Dickie gripped her shoulder and reclaimed his balance.

She bit the asshole's arm and punched him with her free hand. "Don't fucking touch me without my permission!" Screaming at full volume, she released the frustration and indignation coursing through her system.

Dickie yanked free his arm.

Frankie fire off a round, reloaded his shotgun,

pumped the slide, and aimed.

She tensed for an impact.

He returned the barrel toward the ceiling and pulled the trigger.

The bullet surged into the overhead darkness. *Carpentry cast little judgment.*

Before she finished her snide thought, she heard the bullet strike something metal. Releasing her breath, she watched for sparks. When she saw a glowing speck fall like a downed lightning bug, she cupped her hands around her mouth. "Fire!"

"Fire?" Dickie moaned and reached for a pallet. He steadied himself. "There ain't no fire. Shoot her, Brother!"

Smoke's unmistakable scent permeated the air.

Evie wasn't the only Hemlock resident who liked to watch things burn. As soon as Frankie's heated shotgun bullet had clipped a metal pole, the dust-filled warehouse was doomed, but Ann refused to linger and watch the show. Pulling Nathan to his feet, she backed toward the exit as a dull glow rose between two pallets.

Frankie dropped the shotgun and scrambled toward the fire.

Dickie turned toward his brother's weapon.

Gripping her pistol, she slammed the butt into the back of Dickie's head. "Got sprinklers?"

Nathan gripped her shoulder and pulled her back. "No, but I've got you."

She cleared her throat. "When I say run—"

He squeezed her shoulder.

A hundred feet away, Frankie slowly turned, fumbled for the shotgun, and aimed the gun's barrel as if molasses hindered his motions. He raised an arm slowly, inch by inch, as he aimed at her and Nathan.

She saw her escape routes flash before her eyes. Flames burst into sight and exploded a metal canister along the warehouse wall. The fire spread upward and outward through the cotton. One by one, flames closed off their egress.

Frankie parted his yellow teeth in a wolfish smile. No longer timid and unsure, he saw his chance to be the hero.

She refused to give him the satisfaction.

"Get down!" Nathan shouted.

She heard his muffled command through waves of adrenaline. They would be sitting ducks. She had only one choice. Hoping her gun had misfired previously, she raised the piece, aimed for Frankie's chest, and pulled the trigger.

The gun recoiled in her grip.

The bullet hit Frankie in the right shoulder and knocked him off his feet as he pulled the trigger. The shotgun boomed.

Instead of laying her out, the gun fired into the tall stack of cotton on her right. Shreds and fragments blasted from the pallet and swirled like a thick, fiery blizzard. The air was thick with tiny, burning specks and smoking fibers. Burning embers settled on surrounding pallets, and the stacked cotton products burst into flames.

Dickie moaned and struggled to his hands and knees.

"Now, we run!" She yanked Nathan toward the exit. Her steps pounded the concrete floor like rapid-fire machine-gun fire, but Frankie could still catch them.

A whoosh of oxygen rushed into the warehouse to feed the fire. Pallets burst into flames, and the enormous hills of cotton smoldered and carried the inferno throughout the warehouse.

She and Nathan ran flat out for the sunlight.

Frankie reared off the floor and tackled them. He panted like a wounded linebacker bellowing his frustration. The wound in his right shoulder pumped crimson blood and stained his shirt. Drips landed on the concrete.

Nathan staggered off the floor, took Frankie's swing, and rocked back to the floor with a shuddering impact.

She circled Frankie and listened for Dickie amid the spreading flames' pops and sighs. Her lungs burned with each inhalation. She heard a man screaming hysterically and hoped Dickie remembered his stop-drop-and-roll drill. She squared her shoulders against Frankie. Taking his blows would be a losing battle, but at least, he'd dropped his gun. She still held hers. She raised it.

Frankie eyed the piece and stood unsteadily, rocking back and forth and clenching a fist as he readied for a blow.

Lurching forward, she hit him in the throat with her gun. Non-lethal force was always the first means of attack.

He shook off the blow, stepped closer, and swung an enormous fist.

The blow knocked her sideways into burning cotton and hurled her gun through the warehouse. She rolled over the pallet and breathed thick, acrid smoke. Her nerves screamed, and her body ached. Prone, she patted out embers sizzling her skin and watched Frankie's looming silhouette advance through the smoke.

Leaning forward, he kicked her in the chest.

Her ribs cracked, and her vision went black. Gritting her teeth, she raised herself on her right hand. "Is that all you have?"

He sneered and loomed above her. "Ain't so tough now, is you? You put up a pretty fight, though, girl. More than the others."

Her shoe caught fire. She tore off the footwear and hurled it at his face. "Who you calling pretty?"

He batted aside the shoe and swung back a leg.

A second kick would kill her. If Nathan had any sense, he would be halfway to Hemlock.

Frankie's body jerked like somebody stood behind him and unloaded a clip into his back. He turned and ducked Nathan's blows.

She scrambled toward the nearest pallet, yanked a plank off the hot concrete, and slammed the wood into the back of Frankie's head. She abhorred anger, but taking down this clown felt justifiable. He threatened her, Nathan, and people like Jeanne. If she got out of this warehouse and felt regret swamping her endorphins, she would bury her misgivings in the bayou and never look back. The wood cracked against Frankie's skull. She absorbed the impact in her arms and shoulder and dropped the plank to the floor.

His legs crumpled, and he fell face-first into a burning pile of cotton.

Nathan yanked her forward. "Now, we run?"

"Yes!" She gripped his hand and raced through the flames. Her stride ate the distance separating her from daylight, but she stopped short and looked up. The metal along the roof glowed orange through the smoke. If the structure collapsed, flames would boil through the building. "What about Evie?"

Nathan braced his hands on his knees and panted. "I have no idea how we would find her. Do you?"

Helplessness made her consider desperate actions. She squeezed shut her eyes. "The warehouse will crumble. If she's inside, she'll die with Frankie and Dickie."

"I know." Nathan straightened and tugged her hand toward the exit. Tears streamed down his cheeks. "I know."

She wiped a thumb beneath his left eye, turned, and hurled herself out the door and toward the river.

Nathan followed close behind.

His pounding steps drove her through the smoke. Blinking in the bright daylight, she established her bearings. Rows of rusted vehicles looked like a scrap yard, but police cruisers parked along the cracked asphalt roadway flashed blue and red lights stopped. She'd never been so excited to see the po-po.

A fire engine roared to a stop, and firefighters dismounted.

Evie ripped free of Detective Goetz's grip and sprinted across the yard. Screaming, she threw herself into her father's arms and buried her face against his shoulder.

"Evie!" Officer Marcus cupped his hands around his mouth and shouted. "Get back! The site's not safe."

Evie flipped him the bird and continued screaming and wiping away tears of happiness. Crying, she hugged and kissed her father, staggering around him and inspecting his extremities as an afternoon river breeze blew smoke toward town.

After a moment, Nathan braced his hands against her shoulders and started screaming, too.

Ann raised a hand to her mouth with a kind of detached curiosity and wondered if she might be screaming, too, but the moment of happiness belonged to Nathan and his daughter.

Behind her, the roof blew off the warehouse with a deafening boom.

She, Nathan, and Evie covered their ears and turned.

Shooting orange flames and billowing, black smoke swelled into the cloudy, humid afternoon. Fragments of burning cotton drifted around Ann, and heat blasted her back like a furnace. Fire distorted the warehouse and buckled its faltering support beams. Metal screeched and tore. She gripped Nathan's bicep and pulled him and Evie toward the street. "Get clear before the warehouse collapses."

Hands linked, Nathan and Evie ran toward the yard's edge.

Ann followed and stopped short of the police line, breathing hard and giving Nathan and Evie a moment to reconnect. Evie had fallen into Frankie's and Dickie's grasp through no fault of her own. When the time was right, Ann would apologize for taking Nathan's money and his generosity. Hubris had pushed her to help Jeanne. If she had trusted the NOPD, neither Evie nor Nathan would have risked their lives in the warehouse.

"I can see your gears turning." Shooting out an arm, Nathan grabbed Ann and pulled her against his chest. "You're not going anywhere."

"Not for now." She laid her head against his chest and breathed deeply. A smoky veneer subdued Hollywood's gloss, but he still smelled like sage. Whether he wore polished ostrich cowboy boots, crisp jeans, or a white button-down shirt had little bearing on her relief. She listened to his heartbeat and closed her eyes.

He pressed a kiss to her hair.

Opening her eyes, she turned toward him. Bruised and bleeding, his face no longer suggested a boyish appeal. Fear brought a tense, brooding set to his green eyes that might never dissipate. She recognized the feeling and raised a hand to cup his cheek. "We're okay."

Tightening his hold on her and Evie, he swallowed back tears, but one escaped. "I know." He cleared his throat. "Barely."

Dropping her hand, she turned to Evie. "How did you escape?"

"When the shorter guy retrieved your purse, he left open the office door. I made a dash for the exit and called for help. Trust me, you didn't want me to throw a punch on your behalf. I'm an artist. What would I do? Jump on someone's back and strangle them with my smock strings?"

Laughing, Ann exhaled. "Good call, but don't underestimate yourself. You're stronger than you think."

"Right, the next time someone kidnaps you, let them have it!" Nathan shook his head and dropped his shoulders. "Let's stick with bubble wrap. I'll build you a studio in Hemlock. I'll build Huanlong a surgery bay. Whatever it takes—"

"You're so funny." Shaking her head, Evie turned toward the crowd of spectators, police officers, and first responders. She gave Huanlong a thumbs-up.

Huanlong wiped his forehead with a handkerchief.

Ann was pretty sure Huanlong'd been jumping, yelling, and laughing like a madman, too. She also doubted Nathan understood Evie's dismissal. Adrenaline made him hyper, but as the emotion subsided, fear would make him restless.

He rocked back on his heels and scanned the crowd.

She understood his fears and edged closer. At any moment, another Gagne brother might jump from the woodwork and threaten Nathan's family and everything he built.

Instead of realizing that threat, flames compromised the warehouse roof and spread to the warehouses next door. The growing fire intensified as the neighboring warehouse structures caught fire. Explosions and black smoke rolled like heavy thunderclouds brimming with lightning. The combined blazes ricocheted between collapsing buildings like bomb blasts and mortar shells, but Fallujah was a long way away. She knew exactly where she stood.

"Are we burning the entire port?" Nathan asked. "Hemlock's drama doesn't"—he shuddered—"spread. The town's boundaries are so comforting they beckon lethargy. New Orleans is the gateway to the world. How can I leave such a black mark?"

She took his hand and witnessed the inferno at his side. "I doubt we'll burn down the town. Pump trucks can draw water from the river and limit the fire's spread. You're not responsible for the structure's latent energy. Fertilizer, oil drums, and equally combustible wonders predate your arrival."

"But…"

Tat-tat-tat. Boom! BOOM!

She winced.

Nathan raised an arm and shielded his face before slowly lowering it. "I'm more accustomed to blowing fuses."

Laughing, she squeezed his hand. "Are you sure you're okay?"

Raising his face to the sky, he watched ashes fall. "I think so."

The hellish, gray-and-black scene might be the closest thing to a blizzard New Orleans would ever see. The sky looked like the site of a volcanic explosion and held enough ash and cotton embers to make tourists rethink their next Bourbon Street cocktail.

He looked down. "Did we do this?"

"Frankie and Dickie did this." Drawing in a sharp breath through her nose, she measured her words. "They took Jeanne, Lisette, and countless others. I regret their deaths, but faced with losing my life or the people I love, I have no problem with a scorched earth mentality. My decision suits me just fine." She narrowed her gaze. "Nobody in that warehouse was innocent."

He turned, raised her hand to his lips, and placed a kiss on her fingers. "Remind me to stay on your good side."

She opened her mouth to deflect his comment. Having a good side was like having a good hair day. She was who she was, and people could take her or leave her.

"Better yet, say it again." He raised his head. "Tell me you love me."

She leaned close so he could hear her declaration above the fire's crescendo. "I have always loved you. Even when I hated myself for making excuses, I missed you something fierce. I compared every kiss to your kiss. For me, there was no one else. That's why running away hurt so much. I loved you more than I loved myself. Now, I know better. I'm here to fight for both of us. As long as you stay in line"—she took his earlobe between her teeth and softly bit him—"I'll find more productive ways to show my love than kicking your ass."

Laughing, he pulled her into a hug and wrapped his arms around her. "I love you, too. Always have. Always will."

She wiggled out of his arms, wrapped her legs around his waist, and locked her arms behind his head. Instead of waiting for his lead or worrying about who saw them, she kissed him like she would die if she lost contact with his lips.

Evie let out a catcall.

Nathan turned his back to his daughter, spread his hands under Ann's ass, and lifted her higher.

For a moment, she let him take the lead.

He had achieved so much through loyalty and hard work. He deserved to appreciate his success and his vitality. Murder and assault were poor therapeutic devices, but the happiest people she knew in the world had seen their lives flash before their eyes.

Every time she gritted her teeth on deployment, she thought of Nathan and wondered if she should have fought harder to keep him in her life. Today, she had.

Drawing back from his kiss, she cupped his face. Sharing space never felt like an act. They knew each other.

He looked good on regional magazine covers and could pretend nothing happened, but she preferred his newfound wariness. His disheveled, rock-and-roll black hair looked as messy as a raven hit by a heavy-haul truck. At the roots, she saw hints of gray and red peeking through his Hollywood dye job. This might not be the moment to mention it still held cotton scraps. Picking one free, she flicked it into the wind. Cotton fibers were native to Europe and the Americas. Whenever it landed, it would blend in.

Nathan was another matter. He was generous, but he also proved he would fight for the people he loved. More importantly, he listed the reasons he loved her above anyone else. Putting words to feelings gave them power. She believed in his power.

When she stood by his side, wrapped her legs around his waist, or claimed a kiss, she felt his love. The connection was the most powerful feeling in the world. Too bad, her world felt small, and her leave from Valor ended with Paps' death. No matter how much she loved Nathan, she knew he would never leave Hemlock.

Chapter Twenty-Six

Weeks after the ashes settled, Nathan danced in Hemlock's newest event center and held Ann in his arms. Soft music filled the rustic barn, and guests celebrated Evie and Huanlong's wedding. Over the last two weeks, his daughter and his lover had developed a friendship. He should be excited about their smiles, but he tossed and turned, wondering what he'd missed. Now, he no longer had to worry about seeing Evie to the finish line. Her lavish reception united two communities and christened the venue. If nostalgia dragged him toward hard liquor, he focused on the professional photographers shooting pictures to anchor his business' social media posts.

Life went on. Charlet men persevered. He had good reasons to feel effervescent. The building's rough-hewn beams and exposed brick arches lent the venue an established air, and his trained event staff curated magic. The venue could host profitable celebrations. Why did the financial windfall feel less satisfying than he anticipated? Tightening his hold on Ann, he felt like he grasped happiness. As soon as the music ended, she would slip away.

Wondering if he needed distance to remember the mix of vibes vibrating through his soul, he heard the live band played a familiar, lulling Cajun melody and led Ann toward the cocktail patio for a slow dance beneath the stars. Changing his perspective helped him appreciate the venue, but it also let him hold her as close.

She followed, her steps in sync. "What are you thinking about?"

"Curating Evie's wedding pictures for publicity shots."

"Liar." Laughing, she toyed with his hair on his nape.

He probably needed to cut it. In the two weeks since the warehouse fire, time felt like it slipped through his hands. He met his obligations, but he understood why Ann rubbed his shoulders and waited for him to unload his fears. In a moment, he could have lost both her and Evie. Despite the night breeze, he broke into a sweat and shuddered.

"Hey," Ann whispered. "Come back here."

He leaned closer and let her familiar, musky-sweet scent anchor him. After walking Evie down the church aisle, he'd played his part, toasted the married couple's attributes, and signed off on last-minute substitutions. If his baby girl needed him, he was nearby, but her marriage depended on what she and Huanlong put into it. When the last guest left, nobody needed him, and yet, he remained. "I'm here."

"Are you?"

He pulled back and stared into Ann's blue eyes. Behind her glamorous makeup, she was the same woman he'd always loved. She claimed she loved him. Was she soothing his ego? Could he be what she needed?

Flannery neither asked for alimony nor freedom. Holding Ann in his arms, he understood his marriage to

Flannery was a glorified friendship. They made the best of their circumstances. If she lived, he would wish her the best, but he wouldn't bend over backward to make her happy.

Ann, on the other hand, could turn him into a contortionist.

She let herself into his cottage every day and kept the bathroom vanity pin-neat, but everything she brought over would fit into a duffle bag. Fearing she would bolt, he bottled his fears and refused to ask questions about the future. Issues like what she wanted to eat and how she wanted to fuck were gloriously easier. Tightening his frame, he gauged how long the slow song would continue until he had to release her.

"What's wrong?" She looked up. "You're tripping over my feet."

He tucked a long, blonde strand of hair behind her ear. "I'm counting the minutes until I can get you home."

"And then..."

He smiled ambiguously and looked over her shoulder. Stepping on her feet was a minor symptom. Letting her slip away would be as pleasant and self-serving as wiping his ass with poison ivy. He would survive, but he would regret his mistake for the remainder of his life. Too much of his happiness hinged on her unannounced plans, and he was too scared to ask her.

The wedding venue felt alive with the joy and laughter of new beginnings, but when the sun came up, he and Ann would be out of excuses. He needed to know whether she would be by his side on a train back to Colorado.

"When are Evie and Huanlong leaving for their honeymoon?"

"Tomorrow, after the breakfast." He spun her away and caught her back in his arms. "Do you want to join them?"

"Depends." She grinned and rested her hands on his shoulders. "Where are they going?"

"The French Riviera's laid-back capital. She can paint the Mediterranean Sea *and* the French Alps. As long as Huanlong's ass doesn't feature in the picturesque landscapes, I'll add her works to the venue's lobby."

Ann covered her mouth and yawned.

He stopped dancing. "Are you tired?"

She shrugged. "We can't leave until after the newlyweds do."

He wondered if she'd only stayed to support Evie, but worrying over details kept him grounded. The Evangeline had gracious spaces for weddings, receptions, concerts, corporate gatherings, and markets. The venue sat a block from the hotel, shopping, and restaurants along Longfellow Street. Visitors could stay at the hotel, shop at the furniture showroom, select a boutique accessory, or dine in the town's restaurants.

Should he build an ice cream parlor? Did Ann prefer outdoor dining or twenty-four-seven gyms? So much had happened in the last month that his hold on reality felt tenuous and liable to snap. He laced his fingers behind Ann's lower back and followed the song's swaying tempo.

She laid her head against his chest. "This is nice."

Nice enough to stay? The port warehouse fire had incinerated the threats targeting her and his south

Louisiana community. Evie was safe. He'd gained Huanlong as a son-in-law. The kid was earnest and excitable, but he would be a hell of a husband. If Nathan could freeze time at this moment, with Ann in his arms and hope on the horizon, he would do it. "Come on. Let's go inside."

"I like it better outside."

His cheeks heated. "I can't abandon my responsibilities."

"I know." Taking his hand and smiling sadly, she led him inside.

He scanned the room and counted the couples lost in the moment. He was vulnerable to sentimentality, but he manufactured it, too. LED lights embedded in the ceiling lent the room a twinkling effect, but nothing beat the beauty of standing under the stars with Ann. He drew her into another dance.

Ann tilted her head. "Reliving your cotillion days?"

He pressed a kiss to her right hand. "Savoring my time with you."

She laid her head on his chest. "I know the feeling. You love this town."

Did he? Letting the band set the rhythm, he recast his family's association with Hemlock as a symbiotic relationship. Charlet men didn't save Hemlock. People like Guidry, Sam, and Pierre worked hard and persevered. Even Nanette deserved credit for her antiquated determination to hold the line. The town's residents gave him untold opportunities, and he chose his path.

Sometimes, he made mistakes, but he was learning how to correct course. Ann figured out that skill a long time ago. She was nothing like Longfellow's Evangeline, content to sit and wait a spell before working her way along the East Coast. Ann took action. If he wanted to spend his life with her, he would, too.

The band's song ended.

Couples dispersed from the dance floor.

If Ann gave him another chance, then he would follow her wherever she led. Looking for the best place to tell her how important she was, he monitored guest chatter and staff movements. Small imperfections snagged his gaze. "Swan Dance" parties could be beautiful and elegant on the surface, but a hot, swampy mess beneath the water. Even though service directors and lead captains worked out their differences in staff areas, and disagreements were more common than most partygoers thought, operational hiccups should never inconvenience venue guests.

Tonight, Ann wasn't an operative. She was a guest. She shouldn't know about the flies in the food, staff confrontations, or cocktail hour delays. She deserved the same effervescence the wedding guests experienced, too. Keeping his emotions bottled up, he angled her toward a server passing savory delicacies and hoped she remembered this night as a high point of her time in Hemlock.

The lights changed, and Jeanne stepped onto the stage.

Ann waved.

Jeanne winked. "Evie and Huanlong have a special treat in store."

Nanette marched up and yanked his elbow. "What is she doing here?"

Turning from the stage, Ann frowned. "*She* is a

319

talented artist and a wonderful person who experienced horrendous trauma." She crowded Nanette. "Those braids are part of a wig. She has stitches and drains in her scalp, but she still found time to write thank-you notes to everyone who saved her life."

Nathan rubbed his jaw. "I got one, didn't you?

Nanette furrowed her brow.

Ann steered Nanette toward the exit. "You taught me there's always time for a thank-you note, so thank you for everything you've done. Please, stop nitpicking the people who don't fit your mold."

Nathan hung back and wondered how much Ann's velvet-clad lecture cost her. There was telling people off, and there was telling people off with Southern style. Ann preferred brute force.

She planted both hands on her hips. "Instead of remaking citizens to fit your standards, try accepting them for what they bring to the table."

"Jeanne doesn't live here." Nanette crossed her arms and raised her chin.

Ann clenched her jaw. "Lucky her. Living in Hemlock isn't a privilege. It's a linen-draped sentence."

"Well, I never!" Nanette dug in her feet.

Too bad, the dance floor had a fresh coat of wax.

Arms swinging, Nanette struggled to maintain her footing.

Ann caught Nanette's arm and kept her from falling flat on her face. "Stick with the first advice you gave me. Be nice."

Jeanne started an upbeat remix.

Nanette shrieked and slapped a hand to her cheek. "They didn't include me! I'm their leader."

Ann shrugged. "They didn't think you'd approve."

Jerking free her arm, Nanette stomped toward the bar.

The Merrymakers dance troupe paraded onto the dance floor in full regalia. The ladies danced in Mardi Gras parades and organized group activities, but tonight, they entertained wedding guests. Each woman wore flashing accessories and executed choreographed dance steps that would put viral flash mobs to shame.

Wedding guests clapped and cheered.

Nathan crossed his arms over his chest and grinned. Evie hadn't mentioned a thing about Jeanne and the Merrymakers performing. Something about the women's secrecy gave him hope. He didn't need Ann to depend on him, but he wanted Hemlock to make her happy.

The Merrymakers finished their dance. Guests clapped.

Evie and Huanlong hoisted umbrellas and started a second-line dance around the venue's perimeter. The Merrymakers fell into line and tested the limits of their arthritic joints. Staff passed out handkerchiefs. One by one, guests joined the parade and waved handkerchiefs over their heads.

Nathan stood behind Ann and wrapped his arms around her middle. "You've been more involved than I expected." He pressed a kiss to her hair. "Thank you for helping make their day special."

She leaned against him. "You didn't need more worries. You're tough and clever. So am I. We made a great team."

He held his breath and inhaled her perfume. The mindfulness lingering after the warehouse fire felt poised to break free. "I love you so much, but I'm afraid you'll flee."

Turning in his arms, she fine-tuned his bow tie. "I don't see myself staying in Hemlock."

Her voice was barely audible over the pulsing music. He tightened his grip around her waist and stopped masking the flickers of uncertainty that kept him from sleeping. "This is home. I've built my entire life here. The hotel, the community…It's all I've ever known."

She tilted her head. "What about the New Orleans townhouse? Nice? Can't you keep Hemlock in your heart and travel to other places? The world is full of beautiful people. There's just"—she frowned—"not much spy work in Louisiana."

Rubbing a thumb along her shoulder, he felt the faint lines of her compass rose tattoo. She was a combat veteran. Why did he think he could keep her in Hemlock? He cleared his parched throat. "You're good at so many things. Before I messed up everything, who did you want to be? A tumbling coach? I'll build you a state-of-the-art gym."

Laughing, she shook her head. "You can't build me a gilded cage. You can't define my happiness, either. Let me be myself."

The vulnerability of loving her no matter how much she loved him eviscerated his confidence. He should have gotten her a pet. Maybe Kiki, Nanette's ferocious beast, would have kittens. Maybe Evie would ask for a mentor. He scrambled to delay Ann's departure. No matter how she defined herself, he wanted everything she offered and would fight for the privilege of loving her.

She rested her head against his shoulder and

wrapped her arms around his waist.

Feeling the tension in her frame, he shuddered. She loved him but desired something more than he could provide. He wasn't what she needed. Stoicism stole his breath.

"Home is more than just a place on a map. It's where you feel alive and where you feel belonging. I don't feel that here. Maybe I don't have the right DNA to settle beneath an oak tree, eke out a living, and pray hurricanes detour."

He sighed, the weight of her words settling on his shoulders. He had millions at his disposal, but money wasn't what she needed. "Hemlock is more than you remember."

"The town's still not enough."

Panic would be an acceptable emotion, but he swallowed his fears and embraced the keening disappointment and stifling frustration haunting him. Throwing himself into work beat back loneliness, but he would miss her smile for the remainder of his life.

She raised her head and held his gaze. "Come with me."

He swallowed, saw the sincerity behind her offer, and wished he could accept. "Leaving is hard to imagine. My family's been part of Hemlock for generations. Who am I without this place?"

"The man I love." She cupped his cheek. "The man you've always been."

He sucked in a breath. Her feelings thrilled and pained him in equal measures. No matter how many times he heard them, he knew she could slip from his arms and disappear from his life for good. "We're not the same kids."

"No, thank goodness." She lifted her head and met his gaze, her intent tender yet determined. "Memories don't define us. The choices we make, and the actions we take, are the things that influence our futures."

Choosing her might be the hardest thing he had ever done. He led the dance while he waited for her to work out what she wanted to say.

"My mom ran off. My dad succumbed." She cleared her throat and swallowed. "I miss them, but I also miss who they *could* have been. That isn't fair. They would never be those people. Mourning someone's potential is like pinning your happiness on passing clouds, tea leaves, and white gators. Dreams aren't realities."

He doubted Ann wanted to wallow in a murky, twenty-thousand-gallon pool. If a gym and a mind-numbing credit limit weren't enough to tempt her, he wondered if he could provide what she needed.

Most of the women he dated were easy. They loved the gala scene. He could imagine Ann wearing an evening gown with a heavy jewelry that would rest between her clavicles and stake his claim. She would hate the tediousness.

Toying with her pale hair, he resisted an urge to press a kiss against her throat and feel her pulse beneath his lips. Showering her with jewels felt pointless. She was beautiful covered in ash or swaying beneath ballroom lights.

"Do you get what I'm saying?" she asked.

"You're not big into fantasies." After the wedding reception ended, he had several fantasies he would like to play out. Shaking off the thought of Ann spread over his bed sheets, he focused on her statement. "You deal in realities."

"I don't belong here."

He stared and mimicked her stance. "You were born here."

She laughed. "That doesn't mean Hemlock's a good fit. Do I look like a gala queen?"

So much for a gilt collar. He exhaled. If she bolted, at least she would have the decency to tell him goodbye. Following her logic, he searched for holes in her defenses. Life taught her to expect the hard knocks. She learned to take them. What about acknowledging how unique and resilient she'd become? What about enjoying life's simple, gracious pleasures? Passing clouds, tea leaves, and white gators weren't *all* bad.

She laid her head against his shoulder. "I feel selfish asking for more than I have. Paps gave me so much. I should be more like him."

"He loved every minute he had with you." If anyone should channel Guidry Storey, Nathan should. He would give Ann anything she asked for, but he needed her to believe in happiness. How many times had she rallied hope and felt disappointed by people like her mom, dad, and him?

Trailing a thumb along her spine, he thought of her imagining alternate lives, watching them dissolve in the wind, and trudging through her lived experiences. At some point, a person realized time ran out. Optimism kept people moving forward, but acts of kindness and community bonds did, too. For decades, local families worked to change Hemlock for the better. Local companies and community foundations provided resources and passed down generations of love and commitment. People who wanted to contribute to create real, lasting change stayed. His brother stayed. He was free to go. Spreading his fingers along her lower back, he resisted clenching her dress. "Wanting more isn't selfish."

She laughed. "Isn't it? I barely felt like I fit in."

He recalled her daydreams. Floating clouds and random mutations, just like that ridiculous gator. The specimens might be rare and insubstantial, but they were also precious and unique. Surviving her youth made her as precious as the gators he admired. Unless boaters brought the tiny, white hatchlings into sanctuaries, the rare gators became snacks for snapping turtles and wading birds. Hell, other gators were their biggest threats. Paps had done that for Ann. He gave her sanctuary. Now, Nathan hoped for the privilege. He didn't want to cage her in, but he wanted to build a future together. He scanned the room for Nanette and wondered if she would support him. Hardly. Nanette would say, *He'll cheat again. He'll get bored. He'll move on.* She hardly had his back.

He rolled his eyes. Getting bored with Ann would be like getting bored with the wind. At times, the experience could be relentless, but he felt its absence.

Nanette made eye contact, raised her chin, and downed her champagne.

She had more opinions than she had power, but when Ann needed help, she provided an exit ramp. Maybe she'd always known what Ann needed. Influencing her relationship with Ann would be like coaching cheerleading. He put on a good show, but he needed so many cue cards he might as well bow out before the next take. Dipping his head, he pressed his face against Ann's silky, smooth hair. "Did something else upset you?"

Raising her head, she shook it. "No, but you've been busy. I just didn't want to interfere with the wedding prep. You only have one daughter."

"Who's happily married." Pulling back his head, he stopped dancing, considered her angles, and pressed a palm to his chest. "Wait, am I the gator? Am I the one who doesn't fit into your plan? Woman, pin your hopes on me. I'm not going anywhere."

She cupped his cheek. "I know. That's the problem."

His eye twitched. How many times had he caught her looking out the window? He thought he had to marry Flannery and sacrifice his life for Evie's happiness. Asking Ann to sacrifice her life would be just as wrong. Despite his achievements, holding her in his arms felt like his life's greatest privilege. Raising a hand, he stroked her cheek.

She leaned into his touch. "Growing up in Hemlock felt like a circumstantial accident. I need diverse cultures, geopolitical tensions, and big-picture issues. Falling asleep in your arms soothes me, but I don't want to spend my life cocooned in your arms."

He remembered the hot, swirling haze as cotton ashes fell on his skin and choked his lungs. The moment he realized Ann and Evie were both alive, he would have handed over everything he owned to guarantee their happiness. Why was he so dead set on forcing Ann to adjust to his version of happily ever after?

His tuxedo shirt was imminently more comfortable than the feel of ashes sizzling off his arm hairs, but nothing about his feelings for Ann and Evie had changed. They remained the most important people in his life.

The last few weeks, Ann had shielded him so he could maintain his bearings in a topsy-turvy world of forensics and police interviews. She was beautiful, strong, and loyal. Hemlock held his memories, but the town didn't hold his heart. Ann did. He stroked her cheek.

Tears welled in her eyes.

If she thought he could say goodbye, she misjudged how much he loved her. He pulled his handkerchief from his jacket's interior pocket and offered it. He would give her anything. "Another dance?"

She took the slip. "And after the dust settles? Will you visit?"

"You lead, and I'll follow." He held her gaze and took a deep breath. "You're more precious and unique than anything in my life. If Hemlock's not the right place for us, we'll find one."

She blinked. "Anywhere?"

He laughed. Self-importance almost landed him a long, lonely dotage. The mural in the bar should have taught him a lesson. Few people would have noticed something amiss. Capable employees could take his visions and run with them, but if he stayed involved in daily logistics, tedious issues would haunt him until he fixed them. "You'll always have Paps' house, and I'll always have the cottage. The rest of my assets can go to auction. The bills will find me in Hemlock or Timbuktu. No matter where we go, I choose you." He looked deep into her eyes and dropped the tone of her voice. "I love you."

Tears glimmered in her eyes. Wrapping her arms around his neck, she grinned and buried her face against his shoulder. "Good call, *Capitaine*."

Tightening his grip with one arm, he traced the rose tattoo's outline. She would be his past, his present, and his future for as long as she wanted him. He wondered if she would wear his wedding ring. He doubted it. She coveted stuffy ceremonies like he wanted shares in a cotton farm. After their years apart, he wanted a reminder that wishes came true and wondered if he could settle for matching tattoos. It would hurt like hell, but spending another day away from the woman he loved would hurt more. She taught him bravery was choosing her over everything warm and familiar, over everything calm and peaceful, and over everything boring that might have been. She was his success. Loving her would be his life's work— wedding ring be damned.

She raised her head. "What are you thinking?"

He stroked a thumb along her cheek, tucked a strand of hair behind her ear, and took her hand. "The moment I caught sight of you on the football field, I wanted you."

Smiling, she tilted her head. "Liar."

"God's truth." He spun her in his arms beneath the stars and caught her against his chest. Like his love for Ann, the starlight shone no matter where he stood. "Loving you will be the greatest privilege of my life. I wasn't ready for you, but now, I am. Thank you." He pressed a soft kiss against her lips.

She returned the kiss and pulled back. "Late call."

He laughed, tucked her to his side and pressed a kiss to her hair. "Better late than never."

Thank you for purchasing
this publication of The Wild Rose Press, Inc.

For questions or more information
contact us at
info@thewildrosepress.com.

The Wild Rose Press, Inc.
www.thewildrosepress.com